Vengeance Highway, Revision
CalebLott Publishing
ISBN# 978-1-7320906-2-0

Vengeance Highway

(A novel)

By

Caleb Lott

CalebLott Publishing

While inspired in part by true events, the following is a work of fiction. Any similarities to any actual persons, places, events, or circumstances is purely coincidental and is in no way any representation of any real persons, places, events, or circumstances.

To Megan

Vengeance is mine; I will repay, saith the Lord.

Romans 12:19
Holy Bible, King James Version

Chapter 1

1980's

Private detective John Edge drove his navy blue Chevrolet Impala automobile onto the gravel parking lot of the Tangerine, Alabama, Police Department and parked in a space marked 'Visitor' near the front door of the five thousand square foot, brick building promptly at eight thirty on a Monday morning in October. It was cloudy and the temperature was in the mid-sixties.

There were two other cars in the lot; one a shiny, black Ford Crown Victoria, undoubtedly the Chief's vehicle, was parked on the east end, near a window clothed with louvered blinds. The other, a marked Dodge Diplomat, with blue, bubble lights on top, was backed in on the opposite side of the lot, three spaces from the Impala.

Edge got out of the car and looked around, then peered at his reflection in the driver's door window while adjusting his red and white striped tie. He rarely dressed so formally, with neckwear and a jacket, however he was coming to see the Chief of Police about a job and so, on the off chance that the man was impressed by such things, Edge had slipped on a blazer and a starched white shirt over pressed khaki slacks and loafers.

Just inside the front door, Edge stopped and looked right, then left, then straight ahead. The lobby was paneled, doors were on the three other sides of the room, and the black and white checked floor was clean if not polished. There were photographs on the wall directly ahead; one on either side of a glass reception window of the Mayor and a uniformed man that Edge guessed was probably the Chief.

Stepping forward and looking through the three by three foot window, Edge watched as a young blonde, who was seated behind a desk, swiveled right, toward an IBM Selectric typewriter. She bent over the machine, dabbing a bit of liquid paper on a sheet in the roller, and didn't notice Edge, who was close enough to hear her say:

"Shit. Why does this stuff have to dry out so fast."

Her voice was high and soft, typical of a very feminine-appearing woman of her age. Edge noted that she was barely twenty and looked to be slightly over five feet tall. She had an attractive face and blue eyes, as well as an hourglass figure. The name plate on her desk identified her as 'Becky'.

When he cleared his throat, the startled young woman looked up. She smirked at having been caught in a flustered condition but rose from behind the desk, walked to the window, and slid open one of the glass panes.

"Oh, uh, I'm sorry. Can I help you?"

"My name's Edge. I'm here to see the Chief." He paused. "I've got an appointment."

The young woman wore jeans and a white, long-sleeved, pullover shirt with the sleeves pushed up. Her hair was parted in the middle and hung just below her ears, and her nails were painted a dark crimson, as were her lips. She turned her back, and Edge admired the view as she bent at the waist and flipped a couple of pages on her desk calendar. Then she turned sideways while looking back at him, furrowed her brow, and bit the inside of her lip.

"I don't see you on his schedule."

"I don't think he wants me on his schedule."

Chief Tom Strange had contacted Edge on Sunday afternoon, by telephone, and asked him to visit the Police Department the first thing Monday morning. He wouldn't say what he wanted, but he did say it was sensitive. Edge pressed, but the Chief would only say that it involved a death investigation.

"Oh, well, sure," Becky said not knowing how else to respond. "He just stepped out of the office, but I think he'll be back any minute." She looked him over. "You got credentials or somethin'?"

Edge slipped his hand into his jacket pocket and pulled out a leather case that contained his state-issued investigator's permit and his driver's license. He held it up next to his face, and Becky leaned in and examined the two documents closely. Then Edge handed her a business card.

She studied the card, looked up, and said, "Come on in and have a seat. He just stepped down the hall."

Edge took that to mean that the Chief was in the lavatory. He smiled at the euphemism.

Becky walked back around to the other side of her desk and pushed a button on the wall that unlocked the magnetic door next to the window. Edge entered.

He parked in a chair against the east wall and picked up a six year old Time magazine with a picture of a disco ball on the front and began leafing through its pages. Becky went back to her typing but once again cursed lightly after she was forced, following another mistake, to stop and apply more correction fluid. A radio played softly in the background.

In ten minutes, a tall, slim man with a dark complexion and wavy, black hair, who was a live representation of the image on the wall in the lobby, used a key to open the office door and step inside. He wore a short-sleeved, plaid shirt and sans a belt slacks over penny loafers without socks.

"You must be Mr. Edge," he said.

Edge looked up at the tall man, who was at least six foot six. "I am."

The man stuck out his hand, and Edge rose to shake it. His grip was firm and slightly wet.

"Tom Strange, Mr. Edge. Come on in my office."

Edge wiped his hand on his trousers, turned, and followed him through an open door immediately to the right

13

of and behind Becky's desk. Strange turned toward her and said:

"Hold my calls, Becky."

"Yes, sir."

Edge shut the oaken door behind him and then settled into a naugehyde-upholstered chair. He crossed his right leg over his left and folded his hands in his lap.

Strange sat down in an oxblood-colored, overstuffed, leather chair, that perfectly matched his outsized desk and the dark paneling on the walls. Edge looked around the room and saw photographs of Strange shaking hands with several politicos. There was one with the Chief and Ronald Reagan; one with Jimmy Carter; and oddly, one of the tall man towering over a jumpsuited Elvis Presley.

"I hope you didn't have to wait long," he said. His voice was a healthy baritone.

"No, no. I was just catching up on my reading."

Strange nodded and smirked. "I was in the can. It's gotten to where that coffee runs right through me in the mornin'." He chuckled. "You know when you get my age, you never pass up a toilet, and ya never trust a fart."

Edge wondered how old the Chief was. He guessed a well-preserved early or perhaps mid-fifties.

He smiled slightly. "Words to live by."

"You better know it." He paused and rubbed his face, which had turned serious. "I guess you're wondering why I asked ya up here."

Here was Tangerine, a small bedroom community of about six thousand, seven miles north of Mobile, which straddled US Highway 43 as it stretched itself northward from the city, crossed Interstate 65, and then headed toward Washington County. It got its name because of the tangerine trees that were planted there when the town was founded in 1915. It became an incorporated city in 1959.

"Well, you said it was sensitive."

He sniffed. "Well, I think it is. I've got to get some things together before the FBI and the ACLU, and maybe the

NAACP, and them other folks from Washington get down here crawlin' all up in my ass." He paused. "Vic Riley down at the Police Department in Mobile give me your name and said you were pretty good at takin' a look at a death case and makin' some sense of it."

"Vic Riley is prone to exaggeration. I can take a look at a death case, but sometimes the sense of it eludes me – as it does everyone."

He chuckled. "Well, I hope he hasn't wasted your time." He paused and looked upward in reminiscence. "You know, Vic's pushin' sixty. Me and him went through rookie school together close to thirty years ago." He smiled. "He got the gray hair, and I stayed young. He was a crafty sombitch then and, well, he still is." He paused and smiled. "You got any police experience?"

"I was in the French Foreign Legion."

Strange raised his brows. "Oh. I see. Well, I don't know how they look at death cases over there, but if Vic says you can handle the job, I'll take his word for it."

Edge was tired of the small talk. There was no need for apple polishing.

"You got a dead body, Chief?"

He looked away out the window. "Last Friday night, one'a my officers stopped a drunk over on 43 near McDonalds. There wadn't a lotta traffic at that time, but my man said this ole boy was all over the road, so he pulled him over. When he failed the field test, he brought him up here, and he blew a .17 on the GCI (gas chromatograph intoximeter) machine.

"Well, he put him in the cell back there – we got three – did the paperwork, and then went back out on the road. See, the way it's s'posed to work is that after that, on the midnight shift, the officer comes in and checks on the prisoner at the top of the hour, and the dispatcher looks at him on the half hour. She, the dispatcher that is, ain't s'posed to go back into the cell block; she's just s'posed to look at him through the window in the door. If he's movin' about or he's

15

asleep, she goes about her business. If somethin's wrong, she goes back and calls in the officer, and when he gets here, he goes down the hall to where the cells are."

"And he died in his cell."

"Hung his self with his own shoe laces."

"What'd the coroner say?"

Strange picked up a paper on his desk. "Acute asphyxiation by strangulation, by means of a tool (shoe laces) or some other device." He put the paper down.

"Any other injuries?"

"Just a small cut above his right brow."

"You know how he got that?"

"Tom – that's the officer – said he hit his head on the car door frame when he got into the backseat of the patrol car."

"Did your man take his belt?"

"Sure. But, who'da thought he was gonna hang his self with his shoe laces."

Edge nodded. His mind was racing.

"So, why me? Why a PI?"

"'Cause I wanna get a handle on this thing before anybody else gets down here. I wanna be able to tell them what really happened and, more importantly, why."

"You know that the DA or the Sheriff'll do this for free."

He waved his arm. "I know, I know. But they don't work for me. And they write things down." He paused. "What I need is for you to take a look at this thing, kinda unofficial like. See what you think was really goin' on, and then come and tell me. No need to visit the family, go to the hospital, nothin' like that. If I like what you have to say, you write a report, and I'll tell ever'body you're golden – that you're a, uh, an expert in death investigation. In the long run, it'll mean a lot more money in your pocket."

"And if you don't?"

"I shitcan your opinion, and you were never here."

Edge nodded. "This could get expensive."

"No, it won't. I just want you to talk to the officer, talk to the dispatcher, and take a look at the cell. It shouldn't take you more'n a couple'a hours."

Edge nodded again. "Is the officer here now?"

"Tom Strange, Jr. He's in the coffee room. I got him on overtime, so don't keep him long."

"Your son."

"Right."

"And the dispatcher?"

"Rhonda Blackwell. She's on her off day, but she'll be here in about twenty minutes."

Edge took a deep breath and exhaled. "Well, okay. Looks like all I gotta do is read the mind of a drunk."

Chapter 2

Edge found Tom Strange, Junior, sitting at a table in the break room at the northeast corner of the building, near the rear exit; and also near the office of the Tangerine Police Department's only investigator. Strange was tall and slim like his father, and his hair was just as black. His uniform was perfect, and his Corfam leather was shined to a high gloss.

"You Tom Strange?" Edge said as he stood in the threshold.

Strange stood. "Yeah. You the PI?"

"John Edge," he said as he walked over and shook Strange's hand.

Edge took a seat at the table and produced a notepad and pen. He looked around and saw that there was a Pepsi machine on one wall, and a sink and coffee pot on another.

"I guess you know why you're here," Edge said.

"Yeah. That ole drunk hung his self in the jail, and they're prob'ly gonna try to find a way to blame it on me."

Edge looked him over. Strange the younger looked to be thirty, with dark brown eyes and straight, white teeth. He was thin, but fit. The long fingers that protruded from his large hands indicated that with his height, he would have no problem getting leverage on anyone, drunk or sober.

Apprehension painted his face. Strange knew the stress he was about to undergo; interview after interview, interrogation after interrogation, statement after statement; testimony in four or five different legal proceedings; and also the stress of waiting several months – if not years – for a ruling from some government agency whose investigators had never taken a drunk to jail, and, in fact, had no idea of how to go about it. He was not looking forward to any of it.

"Why don't you just tell me what happened."

Strange took a deep breath. "Well, we was out ridin' last Friday night . . ."

"We?"

"Me and Mr. Howell. He's a reserve officer that rides with me once or twice a month. He's about seventy, but he's retired from the Sheriff's Office and is still sharp as a tack; and he just likes to come out and ride. It makes him feel young, you know? I mean, he knows what he's doin'."

"Sure."

"Anyway, we was out on 43 at the McDonald's parking lot, and we saw this car comin' north drivin' real slow in the left hand lane. We got behind'im, and he was all over the road, so I lit him up near the truck stop."

"You say all over the road. How?"

"Well, he crossed the center line two or three times, and he run off onto the shoulder once. When he did, he jerked it back onto the road and crossed the center line again."

Edge made notes. Proving the dead man was drunk was not going to be a problem.

"Well, we got'im to take a field test." He chuckled. "He 'bout fell down twice tryin' to walk the line. He couldn't say his 'ABC's', he couldn't touch his nose, and he couldn't stand on one foot. Anyway, he failed everything, and I put the cuffs on'im. Rhonda – she's the dispatcher – sent a wrecker, and we towed his car. After that, we brought him back to the office. I run a GCI test on'im, and he blew a .17, I think, if I 'member right. So, I put him in jail, in the first cell, closest to the block door."

"He give you any trouble?"

"Not fightin' wise. He just hollered a lot, though; talkin' about how he didn't belong in jail, and he just couldn't go to jail, and how all this wadn't right."

"You figure out why he felt that way?"

"Never did."

"He make a phone call?"

"Nope. We generally don't give'em a call 'til they're sober enough to make some sense with it. Procedure is at least four hours later."

"He ask for one?"

He shook his head and pursed his lips. "Not around me."

"D'ju find out where he'd done his drinkin'?"

"At the Silver Dollar Lounge, down in Prichard," he said.

Edge nodded. "What time'd you stop him?"

"A little after twelve. I was surprised, 'cause it was really slow for a Friday. I mean, I think we had one call right after we come on at ten – a domestic – and after that, things kinda dried up."

Edge wrote. "Okay, so he's in jail, what happened then?"

"Well, we got him in jail shortly after one. Then we went back out, and about one thirty, we get a call from Rhonda tellin' us to come in that somethin's wrong with the plumbin' in his cell. She said water was seepin' out into the hall, comin' from under the cell door. See, she's not s'posed to go through the jail door into the block there, so she couldn't say for sure what exactly was wrong. Anyway, so we come in,

19

and I got the keys from the dispatcher's office and let myself in . . ."

"Was Mr. Howell with you?"

"Yeah. When we got in there, I could see he'd put a bunch'a toilet paper in the commode and stopped it up. The bowl was floodin' and water was runnin' out."

"What'd you do?"

"Well, I wanted to slap'im, but I didn't. I took him out and put him in the middle cell, took the toilet paper away from'im and told him if he had to take a shit, he'd just have to live with a stinky ass until he got out."

Edge smiled. "Was he still hollerin' about not belongin' in jail?"

"Oh, yeah. I asked him, why not? And he just said he had things to do. I told him he was drunk, and if he'd'a killed his self in that car, he'd'a been doin' whatever it was he had to do in the cemetery, six feet under."

"Then, what happened."

"So, I told Rhonda to make a note for the day shift to get somebody out to look at the toilet, and then we went back on the road. I told her that she should check him at two and that I'd be back in to look about him at two thirty. Well, we rode 'til about two twenty, then we come into check on him, and that's when we found him."

"How was he layin'?"

"He was on the floor, face down. What he'd done was to tie two shoestrings together and loop'em around the bunk's bedpost. Then he just set his neck in the loop, and," he snapped his fingers, "that was it."

"You call the medics?"

"Sure. But I knew he was dead when I found'im. He musta done it right after Rhonda checked on him at two. They took him to the hospital, but . . ." He shrugged.

"And he just said, 'I don't belong here,' hunh."

"That's all he said."

"What about the cut over his eye?"

"Oh. Well, whenever I put a prisoner in the back of the patrol car, I always hold their head down so they won't hit it on the door window ledge, but this guy bowed up and threw his head back, and wouldn't let me help him get in. He hit his forehead on the doorpost."

Edge nodded. "By the way, I don't think I asked you his name."

Strange smiled. "George. George 'Boogaloo' Washington; black male; dob: 02-15-54; from Mt Vernon, AL."

"'Boogaloo,' hunh." Edge smiled also.

He dismissed Tom Strange from the break room, and afterward sat and thought about what he'd heard. Boogaloo was drunk. That was it. A drunk was liable to do anything; and what he had going on in his mind about where else he should've been, and what else he should've been doing, went to the grave with him.

Edge didn't perceive that Strange was lying. There were just too many witnesses: the old man, Howell, and Rhonda the dispatcher would both have to be in on the conspiracy. No one gets into the back without a key, and it's a cinch that Rhonda didn't kill Boogaloo by herself.

Heck, he thought, if Washington had lived, when he woke up from his drunk, he would probably have forgotten about all of it anyway. Edge began to see his task as a little hopeless; finding any amount of sense in a gin-soaked mind. He closed his notebook and rubbed his eyes.

Ten minutes later, Edge found Rhonda Blackwell in the Chief's outer office talking with Becky about shopping. She was a pudgy thirty-year-old with a peaches and cream complexion and feathered hair. Edge marveled at her face, one that was completely devoid of any marks; no freckles, lines, or blemishes of any kind. She wore tight jeans and a green, long sleeved, polo shirt.

They repaired to the break room also, and Edge once again took out his notebook. After offering her a soft drink from the machine, he looked at the young woman's blank face.

"No thanks," she said. "I'm watchin' my weight."

"Right," he said. "Rhonda, my name's John Edge. I guess the Chief told you what this is about."

"He just said you wanted to talk to me about that guy that killed his self in jail." Her voice was a soprano, and she made a face.

"Just tell me what happened."

"Well, not much for me to tell, really. Tom and Mr. Howell radioed in that they needed a wrecker and was bringin' in a drunk, or, uh, a DUI. I called the wrecker and then walked across the hall and turned on the GCI machine to let it warm up; 'cause it takes a little time to calibrate. In a little while they got here, and they brought him through the back door." She nodded to the door next to the break room. "When they finished the test they put him in the first cell and left."

"He give'em any trouble?"

"Nope. He was just hollerin' real loud that he didn't belong in jail. He kept goin' on about that even after they left."

"Did he holler for somebody to come talk to him?"

"Yeah, well, I went to the jail door, but I ain't s'posed to go in. I stood there, and he asked me to come in. I asked him what he wanted, but he just said he wanted out, that he didn't belong there."

"What happened next?"

"Well, I checked on him at one thirty, and I could see that there was water runnin' out from under the door, into the drain in the hall in front of the cells. So, I called Tom and Mr. Howell back in, and they went in the cell and found the commode was stuffed with toilet paper."

"Did you go in the cell?"

"No." She shook her head.

"Anything happen while they were in there?"

22

"No." Rhonda Blackwell looked around. "Are you tapin' this?"

Edge shook his head.

"Sometimes, if somebody does somethin' stupid back there they'll slap'em once or twice, but they didn't do that this time."

"How do you know?"

"'Cause I was watchin' through the window; and 'cause I didn't hear nothin'."

"Could they have done it without you seeing?"

She shook her head. "I don't think so."

"What happened next?"

"Well, they put him in another cell, and Tom told me to get the day shift to call somebody to come see about the plumbin'. I checked on him at two, and I could see he was pacin' around in there, like he was real nervous or somethin'. When Tom come in at two thirty, he stopped at the office and got the key and a little bit later he come runnin' out and said call the paramedics."

"How much later?"

"Not more'n a minute or two." She paused. "Then the ambulance come and took him, but . . ." she shrugged, "well, he looked dead to me."

"You ever see a dead body before?"

"Just my granny." She made another face.

Edge dismissed Blackwell and got the day shift dispatcher to show him the jail. It turned out to be three identical eight by twelve foot cells each furnished with a metal bunk and a stainless steel commode. Each toilet had a sink built in, above the toilet tank. There was a shiny piece of aluminum affixed to the wall above the sink that served as a mirror.

Edge walked inside the middle cell and took a look at the bunk. It sat no more than a foot off the concrete floor and was bolted to the cinderblock wall. Inside the first cell, he could see what looked like two full rolls of toilet paper stuffed into the bowl.

After the tour, Edge got himself a soda out of the break room and went back to Strange's office. Becky said the Chief was out but would be back in a minute. She told Edge to go ahead and wait in the inner office if he wanted. Edge went inside and sat down in the same naugehyde chair as before. Becky left the office door open.

In ten minutes Strange returned. He shut the door and took his place behind the desk.

"Man, I gotta ragin' case'a di'rear. I been runnin' all mornin'." He paused and licked his lips. "Well, what'cha think?"

Edge took a deep breath and exhaled. He didn't know if what he was about to tell Strange was the truth, but he had tried to put himself in Washington's mind and come up with a reason for what the drunk man had done, and what followed was the best he could do.

"Honestly, and this is purely conjecture on my part, but I think this was an accidental death. I think the man was trying to escape."

Strange's brows went up. "How so?"

"Well, this guy, 'Boogaloo,' comes in agitated. He's not fighting, but he lets everybody know that he don't belong in jail. For some reason, probably a good one in his own mind, he doesn't want to be in jail, and he doesn't think he belongs here. He doesn't fight about it, but he's clearly upset. He even tried to get the dispatcher to come in and talk to him about it." He paused. "That thing with the toilet paper, that was just to get somebody to open the cell door. He probably thought the woman, uh, Rhonda, would do it, so he could get the jump on her; but when the *officers* came in to check out the plumbing, he lost his opportunity.

"When they moved him to a new cell, he had to have another way, a more serious reason to get'em to open the door so he could make a break for it. The only way was to make'em think he was tryin' to kill his self. That way he could run past'em out the jail door; or, maybe even get away from the medics in the ambulance.

"So, he takes out his shoe laces, makes a loop over the bedpost, and sets his neck inside. He was sure the girl would check on him then. But he probably thought it would be sooner than it actually was."

Edge paused. Strange was enthralled.

"He put his neck in the loop. There was pressure, but he thought he could raise himself up before he passed out; that is, if he thought about it at all." He paused. "He was out before he knew it. It only takes a few pounds of pressure on the carotids to get'chu to you to pass out – you know, like with a sleeper hold; and thirty seconds later, he was too out of it to wake up. In three minutes he was dead." He paused. "He just didn't think he belonged in jail, and he wanted to make a break for it."

Strange shook his head. "I'll be a son of a bitch."

Edge smiled. "That what you were looking for?"

Strange smiled and nodded. "Sure is; and in record time, too." He reached into his lap drawer and pulled out a check book.

"Will five hundred be enough?"

"That's very generous."

"Believe me it's worth it." He started writing the check. "Now, I'll have something to tell those know it alls when they ask how this could happen. I can tell'em it was all just one big, unfortunate accident."

"And that'll get'em off your back?"

"More so than if I couldn't tell'em anything."

"Well, the key was that toilet paper. That was just to get the woman in there with him so he could jump her and run off."

Strange pointed his pen at Edge. "*That* is a very good point."

Edge sat back and watched while Strange finished the draft. He almost felt guilty. It seemed too easy, but really, there was no other explanation that would hold water. Boogaloo's family would never countenance a suicide theory; no one ever believes that a family member wants to kill their self. 'Attempted escape by diversion' was the only other plausible conclusion. Edge shut his eyes and waited.

The noise they heard coming from the outer office wasn't sustained, but it was loud. They both looked up when they heard what sounded like a man yelling, out in the lobby. Edge turned around in his chair.

"I've got to see the Chief, I tell ya! I need help. He's gotta help me!"

The words were muffled but audible. Strange shook his head.

"Who's that?" Edge said.

"Aw, that's Otha Harbin," he said as he rounded his desk and walked to the door.

In the outer office, Becky was on her feet and backing away from the reception window, a nervous look on her face. Strange walked over and opened the magnetic door. A disheveled man wearing dirty jeans and a long sleeved plaid shirt was standing in the front hall, directly in front of the three by three glass window.

"Here, now. Shut your mouth, Otha." Strange said angrily. "What do you want?"

"I gotta talk to you, Tom. Have you been readin' what they're sayin' about ma boy?" He was on the verge of tears.

"Otha, I told you that's the Sheriff's case. I can't help ya. Now, get outta here 'fore I put you in jail."

"Please, Tom. I've known you for years. Ain't there somethin' you can do?"

Strange said nothing for half a minute. He snorted and nodded toward his office door.

"Come on in."

The two walked past Becky and into the big office. Strange took his place in his chair, and the man called Otha Harbin stood up next to the corner of his desk.

Strange looked at Edge. "Otha's boy was murdered about a month ago; out in Grand Bay. That's about as far from Tangerine as you can get in this county." He looked down and finished signing the check.

"Please, Tom."

Edge could see a tear in the corner of the man's eye. Clearly, he was in pain.

"You hear about his case?" Strange said to Edge as he handed him the check.

Edge frowned as he took the note. "You know, I think I did. A boy and a girl shot in a car?"

"That's . . ."

Strange stopped in the middle of his thought and held up his hand. He looked up at Harbin.

"Otha, have a seat. I think I've found just the man that can help you with your son's case."

Chapter 3

It was the next day when Edge met Otha Harbin in his office, a sixteen by twenty foot space at the rear of Attenborough, Lawson, and Associates, LLC, on Congress Street in downtown Mobile. Edge was behind his desk, and his newest client was in a wooden chair in front of him.

Harbin was gaunt but wiry. Edge pegged him at forty or forty-five, with thinning brown hair sprinkled with a few flecks of gray. He was in a clean, albeit wrinkled, white shirt and tan Dickeys work pants; and though the boots he wore, lace up work boots, were not clean, they did have most of the dirt knocked off of them.

He was the picture of a man in the throes of a terrible, month-long sausage grinder, with no end in sight; by that it is meant that his eyes were red rimmed, with dark circles underneath, and he was perpetually on the verge of tears. His blank, beaten face had about a five day growth of beard, and he continually wrung his hands and then wiped his face as he leaned forward in his chair.

"How can I help you, Mr. Harbin?"

"Well, you told Tom yesterday that you'd heard'a my boy Ty's case. He was shot out in Grand Bay, at the exit ramp at Grand Bay-Wilmer Road." He paused as a sob crept into his throat. "He was shot in the head." He paused again. "Slaughtered. Shot down like a dog."

The terms he used to describe the death of his son sounded as if they were designed to elicit from his own self, more than from his audience, an emotional response; as if he was trying to make himself cry. Crying would impress Edge, and let him know how much he loved the boy. Then again, perhaps Harbin was using his emotions to punish himself for something that he felt he had done to cause his son's death. Edge couldn't tell which.

"Wasn't there a girl with him?"

"Yeah, uh, his girlfriend, uh, Carla. They was s'posed to be goin' to the football game out there. They found'em on Saturday mornin' on the ramp headin' back to'ards town." He stopped and looked away, fighting back tears.

Edge said nothing for a minute. Then:

"I'm sorry for your loss."

Harbin nodded. "They was just two kids. I don't even know . . . I never got to say . . ." He bowed his head.

Edge nodded. He'd seen grief like this before. Oftentimes, survivors try to work themselves into as much of an emotional state as they can. Some are trying to get it all out as soon as possible so they can get on with their lives. Others are in love with the pain and want to make it as intense as it can potentially be, and last as long as it can. Edge believed that kind of masochism bordered on the pathological. He didn't know what to say, so he said nothing.

"I been to see the DA; and Tom, you know about that; and the Sheriff, too. The Sheriff says that his people is workin' 'round the clock' to solve the case, but . . . ."

"I understand."

"His mama's 'bout to die. I think she's gonna have a nervous breakdown. I been runnin' 'round here and ever'where, tryin' to find out what happened, to see if anybody knows somethin', but I just can't find out nothin'."

"Do you know who shot your son, Mr. Harbin?"

"That's just the thang. I got no idea. He was a good boy; he didn't have no enemies. I mean, he was goin' into the Marines, for heaven's sake."

"Was he in high school?"

Harbin shook his head. "No. He finished two years ago. He works over at the syrup plant in Chickasaw."

"How old was he?"

"Twenty-two."

"Was his girlfriend still in high school?"

"Yeah. She goes to North Mobile County High. She's in the twelfth grade, I thank."

"Was that something they normally did? Go to high school football games, I mean?"

"Well, no, not usu'lly. She wanted to go 'cause it was the first game of the season, of her senior year, and all. He told her he'd take her. I told Ty to get her home 'fore too late. He asked me what time, and I said, well, whatever time her daddy says, but, since she's in school, I thought about eleven."

"When he didn't get home, did you call and report him missing?"

"I called the Sheriff's Department on early Saturday mornin', but they told me he had to be gone twenty four hours 'fore they could take a report."

Edge nodded. When he spoke, he spoke slowly.

"What do you want me to do, Mr. Harbin?"

"I wanna hire you. Tom says you're real good at what'cha do, and, well, I got some money. I got two thousand dollars saved. I was gonna buy a new truck; and I just sold my

29

lawn mower. I done talked to Carla's daddy, and he says he'll help out."

"Mr. Harbin, I think you know I can't get involved in this case for a couple of very good reasons; the first being that the Sheriff might throw me in jail if I do." He paused. "I mean, as long as the case is active, they'll . . ."

"But, they're sayin' all these things about ma boy."

"Who?"

"The paper; the 'tectives."

"What things?"

"That he was killed over drugs." He set his mouth in a determined line. "My boy don't take no drugs. And they said he was messin' with a gang. Let me tell you, Mr. Edge, my boy don't use dope, and he wadn't in no gang, neither." He paused. "They're makin' out like this is just another dope killin', and that ain't so. My boy was a good boy, you can ask his mama. He was goin' into the Marines. Would he be usin' dope if he was goin' in the service? They wouldn't let'im in."

He was right. They wouldn't take him if he turned in a tainted urinalysis. But that didn't mean he wasn't into anything else that could hang him up, Edge thought.

"I know they ain't puttin' nothin' into findin' out who killed my boy." He gritted his teeth. "It just makes me so mad."

Edge exhaled deeply and looked away. He didn't want to get on the bad side of the Sheriff, but, he could always use another two grand. He thought about who he knew at the Metro Sheriff's Department and whether or not they would mind him looking into this case. Until he found someone, discretion would be the watchword.

"Okay, Mr. Harbin. I'll make a couple of calls, on two conditions."

"Anything."

"Leave Tom Strange alone. He can't help you. If he does, his name'll be mud with the Sheriff, and he'll never get anything else from him, ever again."

"Sure, sure, okay; no problem. Fine. I ain't never heard'a the man."

"The second thing is, you don't tell nobody, and I mean nobody, about me and what I'm doing – not even your wife. It gets around that I'm asking questions then I'm off the case, you understand?" He paused. "I'll call you and let'cha know if I find out anything, but until then, you ain't never heard *my* name either. Got it?"

"Sure, sure." Harbin reached into his front pants pocket and pulled out a roll of twenties. "How much?"

Edge looked at the money. "Just five hundred to get me started. I'll let you know if I need more."

Harbin peeled off five twenties, a couple of fifties, and three, crisp hundred dollar bills and handed them to Edge.

"Please. Please help me," he said. Edge could tell he was still on the verge of tears.

"I'll do what I can. In the meantime, I'm tellin' you. Don't say anything to anybody." He paused as he put the money into his own pocket. "Now, tell me about your boy."

Two hours later, Edge knew everything that Otha Harbin wanted to tell him about Tyrone Lester Harbin, twenty-two years of age, a loading dock operator at the Mapletree Syrup Plant on Telegraph Road, in Chickasaw, Alabama.

Tyrone graduated from North Mobile County High in Saraland; though he was not a particularly bright student. He played JV football and freshman basketball and liked English, his father said. He had been left back in the first and second grades, not mature enough, according to his first grade teacher; and that was why he was twenty-two and only two years out of school.

He'd gotten the job at the syrup plant through the state unemployment service. Ty Harbin, according to his father, had never been late to work, had never been in any fights with any other employees, and had never used a sick day.

Ty knew Carla Morgan from school. They were in a History class when she was a freshman and he was a senior, and they had somehow hit it off. Harbin had made a 'D' in the course, but he and Morgan had been dating off and on ever since. It seemed to Edge to be an odd match. Harbin said that Morgan and her family were upper class; that they owned several hundred acres off Celeste Road in Mobile County. But by all that Edge could determine, the Harbins were, in the recessive economy of the times, just barely making ends meet.

According to Otha, Ty Harbin had plans to join the Marines, and had even taken the physical. His goal was to make himself eligible for the new Montgomery GI Bill of Rights so as to further his education. With that idea in mind, he began to see Carla Morgan steadily, and the two were talking about marriage.

That's never gonna happen, Edge thought. If Morgan's family had what Harbin said they had, there was no way they were gonna let her marry down, into a family like Harbin's. In fact, her parents probably had done what they could to bust the two of them up. They might even blame him for getting their daughter killed.

Edge ended the interview by getting from Otha a list of friends and acquaintances of his son.

"But, who was his *best* friend?" Edge said.

Harbin looked away. "I guess that'd have to be Timmy, Timmy Hankins. He grew up down the road from us, back when we lived in Creola. Him and Ty went through school together and hung out a lot, up until I moved us down to Chickasaw, that is." He paused. "I guess Timmy'd know him better'n anybody." He supplied the name of the trailer park and the lot number where Hankins lived.

"Okay, I'll start there," Edge said. "But remember, you keep your mouth shut." He shook his finger at the man.

"I will. I really will."

Edge looked at him thinking that he may already be talking to the front page of the local newspaper.

Chapter 4

Edge found the Shady Acres Trailer Park on Salco Road off Highway 43, just north of Creola, Alabama, at eight thirty the next morning. It was a rundown community of about twenty-five mobile homes of varying degrees of repair on either side of a narrow, dirt drive. Shade trees overcast the lots and made for a cool atmosphere on that humid and warmer than average October morning.

Lot eleven was about two thirds of the way down on the left side. Edge parked the Impala out front, on the shoulder of the road. There was a makeshift clothesline – an insulated wire strung between two oaks – in the side yard next to a seventy-two foot, single wide mobile home. A half a dozen shirts and several pairs of undergarments were flapping in the breeze. The trailer was white, but moldy, and the shutters were green.

Standing at the door and listening, Edge could hear a television playing – the *Price Is Right* – and a dog barking. He knocked three times.

Heavy feet lumbered to the door, and in seconds it swung out. Edge stepped down to the bottom concrete block that served as a step and looked up as a round woman with flyaway hair and a tattered housedress peered down at him.

"Hey. Timmy Hankins here?" Edge said.

"Who wants to know?" The woman's voice was tired and phlegm throttled.

"A friend'a Ty Harbin's."

"You don't look like no friend'a Ty's. 'Sides, he's dead."

"Is he here?" Edge said in an exasperated tone.

The woman looked him up and down. She turned away from the door.

"Timmy!"

33

In a minute the woman backed away and a tall, gangly male stood in the threshold. The woman looked out from around him.

"Yeah?" the boy said.

"You Timmy Hankins?"

"Yeah."

"My name's Edge. I'd like to talk to you about Ty Harbin."

Hankins looked him up and down. "You the law?"

"Nope. Private." He held up his state-issued credentials. "Can we talk?"

The boy leaned in and looked at the leather case. "Yeah, I guess. You wanna come in?"

Edge looked around. "I was thinkin' about maybe gettin' some breakfast."

"You buyin'?"

Edge nodded and smiled. "Sure."

"Well, fuck, yeah. Let's go."

Without hesitation the boy bounded off the steps and toward the Impala at a trot.

"Bring me somethin'," the woman yelled behind him.

Twenty minutes later they were at the Waffle Hut on Highway 43, in Tangerine. Edge chose the corner booth, in front, next to the picture window. He sat with his back to the wall and took the measure of Hankins.

Though he was thin, almost emaciated, and his t-shirt and jeans hung on him, his hands and feet were huge and his bones thick. He had dark circles under his eyes, his jaws were sunken, and his pock marked face framed a mouth full of badly deteriorated teeth. From the looks of him, Edge guessed that he was grossly malnourished. No wonder he was so eager to leave home with a complete stranger just on the promise of a meal, he thought.

The waitress came and Hankins ordered the lumberjack special: three eggs sunny side up, rib eye steak,

34

bacon, biscuits, grits, orange juice, a glass of milk, coffee, and a sweet roll. Edge ordered coffee and a glass of water.

"You a real PI?" Hankins said after he had drained half of the water glass.

"Yeah."

He smiled and looked away. "Man, I'd love to have that job. I'd knock the shit outta all them dudes."

"What dudes?"

"You know, dudes I don't like."

Edge chuckled. "Well, it ain't quite that simple."

"I seen it on TV."

"You gotta TV?"

"Yeah. Me an' Mama got a portable that sits in the livin' room. She got it when the folks that was livin' nexta us moved out. They left it out by the dumpster."

I bet they just barely have electricity, Edge thought. "Well, good. That's good."

The waitress brought the drinks, and Edge creamed his coffee heavily. Hankins turned the milk up and drank it without a breath. When he was finished, he wiped his mouth on his forearm.

Edge looked at him. "Get some more, if you want."

Hankins turned around and looked toward the waitress. He held his glass high.

"So, Timmy. How long have you known Ty Harbin?"

He put down the glass. "You know he's dead, right?"

"I know. You know who killed him?"

He shook his head. "No. Ty was a pretty good ole dude. I don't know nobody that was put out with'im. He was gonna join the Marines."

"So, I've heard. How long did you know him?"

"Since grade school. Me'n Mama moved here when I was in third grade; after Daddy run off."

"Tell me about him?"

He shrugged. "Well, there ain't much to tell. We went up through school together. We had gym together every year;

really, we had most all our classes together. I guess it was 'cause our names both started with a 'H'."

"How'd he do? In school, I mean."

"You mean grades? Well, we wadn't no geniuses, but we got by; 'Cs' and 'Ds', mostly. I think he flunked math and had to go to summer school one year."

"Ty drink?"

"Well, yeah. He'd sneak a beer ever' now and then. His mama didn't like it, so he kep' it hid."

The waitress brought the food, and another glass of milk, after which Hankins dug in. He ate like a hyena as he tore into the steak, which he stabbed with a fork and ate from the outside in.

"Drugs?"

He shook his head and talked with his mouth full.

"No, well, not to use. He was tryin' to get into the Marines. But . . ."

"He sold."

"Just some weed, ever' now and then. He's gotta place back off in the woods near where he lives, that he grows it. Just a few stalks, not what you'd call a major operation."

"Why'd he get into that?"

"I don't know. I guess, mostly, it was to pay for that girl he was seein'."

"You ever meet her?"

He shook his head as he took a big bite of biscuit. "Once. He didn't usu'lly bring her around me. He told me her and her people had money, so he kep' her away from all'a us. He sold weed so that he could keep that car runnin', and have money to feed her and take her to the movies."

"What kinda car did he have?"

"It was a four door Buick; a '73 LeSabre. It's got a cassette player and some real good speakers."

"Was that what he was drivin' when he was killed?"

"I guess so. He took good care'a that car. It looked real nice."

"Think anybody'd kill him for it?"

36

"I don't know." He paused and frowned. "No, I don't think so. I mean, kill for a car? That sucker was twelve years old."

"He ever go to bars? Hang out? Get in fights, maybe?"

"Nah. Ty was a real calm dude. He never went to bars. He was too afraid that girl's mama and daddy'd run him off if they found out he was a carouser. He said he wanted to marry her."

"How about in high school?"

"No. He was calm then, too, 'specially after the accident."

"What accident?"

"The huntin' accident."

Edge raised his brows. "Tell me about it."

Hankins emptied his mouth and took a swig of milk. "Ty had this friend, see; Terry, uh, Terry Sawyer, from down in Chickasaw. They hung out 'cause he had a lotta classes with Ty, just like me. Terry liked to hunt, so he was always talkin' to Ty about Ty comin' with him to his daddy's huntin' camp up in Clarke County. So, one day, Ty went with him."

"Terry's people have money, too?"

"They do alright, I guess. His daddy owns some kinda business."

"When was this that they went huntin'?"

"Seven or eight years ago, I think. I know it was right 'fore Christmas."

"What happened?"

"Well, the way I heard it from Ty was that they had set up and spent all day in a shootin' house, but they didn't see shit. So, 'bout three o'clock Terry says, 'hey, let's go over the hill and down to the creek and see if we can spot somethin' movin'".

"So, Ty said when they got up to the crest, they heard somethin' in the brush, so they split up, and Terry went down to the creek and left Ty up on the hill, so's Terry could run the deer to'ards him. Well, Ty saw somethin' runnin' through the

37

woods, and, you know, he just got excited and lost his head."
He paused. "It warn't no deer. It was Terry. What is it they
call it, 'buck fever'? He gotta case'a that."

"He killed him?"

"Graveyard dead."

"How'd Terry's family take it?"

"Well, it's been six or seven years, so, I mean, I guess
they got over it; all 'cept his daddy. I heard he ain't never
really put it behind him. Last thing I heard was he was still
pretty stoked about it."

"Where's that comin' from?"

"You know, just talk. I hear things." He paused.
"Anyway, Ty wadn't the same after that. He was kinda quiet
and never mixed with too many people. He quit football and
just used'a keep to his self."

Edge nodded. He was thankful that at least one lead
had come out of this ten dollar breakfast.

"How about this girl? Ty say anything about her
daddy not likin' him? Maybe wished she'd see another boy?"

"Ty said her mama and daddy didn't like him at first,
but he thought they was warmin' up to him." He paused. "He
did say somethin' about some dude at North Mobile that he
thought was tryin' to move in on her; said he played football.
Ty said he thought he was gonna have to kick the boy's ass."

"That ever materialize?"

"Not that I know of.

"When was all this goin' on?"

"It was kinda recent, I think. Anyway, I heard the boy
was a big dude; played tackle or somethin', and he takes
steroids, too. He might'a been hard for Ty to handle." He
paused and took a drink. "You know, this chick's at school all
day, and Ty's up at the syrup factory; and you know how
women are, always flirtin' around tryin' to get somebody's
attention."

Edge smiled. Pretty insightful thinking, he thought.
Edge asked, but Hankins didn't know the football player's
name.

"Was she and Ty gettin' it on? I mean, she wadn't pregnant, was she?"

Hankins chewed and thought. "Well, yeah, they was fuckin', but, I don't think so. Ty said they was careful."

"What about his supplier? A few stalks wouldn't keep his business goin' for long. Did he get product from somebody else?"

"Once or twice, I think he bought from a black guy in Mobile Terrace. His name was, uh, uh, Mule Head, I think."

"Mule Head? You know anything else about him? His real name?"

"Nope."

Edge exhaled. "How come you never got in the weed business?"

"Me? I don't wanna go to jail. It'd be just my luck I'd sell to a narc."

Edge nodded. "You work?"

"Yeah, well when I can get a ride into Mobile, I work down at The Met, in Springdale."

Edge knew the place. It was a former disco and party club located inside one of the city's two shopping malls. He'd heard it was about to go out of business.

"What do you do there?"

"On Saturday and Sunday mornin's I come in an' clean up; you know, after the night before. You find a lotta interestin' shit when you're cleanin' up."

"Yeah? Like what?"

"Like money, mostly. When the people are fuckin' in the back rooms, a lotta times money falls outta their pockets."

"Oh, yeah?"

"Yeah. And I find keys, and drivers licenses, and, once, even a passport."

Edge chuckled and smiled. "Okay. So, was there anything else goin' on in Ty's life? Maybe some deal gone bad? Somethin' like that?"

Hankins shook his head. "Not that I know of. I'll think on it."

"Okay." He looked at Hankins' empty plate. "You full?"

He smacked his lips. "I could eat a piece'a pie."

"How come you're so hungry?"

He shrugged. "Food stamps don't go real far."

Edge smiled and called the waitress over. "Okay," he told Hankins. "Order a piece'a pie." He paused. "Oh, and get somethin' for your mama, too."

Chapter 5

Edge spent the rest of the morning at his office with his feet up, thinking. He believed he had Tyrone Harbin pegged and could guess what was going on in his world

Harbin was a climber. He had taken a look at his own family and the life into which he had been born, and how he'd been raised, and realized that it was not the life for him. The rich girl, the wealthy hunting buddy, the Marines, even the marijuana side hustle were all designed to get Harbin up in the world – up and out of Chickasaw, Alabama.

That was *his* motivation. Now, Edge thought, to find out who wanted to stand in his way; who wanted to stop him from his upward mobility. There were people coming in and out of his life on a regular basis, and Edge didn't think he'd have too much trouble locating and talking to them.

At least he had a few places to start. This football player who was moving in on Harbin's girl was intriguing; especially the fact that he might well be using anabolic steroids. Edge had heard about something new called, "roid rage,' a syndrome that inclined a user to easily lose control of his temper and become prone to fits of violence. A football player, large, strong, and willing to mix it up anyway, who was under the influence of the drug, could reasonably be expected to fall victim to the effects of it. Still, killing Harbin, and the girl? With a gun? This murder, depending on the scene, sounded a bit more adult than some high school kid with a bad temper and a crush on a girl. It sounded like a hit.

Edge knew that at some point he would have to notify the Metro Sheriff's Department and their politically pragmatic chief executive that he was looking into the case; if for no other reason than to keep his license safe and his livelihood secure. He sat at his desk and tried to think of someone over there with whom he could talk honestly.

The only name that came to mind was Nathan Randall, a lieutenant in the criminal investigation division. Edge had the opportunity to interact with Randall on at least one occasion that he could recall: the death of a baby found in a creek in the western part of the county. A high school girl had given birth in a vacant trailer nearby, and the baby's father had immediately taken the child from her and drowned him. Edge had worked for the parents of the girl in an effort to keep her out of jail. His contribution consisted mostly of telling her to get a lawyer and to keep her mouth shut.

Maybe he could talk Randall into a look at the file, and, more importantly, the photos, so he could at least know what he was looking for. He was ready to trade the least promising of his leads – the one involving Carla Morgan's father – for some help. Edge decided that he would work until the five hundred ran out and then have another talk with Otha Harbin.

That afternoon, at about two, Edge parked on Church Street, on the south side of the county courthouse near the parking lot that backed up to the entrance to the George C. Wallace Twin Tunnels. He stepped out of the car and into seventy degree weather and walked across the street toward the Metro Sheriff's Department.

Edge found the second in command of the Department's Detective Division in a small office off the left side of the only hall, about halfway down, next to the Records room. Edge stood at the threshold and knocked.

Nathan Randall was an average-looking man with short, brown hair and wire rimmed glasses. His rosy cheeks and round face, as well as his puffy midriff, gave him the look of a well-fed cupid. He was dressed in a white shirt and dark slacks held up by multi-colored suspenders.

"Have a seat, Mr. Edge. I haven't seen you in a while," Randall said. His voice was calm and precise.

"I think it was that dead baby case out west."

"Right, right. You worked for the girl's family, didn't you?"

"Well, I wouldn't exactly call it work. I just told her to shut up until her lawyer got there."

"Well, you did a good job. She kept her mouth closed long enough to cut a deal. The boy went away for a while, but the girl stayed outta jail."

"Well, seems only fair." Edge smiled. "She did do most of the heavy lifting – the pregnancy, I mean. She deserved some consideration for that." He paused. "At any rate, I hope that case didn't leave you with a bad taste in your mouth – about me, I mean."

"Oh, nooooo. Live and let live, I always say. No jury was gonna convict her anyway; after her layin' there and givin' birth." He shook his head. "There was no way she was gonna do any time. We got all we could get, which was probation." Randall smiled. "Now, sit down and tell me, what can I do for you?"

Edge took a seat in a wooden chair and settled in. "Well, it's like this. I've been asked by the family of Tyrone Harbin to take a look at his case. His daddy's got some silly notion in his head that the Sheriff isn't doing enough to get this thing put together." Edge paused and smiled. "I don't know where he could'a got a darn fool idea like that. I told him he was crazy, that you folks were doin' all you could, but he just wouldn't take my word for it." He paused. "You know, some people just can't be reasoned with."

"I see."

42

Randall sat back in his chair with an amused look on his face. He paused to choose his words carefully. Knowing that what he said might get back to Otha Harbin, and ultimately to the newspaper, he wanted to be circumspect. It would be election time soon, and though the Sheriff was thought to be a shoo-in, any negative publicity would not be welcome.

"You know, John. Can I call you John? I'm actually glad that Harbin's got you working for him. He was down here every other day, raising all kinds'a sand and showing his grief – and his ass. Honestly, he was getting to be a nuisance. Hiring you is actually a good thing. At least with you on the payroll, he'll think he's doing something." He paused. "You know, these cases can sometimes take years to break. I'm sure that Harbin doesn't have the patience to wait that long. He'll drive himself crazy – and us too – obsessing over it."

In a roundabout way, Randall had just given Edge his blessing to investigate the case also. Edge saw it as a major hurdle out of the way.

"See, now, I knew we could help each other," Edge said.

"Well, 'help' is a complicated term. What'd you have in mind?"

Edge smiled. "I get a look at the file, or at least the scene photos, and in return, I go about my business and keep Harbin off your back."

"What about leads? T.T.'s not just gonna let me turn the file over to you, without anything in return."

Thomas Talmadge 'T.T.' Lawrence was the Sheriff of Mobile County. He was a 1960's era, University of Alabama football offensive tackle that hurt his knee in his junior year and had to quit the team. But he finished his degree in Physical Education, and after he did, he came home to Mobile and opened a grocery store, 'The Food Dynasty,' which had expanded into a chain with six locations. He was six foot six, he weighed almost two hundred and seventy five pounds, and though the hair on his head was still thick and full, and his arms and shoulders looked as if he could still move a linebacker, he was beginning to show his age; by that it is meant that his mane had tinges of gray in it, and the crow's feet at the corners of eyes were becoming much more pronounced.

Then, ten years ago, with no law enforcement experience whatsoever, Lawrence used the notoriety of his athletic career and his grocery chain as a springboard to election for sheriff, defeating, without a runoff, a half dozen challengers in the Democrat primary.

Lawrence won on a platform of trying to bring business principles to bear at his office. Among his new ideas was a system called ProClient. He paid twenty-five thousand dollars to purchase the plan, which was designed to encourage deputies to start dealing with complainants as 'clients' rather than victims or witnesses. He wanted his employees to 'sell' residents on accepting advice and counsel rather than results, i.e., placation rather than resolution; by convincing them that just by showing up and listening, the Sheriff was meeting his obligations, and their needs. That way the people would not expect arrests, which, most of the time, didn't happen anyway, and would instead be satisfied with attention and good will. It was all designed to give people a more palatable product that they could live with, and to give the Sheriff a better chance at re-election.

"What about'em?" Edge said.

"If you get anything that could be of help to us, I know that the Sheriff would certainly want to know about it."

"I'll be happy to pass along to you anything that I feel is relevant to the case."

Randall smiled and shook his head. "Well, that sounds good, but, I think you know that it'll have to be a little more than just what you think is 'relevant.'" He paused and smiled. "T.T. would never forgive me if you put this thing together before us." He paused again. "Consider this: you get a look at the photos, and in return you take on one of my deputies as a partner, who'll, of course, keep me informed of your progress."

"A spy?"

"Oh, no. Not a spy; kind of an intermediary to facilitate information sharing. She would let you know what's going with our end of the investigation, and, of course, she would inform us on how things are going with you."

"She?"

"Right." He paused. "And, if, or when, you come up with something, and it should happen to make the press, then the presence of a female will demonstrate to his constituents the Sheriff's commitment to diversity."

Edge smirked. "I don't know. I prefer to work alone. Besides, people that work with me don't always come out smellin' like a rose," he said remembering the Wyatt case.

"Oh, don't worry about that. The young woman I've got in mind can handle herself, reasonably well. I'm thinking of a couple of people, actually." He cleared his throat. "Well, that's the deal," he said matter of factly. "Take it or leave it. Otherwise, you'll be on your own, and if you get in the way, well . . . ." He shrugged.

Edge looked away and snorted. This case, two kids – one, a rich, teenaged female – was too high profile and too intriguing to pass up.

"I can't very well say, no, now can I. Not with a threat like that attached to it."

Randall smiled. "Great. I knew you'd see it my way. Just give me a couple'a days, and I'll call you and let you know who you'll be working with."

Edge nodded. He'd been a party to these arranged marriages in the past. Sometimes they went well, sometimes they didn't.

"Okay. But in the meantime, can I at least talk to the first deputy on scene out there?"

Randall thought for a minute. "I don't guess that'd do any harm. Her name's Amy Austin."

"Her? You guys are just overrun with females around here."

"We've got one on every patrol shift and three in the Detective Division." He paused. "T.T.'s trying to, you know, broaden the department, if you'll pardon the expression. It's supposed to make the people that call us feel better in the midst of their calamity."

"How stylish."

"Yeah, well, Austin's one that doesn't really fit the Sheriff's mold. She's turning out to be a real police officer. Right now, she's in hot water."

"What for?"

He smiled. "You'll get a kick outta this. She picked up a guy for drunk down on Dauphin Island, and, according to her statement, he was giving her a lotta lip on the way to jail. Well, she got about halfway up Rangeline Road and decided that she'd had enough. She *says* she had to brake to avoid a dog in the road. You can guess what happened."

"The drunk ate a faceful'a cage." Edge was talking about the metal partition between the front and backseats of the patrol car.

"Right. She had to make a stop by the hospital before she could get him on docket."

"Sounds like my kinda woman."

"T.T. wasn't too happy. He's got her on a twenty-nine day suspension."

"What then?"

"I don't know; maybe a trial board." He paused and pursed his lips. "He might even try to fire her. She doesn't really fit his idea of a 'ProClient' deputy."

Edge nodded. She sounded to him like she might be the only female around the department that might know what she was doing.

"Anyway," Randall said, "I'll call her and tell'er you wanna see her. Then I'll call you in a couple'a days and set you up with a partner. In the meantime, you can meet me out at the substation tomorrow morning. I'll have the file." He paused. "Oh, and by the way. I know that you've got something on this thing already, so," he waved his hand in that give it to me motion, spill."

Edge smiled. "Well, the only thing I've been able to find out is that the girl's father didn't really cotton to the idea of her marryin' a poor boy from Chickasaw. Have you checked him out yet?"

"Kenneth Morgan? I don't think . . ."

"Just see what kinda work he does. If it's something that has to do with a union, or anyone that could otherwise be called the 'criminal element,' well, those kinds of shady characters might be worth lookin' at."

Edge started out thinking the lead didn't mean that much, but as he recited it to Randall, it began to sound more and more viable. He wondered if he should have kept it to himself.

Kenneth Morgan certainly wouldn't have offed his own daughter just to get rid of an unwanted suitor; but mistakes do happen, and whoever he hired to do the job might've gone too far. Edge made up his mind not to *totally* abandon the idea.

"Okay," said Randall. "Just tell Harbin to go through you if he has any more questions about the case; you'll be kinda like a liaison, you know?"

Edge nodded and smiled. "A liaison, hunh. Sounds very diplomatic; too diplomatic for a man whose son has just been murdered."

Chapter 6

At about four that afternoon, Edge was standing in a second floor hall on the north side of the Airmont Apartments on Bel

Air Boulevard, a two hundred and fifty unit complex located across the street from the city's largest shopping mall.

Airmont wasn't the nicest community in town, but it was close. The buildings were recently constructed, the grounds were immaculate, and it was located in an area convenient to shopping and business.

The carpeted hall had a peculiar odor to it; as if someone had just recently come along and hosed the place down with deodorizer. It wasn't the worse thing Edge had ever smelled, it was just out of the ordinary. Looking around, he noticed cheap paintings on the walls and hanging lights about every fifty feet, giving the place a bit of a downtown hotel feel, rather than the suburban apartment complex that it was. Edge found Amy Austin's door about halfway down on the north side.

The person that answered Edge's firm knock appeared as if she had just gotten up. She smelled of beer, and she leaned against the door frame to keep herself from swaying. Edge looked at her with amusement.

"You Amy Austin?"

"Yeah. You Edge?"

"Yeah." He looked past her. "You gotta few minutes?"

"Sure. Why not. I ain't got nowhere else to be."

Austin stood aside, bowed, and waved her arm in mock welcome. Edge walked past the young woman, who was wearing only an oversized man's dress shirt. He looked down and admired her sturdy, tanned legs.

"Just sit down anywhere," she mumbled. "You wanna beer?"

"No, thanks," he said as he parked in an obviously expensive club chair. Austin walked toward the kitchen.

In fact, as he regarded the room, he could tell that all the appointments appeared to be high quality; from the leather chairs, to the sterling silver wall hangings, to the mahogany entertainment center that featured a large television with what looked like some type of gaming device attached to it. In addition, there was a component stereo system behind glass in a rolling cabinet, over against the wall near a north side window.

Austin returned with a Miller High Life, and a napkin, and sat down on a leather couch. She popped the top on the pony-sized bottle and took a long pull.

"Nice place you got here," Edge said. "Been here long?"

"Just since I came to town." She took another swig.

"Classy," he said as he looked around the room then back at her.

"Don't be too impressed. Daddy bought most of it." She herself paused and looked around. "I guess I'll have to give it up if I . . ." There was a sob on the end of her words.

Edge thought for a minute. "Oh. You mean that drunk thing? Na, don't worry about that. You'll beat it. From what I know about the Sheriff, he won't get rid'a you. He'll keep you around – for looks if nothing else. You might be workin' in the jail, but you'll be around. A lotta guys have done a lot worse."

Edge spoke with an eye on encouraging her. She didn't look encouraged.

He looked around the room again. "What's that thing over there?"

"What?" she said.

"That console attached to the TV."

"Oh, that's somethin' new. It's a game, uh, Pong, they call it. Kinda like table tennis, 'cept on a TV screen."

Edge smirked. "What will they think of next."

He looked at the young woman and noted how that when she was cleaned up, she was probably a knockout. Austin was in her early twenties; a shade over five feet tall, with full breasts, a flat middle, and muscled legs. She had dark brown, Pixie-cut hair over brown eyes, and dark brows and lashes. She sat with her legs tucked under her, the way that women do, and slugged her beer with enthusiasm.

"You might wanna lay off those," he said.

49

"How come?"

"Well, they're fattening, for one thing; habit forming for another."

She took a deep breath, looked away, and belched. "Who cares. I'm gonna lose my job anyway."

"Yeah, but you'll have to do something after that; maybe hunt up a man to pay your bills. Nobody's gonna want a porker."

"Fuck you."

"I'm just sayin'."

"Yeah, well, don't say. Just tell me why you're here wakin' me up from my afternoon siesta."

"Randall didn't tell ya?"

"He just said he was sendin' some PI to see me about a case. This about some car wreck or somethin'?"

"Unh, unh. It's about Ty Harbin and Carla Morgan; the two kids killed out on I-10 in Grand Bay. I understand you were the first officer on scene."

She paused and looked up. "Oh. Yeah. Uh, I met the paper guy out there. He said he noticed'em when he was gettin' on the interstate to drive up to Mobile and pick up his newspapers."

"What time was it?"

"About three."

"Go on."

She raised her brows and shrugged. "Well, there ain't much to tell, really. The boy was in the driver's seat, shot in the head, it looked like. The girl was in the passenger seat, well, kinda halfway hangin' out the door."

"Was the engine running?"

"Nope."

"By the way, this was at the Grand Bay exit, right?"

"Yeah, on the eastbound on ramp, off Grand Bay-Wilmer Road. The car was about a hundred feet down the hill, parked on the shoulder; about twenty feet from the pavement."

"The passenger door was open?"

She took another pull on the bottle. "Not very much. It looked like she mighta been tryin' to make a break for it, but she didn't get too far."

"How long had they been dead?"

"I don't know. Not long, I don't think. I touched his neck and it wadn't feezin'."

"What about this newspaper guy? He seem okay to you?"

She took a deep breath and exhaled. "Yeah. I took his name and address and all that, and he hung around 'til the detectives got there. He wadn't nervous or nothin'. In fact, it didn't look like he was even sweatin', and it was pretty warm out there."

Edge nodded. "See any weapons around?"

She shook her head. "Nope."

"How 'bout drugs or alcohol?"

"Well, I really didn't get close enough to check. I think there was a beer bottle in the back floorboard, and maybe a roach in the ashtray; but, like a kilo, or somethin', well, no. I didn't see it."

Edge nodded while he took notes. All she was telling him was what he could see in the photographs the next day.

"Anybody else around?"

She shook her head. "It was pretty deserted; except for the Blue Moon, down the road. There were still a few cars down there."

The Blue Moon Lounge was the closest bar to the murder scene. It was a red neck joint inside a nondescript building on the Grand Bay-Wilmer Road, about a quarter mile south of where the victims were found.

"How 'bout the truck stop?"

"Well, it was full, like it always is. I didn't go down there. I figured that was a job for a detective."

"Anything else that I haven't asked you about?"

She looked down and closed her eyes. Edge thought she was going to nod off.

She made a face. "There was a shell on the seat between'em."

"A cartridge?"

"Yeah."

"Like a shotgun shell?"

"No, no, a spent cartridge."

"What, like a pistol hull?"

"Yeah. But it was like a rifle shell."

"Either of'em shot with a rifle?"

She shrugged. "I don't know. Maybe. The boys head was pretty messed up."

Edge nodded and started cleaning up his notes. She watched him while at the same time draining the bottle of beer. When she finished, she sat it down on the coffee table and wiped her mouth on her sleeve; but, even in her inebriated condition, she had the wherewithal to place a napkin under the moist bottle.

"So you're workin' on this murder, hunh?" she said.

"I am."

"I guess you're workin' for the girl's family. I heard she was fixed."

He looked at her but said nothing.

"Right." She nodded once. "What's it like? I mean, how's it feel, bein' a PI?"

"About like you think; a whole lotta talkin' and a whole lotta thinkin'."

"Anything like on TV?"

"Only if I'm fallin' down on the job."

"How do you mean?"

"I mean that if I talk to the right people and say the right words, people will tell me what I want to know. If I don't, then maybe I don't find out anything . . . or I have to find out in other ways."

"You mean like kickin' ass?"

"Maybe." He paused. "Why all the questions?"

She looked away at the floor. "Look," she lifted her brows and cleared her throat. "I was just thinkin'. I got some

52

time on my hands right now, and who knows if I'll ever get back to work at all, and . . ."

"No."

She looked at him. "Come on. I could be a big help to you."

"How? I already know how to lose my temper."

She froze. He was silent also. It was a remark he shouldn't have made.

"That was a low blow," she said looking away again. He thought he detected another sob in her voice.

"Look, I can't pay you; and, besides, Randall's already got somebody to work with me."

"Oh, don't worry about money. My family's loaded. They been takin' care of me right along while I been slummin' it with the cops. Really, Daddy's kinda glad all this happened. He wants me to go to law school." She paused. "It would be like, just for grins, you know? And I've still got some friends at the Department, so I can help out with information and runnin' tags and shit."

He looked at her, hard. "I don't do this for grins."

"You know what I mean."

He took a deep breath and exhaled. "Look, it's an idea. But, like I said, Randall's already huntin' me up somebody to work with. I gotta go with whoever he says. It's part of our deal."

She smirked and looked away. He began to notice a 'Lucy Ricardo' look in her eye.

"Just hold that thought," she said. "I gotta make a phone call."

He looked at her, but said nothing. She got off the couch, walked down a short hall, and turned into what he thought was probably her bedroom. Edge watched her with interest.

Five minutes later, she returned with a smile on her face. She replaced herself on the couch and once again tucked her legs up under her.

"There. That ought'a do it."

"Do what?"

"I called Daddy. He's gonna call the Sheriff and fix it all up."

"Fix what up?"

"You know, he's gonna talk to the Sheriff."

"What's he gonna say?"

"Well, he's got 'other ways' of gettin' things done, too; jus' like you."

"A donation."

"I guess; whatever it takes."

Edge smiled and shook his head. "You'll have to stay sober."

"Sure. Agreed."

"And you'll have to keep your mouth shut."

"Well, that might be a little harder to do." She paused and smiled. "But, I'm a pretty quiet drunk."

He took out a business card and scribbled his office address on the back.

"Okay," he said with a reluctant tone. "If you're the one, meet me at my office tomorrow, at noon." He paused. "If you're there at five after, you'll be too late."

The next morning, Edge met Randall at the Sheriff's substation on Old Pascagoula Road, about two miles west of Interstate 10. It was about a three hundred square foot storefront, next to a convenience store and a video rental place. It contained two desks, a couple of filing cabinets, a toilet, and little else. It was a place for supervisors to review reports and for deputies to drink coffee, and it gave the Sheriff a presence in an area of the county that he very seldom visited.

The caretaker was a county employee, Arthur 'Rocky' Allen, a World War II veteran who had a thick head of silver hair and a big smile. He was a political crony of the Sheriff's from back when Lawrence first got into politics. Allen had in the past worked at the paper mills in north Mobile County and was responsible for securing the union vote at election time. Allen's payback was a janitorial position at the Department that allowed him to keep getting insurance after age sixty-two, but before Medicare could kick in. Edge knew Allen and liked him.

Edge parked the Impala in a space in the middle of the parking lot next to a brown and tan, marked sheriff's vehicle. He bought a soft drink at the convenience store next door, then entered the office to find Randall seated at the desk along the north wall with a file folder, as well as a cup of coffee, sitting in front of him. Randall's eyes followed Edge as he walked into the room and took a seat near the front of the desk.

Edge looked around.

"Where's Rocky?" Edge said.

Randall glanced over toward the rest room. "In there."

They heard the toilet flush, after which the door opened, and Rocky Allen walked out of the restroom carrying a mop. Edge spoke.

"Hey, Rocky. How are you doin'?"

"Good morning, Mr. Edge. If I was any better I couldn't stand myself," Allen said. "You here on some hot case?"

"Oh, you know it, Rocky. I'm just here cleanin' up one of the Sheriff's messes."

Allen laughed out loud. "Well, a lot of us got that job." He smiled as he lifted the mop and looked over his shoulder at the restroom. Then he glanced at Randall. "I think I'm gonna leave you two alone and go get myself a biscuit."

"Good to see ya, Rocky," Edge said.

"Ya'll be careful out there."

Allen left, and Edge looked down at the file on the desk in front of Randall. "That what I came to see?" He nodded toward the paperwork.

Randall nodded. He opened the file, and slid a stack of eight by ten glossies toward Edge.

John Edge began to thumb through the photos. They were in color, but dingy, like whoever developed them didn't know what he was doing.

The first few images set the scene. It appeared as if Harbin's blue Buick was parked off the right edge of the eastbound ramp about a hundred and fifty feet east of the Grand Bay-Wilmer Road. Hankins was right. Harbin's car was a peach. It had shiny mag wheels, a whip antenna, and some aftermarket striping over a metallic finish. Edge looked closely.

The two rear doors were closed, but the front passenger door was slightly ajar. The girl was part way out the door, her head and shoulders hanging out but not touching the gravel pavement. There was blood on her face and neck, and the front of her clothes.

The driver's door was closed. Harbin's head was leaned forward on the steering wheel and there was a massive amount of blood on his shirt and pants. Both the victims wore jeans and short sleeved shirts; both were dressed for a warm, south Alabama night in early September. Morgan wore tennis shoes and Harbin some type of crushed leather, casual shoe.

There were various other shots of the interior of the car. Edge noticed a tape half in and half out of the cassette player. He held the print up close to his face. It was the album '*Major Moves*' by Hank Williams Jr.; an appropriate choice of music for Harbin who gave all the appearances of being countrified. Edge looked closer.

"What's that in the ashtray?"

"It's a roach. Looks like they shared a toke before they died."

"Or she did. I heard he didn't use."

"If you believe that, I've gotta bridge in Brooklyn to sell ya."

Edge smirked. "You're gonna disappoint his old man with that opinion." He paused. "What about the autopsy report?"

"Alcohol and cannabis in him, alcohol in her. We think he was he was just getting in the mood; you know, waiting until after he got her home, or wherever he was intending to have sex with her."

Edge nodded. "Anything in the back seat?"

"No, just a little sand on the floorboard, and a beer bottle. Otherwise, clean."

"No prints on the bottle?"

"Not a one."

Edge looked back at the photographs once again but couldn't locate the spent rifle cartridge that Austin claimed to have seen. He decided not to ask Randall about it.

"Looks like two guys got in behind'em," Randall said, "the Harbin kid was shot first; the girl tried to make a run for it and got it going out the door."

Edge bit the inside of his lip. "Yeah, could be." He studied the photos. "What kind of weapons?"

"A forty-five in the back of the boy's head. The girl got it with a shotgun."

Hmmmm, Edge thought. Two men. One used a pistol, the other a killing weapon that would leave no doubt – and no trace. The one that killed the girl had thought it through.

"You recover any slugs?"

"One forty-five bullet from the boy. It looks like whoever it was picked up the brass. There were some pellets in the girl."

"Any tracks?"

"Not on the roadway."

Edge nodded. At least there was a forty-five bullet to compare. Blood on the clothes would be long gone. Finding evidence of the circumstances surrounding the shooting would be more important than finding clues to the actual shooting itself. If the guys that did it are smart, he thought, those guns are in the Gulf of Mexico by now.

Edge laid down the stack of photos. Randall cleared his throat.

"Now. Did you get by to see Austin yesterday?"

"Yeah, yeah I did."

"Well, I don't know what you said to her, but I gotta call from T.T. this morning. You wanna know what he said?"

He smiled. "I can imagine."

"He said that Austin was reinstated and that he had no objections to her working with you on the Harbin homicide. He even issued her an unmarked car." He paused and a smile crossed his lips. "That a surprise?"

"Nope. Money talks, bullshit walks."

Edge was not altogether disappointed in the turn of events. At least with Austin he'd have something nice to look at while on stakeouts. And with her recent history, he was sure she was willing to inflict pain if she had to. He raised his soft drink bottle and toasted Randall.

"Here's to a fruitful relationship."

He took a pull and stood up. Randall raised his hand.

"Oh, there's one more thing."

He laid down a deputy sheriff's badge and a reserve officer ID card in front of Edge.

"What's this?"

"The Sheriff and I talked it over, and he wants to swear you in as a reserve deputy. He thinks it'll keep you outta trouble."

"You mean it'll give him the credit when I break the case."

"Ha, ha. Well, whatever gets you through the night, Edge. Raise your right hand."

"This a dealbreaker?"

"I'm afraid so."

Edge smiled and picked up the golden, six-pointed star and looked closely at it. It was completely without blemish and the overhead lights beamed off the finish. There was state seal of Alabama in the middle and the words, 'RESERVE DEPUTY' in black letters around the top of the circle strap, and 'MOBILE COUNTY, ALA' around the bottom.

"I don't need this. Besides, I might not be on the case that long."

"Just humor me."

Edge raised his right hand and was sworn, and then reached down and picked up the ID card. He smiled and shook his head but said nothing else as he turned and walked out the door.

Chapter 7

Edge was in his office with his feet up on the corner of his desk when, at two minutes after noon, there was a knock on his door. With some effort he rose and walked toward the entrance with his hand on the forty-five in the holster at the small of his back. He looked through the peep hole and saw Austin standing, coffee cup in hand, on the concrete stoop. Edge turned the lock and opened the door.

"You're late," he said.

"You said five after." She held out her hand, "Here. I brought coffee." He took the cup but did not drink from it.

Edge stepped back, and Austin stepped over the threshold. He stopped and leaned forward.

"Breathe," he said.

She exhaled loudly without complaint. Edge sniffed suspiciously. He thought he caught a hint of beer.

Austin realized what he was thinking. "Don't worry. Nothing since last night." She held her arm out straight to demonstrate that it didn't shake. "See, I'm stone cold sober."

"Bullshit."

"I am," she protested. "Besides, you agreed with Randall to this deal. You're stuck with me."

He looked at the coffee. "You just get up?"

"No. I've been up for hours."

Edge replaced himself at his desk, and Austin took a seat in the wooden chair across from him. She was dressed in short blue blazer over a white oxford shirt, jeans, and Timberlands.

"Did you take a look at the file?" she said.

Edge sat with his eyes closed. "Just the pictures."

"Well?"

"Well, what?"

"Well, what did you learn?"

He smiled. "Oh, I don't know. Harbin and the girl got creamed, I guess." He paused. "You see it differently?"

She smirked. "Is this how this thing's gonna go? You makin' fun'a me?"

He opened his eyes. "Well, what do you want? I can't look at pictures and tell ya who killed'em."

"Okay, okay." She paused. "So, what do we do first?"

"Just be patient. I'm thinking."

They sat in silence for three minutes. Then Austin spoke.

"I talked to the Sheriff."

"Yeah?"

"Yeah. He said that he knows the dude that I arrested, and that he's some muckety-muck down on the Island. He said that's why he just can't let me off with a warning about what I did; this guy's pushin' real hard to get rid'a me. The Sheriff said that he really wants to keep me around, that he's on my side, but . . ."

Edge nodded. "I know. Politics."

She nodded also.

"Well, get used to it. And don't believe that business about T.T. bein' on your side. T.T. is on his own side. He'll cut you loose in a second if he has to."

"That's what Daddy says." She paused and looked away. "So, the Sheriff said that my time off so far would serve as my punishment, but that he could revisit things at a later date. Meanwhile, I wasn't to do anything like that again."

60

Edge exhaled. "By the way, how much did your Daddy give him?"

She raised her brows. "What?" He didn't repeat himself. "Five thousand," she answered softly.

He chuckled. "Wow. I'm impressed; and flattered."

"How so?"

He smiled. "That he'd pay that much to provide you the opportunity to work with me."

Out the door and across the street, in the parking lot next to Edge's Impala, Austin pointed at her vehicle, a Ford.

"My car or yours?" she said.

"Let's take yours, at least until you try to kill me. Then, we might change."

She smirked at him and reached for the door handle. "Don't squawk. It's county gas."

Inside her government-owned Crown Vic, Edge belted himself in place. He looked at his new partner.

"Well, you got any ideas? I mean, where do *you* think we ought'a start?"

She looked at him. "Randall told me that we were to run down your leads only."

Edge smiled. "Well, okay. Let's just run down my leads only." He paused. "You're not just here for window dressing, are you? I mean, you got'chur gun and your badge, right?"

She smirked. "Don't worry. I'll do my part."

"I mean, it's beginning to sound as if you're just here as, well, you know, as payback."

"I can do my job; no matter how I got here . . . or what they think of me."

"What do they think of you?"

"They think I'm a woman . . ."

"Well, they've pretty much nailed that part of it, haven't they?"

"You didn't let me finish. A woman who can't do police work."

61

"Well, they shouldn't feel that way. Sounds to me like you do your police work a little too well." he said.

She looked at him with brows raised, thankful for his encouragement.

"Where to first?"

"Well, not knowing what these clowns have already done, let's head toward the scene of the crime. Think you can find it?"

She glared at him. "Oh, please."

Chapter 8

They were in Grand Bay, Alabama, in the southwest corner of the county, not far from the Gulf of Mexico, in about twenty minutes, and at the interstate on ramp in five more. Austin parked the car about a hundred feet east of the Grand Bay-Wilmer Road.

Edge looked around. To the south, down the hill off the interstate right of way, past a six foot chain link fence, was a thick stand of trees. In front of them, to the east, was the highway. To the north, it was downhill to the eastbound lane of the interstate, then across the pavement to a clear median. Farther north was the Truck Stop. Behind them, across the Grand Bay-Wilmer Road was a Chevron station, and further to the south, a bar, the Blue Moon Lounge.

"I don't see our killers going down that hill to the woods," Edge said thinking out loud. "And running across the interstate makes them conspicuous – and, it's dangerous." He paused. "So, I'm thinkin' our perpetrators parked behind them and walked up; which means our victims had to have some reason to stop, like they were either blocked from leaving or . . . or they were here to meet their killers. If that's so, then they knew who they were. That narrows the field quite a bit."

Inexplicably, Austin was taking notes.

"What are you doing that for?" he said nodding at her pad.

"Just tryin' to keep a train of thought."

He smiled while remembering her duties as a snoop. "Well, just don't write down everything I say. I wouldn't want some of it to get back to T.T."

She smirked. "Don't worry."

Edge looked back over his shoulder. "Let's go over to the Blue Moon and see if anybody's there."

"Are you sure? It's one o'clock in the afternoon."

"I know, but there'll be somebody around. Someone's got to come in to meet the beer guy and count whatever money didn't get stolen the night before."

She nodded and backed the car up the hill. In three minutes they were at the gravel parking lot around a light blue, cinder block building with no windows. A sign next to the front door said: 'Be 21, or be gone . . . to the Blue Moon, Alice!' Edge smiled at the reference.

At the door, Edge pounded. They heard nothing, but in thirty seconds it opened.

A short, thin woman with stringy hair and glasses on a chain stood before them. She had on a clean pair of jeans, a red and white pullover shirt, and sandals. Her face was suspicious.

"Yeah?"

"My name's Edge, and this is Detective Austin, from the Metro Sheriff's Office." Austin held up her star. "Can we talk to you for a minute?"

"What if I say 'no'?"

"Well, then, Ms Austin here will have to announce an inspection of your liquor license, and will demand entry. If she doesn't get it, she'll call about a half dozen of her colleagues out here and break down the door." Edge smiled broadly.

She stared at the badge, then, reluctantly, stepped aside and admitted them into the surprisingly well-lit interior.

The woman turned and walked behind the bar. The two investigators took seats on two stools in front of her. The thought flashed through Edge's head that she might be positioning herself in front of a shotgun hidden under the counter.

"Look," she said, "you're in now, so, why don't we just forget all about that liquor license business, okay?"

"Oh, sure, sure," Edge said. "We just need a few answers. We're not lookin' for trouble." He paused and jerked his thumb over his shoulder toward the interstate. "We're working on the case of the two kids shot, up on the ramp about a month ago. Are you the owner?"

The woman's face softened. "Manager. Sadie Huff. Yeah, I heard about that."

"Were you working that night?"

"I usually work on Friday nights, so, yeah, I'm sure I was."

"What I wanna know is did anything happen that night? Any trouble? Any hitchhikers or bums off the highway come in? Anybody new that you hadn't seen before, maybe a pair of men that just stopped in for a beer? Maybe somebody askin' to use the phone, or needing directions?"

"Wow. Well, let me see." She closed her eyes and tilted her head back. "I really don't remember anybody new. Our crowd is pretty reg'lar." She paused and said nothing. "Seems like Hardy come in and asked to use the phone. But he's been around here before."

"Did he call anybody?"

"I pointed him to the pay phone over by the bandstand. I don't let nobody use the phone behind the bar. No tellin' who they're callin' and what kinda 976 bills they're rackin' up."

"Did he use that phone?"

"Not that I saw."

"What's the number, anyway? Just for grins."

Austin scrambled to get out her pen and pad. Huff looked up again and closed her eyes.

"It's 865-somethin'." She thought a minute and then recited the last four digits.

"You know this guy's name?"

She looked up again. "Hardy? Yeah, well, I mean, I think it's Hardy. That's what he calls his self. Don't ask me what his last name is, 'cause I don't know, but I think he works down at the Daily Double."

The Daily Double was a lounge on Theodore-Dawes Road, not far from the Sheriff's substation, across from the dog track. It was of the same class as the Blue Moon.

"What's he look like?"

"Oh, Hardy's about five eight or nine, kinda thin. He's got blond hair and blue eyes; he looks about thirty-five or so."

Imagine this woman knowing the eye color of a drunk, Edge thought. Clearly, she knew more about this Hardy character than what she was telling.

"What's he do at the Daily Double?"

"You know. He picks up the parking lot, brings in cases'a beer and stuff."

"For a few dollars and a few brews?"

"Sure. I gotta couple'a guys that do the same thing for me."

"So, you think he might'a been here the night of the murders?"

"I'm not for sure. I think he lives around here. He just comes in when he thinks he can bum a free one. Sometimes, if I got some work, I give it to him just to keep him outta mischief."

Edge nodded. "Okay. Anything else? By the way, what time do you close?"

"On Friday? We stay open 'until.' See, we're a private club."

Private clubs were not covered by the normal ABC (alcoholic beverage control) rules. Any club that collects dues and can produce a membership list and some bylaws can stay open as late as it wants; around the clock, even.

"When did *you* leave?"

"Prob'ly two or so." She smiled revealing a gap in her front teeth. "I got to get my beauty rest. Plus, I come in on Saturday to do the books and make out payroll."

"Did you see a blue car parked on the ramp when you went by?"

"Oh, I don't go home that way. I live in the Bayou."

Edge nodded again. She was talking about Bayou La Batre, Alabama, a small town to the southeast. She would have left the bar heading south and would not have gone past the on ramp.

"I told most'a this to those other detectives that come by."

"You tell'em about Hardy?"

"No, I don't think so. They didn't as' me."

"Good."

In the car, Austin started the engine. "You don't think this Hardy killed'em do ya?"

"No. But he might've seen something. He might'a been out in the parking lot pickin' up trash. Actually, that, in and of itself, is pretty unusual for a bar. Unless there's about to be a fight, nobody comes out into the parking lot; too many chances for the law to come by and make trouble."

"What are the chances of Hardy bein' sober enough to notice anything?"

"Probably pretty slim. But, maybe whoever we're lookin' for stopped for some reason, or were speedin' by on the road, or doing something to attract attention. If so, he might remember it." He paused. "Look, it's just a thread. We've gotta pull it."

She nodded. "Okay, where to, now?"

He looked around and thought. The Chevron would have been closed at the time of the murder and there were no other businesses around.

"Go on over to the truck stop."

"Is there a lead there?"

"Nope. Just a sandwich. I haven't had my lunch yet." He paused. "Oh, and by the way, give the Blue Moon to the ABC boys. Let *them* come out and check her license."

They parked out front near the entrance to the retail store portion of the Allied Truck Stop; where the showers were, and where they sold the maps and other sundries that truck drivers use to make sitting in the cab of an eighteen wheeled truck for ten hours at a time a bearable experience.

Inside the restaurant, Edge ordered a BLT and a cola, and Austin ordered a chef's salad with Thousand Island dressing. Edge told the bleached blonde, middle-aged waitress to send over the restaurant manager. Richard McGarr found their table in five minutes.

"What can I do for you folks?" McGarr said.

He was a round man with brown hair and a mustache, and a big smile. His white shirt had what looked like an oil stain on the front, and his brogan shoes were dingy.

"My name's Edge, and this is Ms Austin from the Metro Sheriff's Office. Can you sit for a minute?"

"Sure."

McGarr found a chair and pulled it up to the end of the booth. His face was apprehensive.

"What's up?" he said.

"We're workin' on the case of the two dead kids over across the highway."

"Oh, yeah, right. I was wonderin' when you guys was gonna come over here."

"Nobody's interviewed you yet?" Edge said.

"No." He looked around. "I been expectin' somebody to come by, on the night shift, I mean, and I been askin' the girls. But nobody's been here yet."

Edge looked at Austin. "Make sure you write that down." She had taken out her pad, and he pointed at it. Then he looked back at McGarr. "Were you workin' that night?"

"I wadn't, no, but Joan, the night manager next door at the truck stop was. She told me some'a the truckers come in talkin' about it; you know, seein' all the cop cars and the lights out there."

"Did anything unusual happen that night?"

"Well, not about the murder, no. But there was some drivers that was talkin' about a trucker that was drivin' crazy, runnin' people off the road, and wavin'a gun."

"Did they know who this guy was?"

"Well, no, not by name, but they wrote down the information off his truck and give it to the Highway Patrol."

Edge nodded. Austin wrote. "Did they say which way he was going?"

"Ah, west I think. He didn't stop here."

"Did they say what kind'a gun he had?"

"They said it looked like a forty-five."

"Anything else?"

"Nothin' worth mentionin'. Like I say, Joan was the night manager on duty. I come in at six and things were still goin' on up the hill there." He motioned toward the murder site.

McGarr nodded at Austin's salad. "How's that salad there, little lady?"

She looked at him with distaste. "It's fine, sir; mostly lettuce, just like I like it."

Edge expressed their thanks and continued consuming his sandwich. Austin slathered her salad with more dressing and attacked it with vigor.

"How about that?" she said between bites. "They didn't even come down here to talk to anybody."

Edge was in no mood to criticize anyone else's work. "Well, you know, these truckers come and go. If there was anybody here that saw anything, they're prob'ly on their third or fourth trip across country by now."

"Still."

"It's alright. We're going to get a lot of information, some of it useful, some not. Don't get too impressed by what your colleagues *didn't* find out."

Chapter 9

"Where to now?" Austin said when they were back in the car. "Looks like we got more leads than we know what to do with."

He chuckled. "Really?"

"Sure. We can find Hardy; we can run down this trucker; we can go talk to Joan, the night manager; we can . . ."

He smiled. "Imagine that. More leads than we know what to do with."

She snorted. "Don't make fun of me."

He chuckled. "I'm not. It's just that I find it humorous when people make a big deal out of stating the obvious."

"Well, there are not usually so many leads on cases like this, are there?"

"Most of the time, there are more than you have time to run down. You have ta prioritize." He paused. "They're all gonna have to be run out, eventually; especially, if you write them down in your book."

"Why's that?"

"'Cause if you go to trial, a defense lawyer'll ask you about'em. These people could all be considered sources of 'exculpatory' evidence." He paused. "You know what that means?"

She smirked. "I went to college."

"Where?"

"John Jay in New York."

"Wow, that's pretty high toned. Who's got the money in your family? Mama or Daddy."

"Oh, Daddy." She paused. "But, I got some too."

"You?"

"Well, just what I inherited from my Nana."

He raised his brows. "Pretty and rich. So, what's a nice girl like you doin' in a place like this?"

"Well, it's kind of a short, long story. Mom and Dad are divorced. My father bought some property down on Orange Beach after the hurricane came ashore, uh, Hurricane Frederick. He's been developing condos down there since '80." She paused. "I came down here to be close to him."

"How long they been split up?"

"Well, they separated about ten years ago. They've been back together kind of off and on since I was fourteen. He hung around home to watch me grow up and kinda stay in my life. Then after they got divorced, he came here after I went to college."

"Mama still live in New York?"

"Connecticut, uh, Greenwich."

He pondered his next question. "So, deputy sheriff was the only job you could find?"

"Oh, no. I've always wanted to be a cop. I went to school for it."

He measured his next words carefully. "Significant other?"

She looked at him and smiled. "Yeah. Pat."

"Oh, I see. Pat. Okay, I can take a hint."

She raised her brows. He smiled at her. She started the car, backed out, and drove in silence toward the interstate.

"I said, where to now?"

"Go on up to the Daily Double. We might as well try to find this Hardy character while we're out this way."

The Daily Double was a wooden building, red, with two dice painted on the wall next to the front door, right above the name. At two thirty, they parked in the gravel lot, at the end of the building near a large oak tree. There were two other cars and a pickup truck present.

Inside, Edge stopped at the threshold to let his eyes adjust to the lack of light. Austin ran into his abrupt stop. He surveyed the room.

There was a grubby blond man at the end of the bar under a Pabst Blue Ribbon light, a red haired woman with her sleeves rolled up behind the bar washing dishes, and a male/female couple sitting at a table near the deserted bandstand.

At the bar, they took seats. The woman walked over.

"What can I get'chu folks?" she said. She had a bouffant hairdo and her polyester blouse had the top three buttons undone.

"Just a little information." Edge paused. "We're lookin' for Hardy."

Almost imperceptibly she cut her eyes toward the man at the end of the bar. Then she took out a towel and began wiping the bar. The non-verbal communication was unmistakable.

"I don't think I know'im," she said.

Edge smiled. "Bullshit."

At that moment the grubby blond man rose to his feet and began a fast walk toward the door. Edge rose also.

"Hold up, Hardy. We just wanna talk."

Edge had told himself he was getting too old to chase hoods on foot. But, he had Austin with him, and she was much younger, so it was time to see what she could do. The dirty man took one more step then bolted for the door, with Edge and Austin in close pursuit.

Edge hit the door in full flight but was surprised when, ten steps into the parking lot, Austin passed him. He slowed to a trot and watched as she hurtled after Hardy, into the woods adjacent to the east end of the property.

For an alcoholic who so obviously neglected himself, Hardy could fly. Amazingly, Austin kept within about ten steps of him. Edge, thinking that Hardy could not go too far into the thick stand of trees without getting bogged down and turning for Theodore-Dawes Road, started making his way to the pavement to set up, waiting for him to break out of the thicket.

Sure enough, the blond man hit the shoulder of the road ten yards ahead. With a quick burst, Edge had hands on Hardy's shoulders, and the two fell to the ground in a tumble, with Edge on top, and Hardy face down in the gravel. Austin burst out of the undergrowth and was with them in seconds.

"Calm down, Hardy," Edge said.

Edge managed to pin his arms behind his back, and Austin produced handcuffs. In short order, the dirty man was restrained.

"You're under arrest," Austin said while panting heavily.

Edge stood and lifted the man to his feet. "What'ja do that for, Hardy? We just wanted to talk."

"I don't know. I, I, uh, I guess it was just force'a habit." He looked at Austin. "How can you run so fast? I ain't never had a girl catch me."

"I was a sprinter in high school. You're not even in my league."

Edge laughed. "Just goes to show'ya, Hardy. Ya never know who you're dealin' with."

They walked Hardy back to the parking lot and leaned him against Austin's car. She patted him down and found one joint in his right front pants pocket.

"What'chu guys want?"

"What's your last name, Hardy?" Edge said.

"Eubanks. I gotta cousin that works at the Sheriff's Department. Will, Will Eubanks."

"We don't want nothin', Hardy. We just wanted to ask you about bein' at the Blue Moon about a month ago on a Friday night. Were you there?"

"I don't know."

"Sure you do. You go there every Friday night." He paused. "It was the night them two kids was killed."

"Oh."

"Oh, is right. Now, what do you know?"

"You mean about the night them two kids was killed?"

Edge slapped him on the side of the head. "You heard me."

"Owwww. Quit it."

"Talk."

"Well, I might'a seen somethin'."

Edge's face was deadpan. "Yeah. What'd you see?"

He looked over his shoulder at the handcuffs on his wrists. "Maybe, if ya'll take these off, I'll tell ya."

Edge looked at Austin. "He's your baby."

"I already told him he's under arrest."

"Well, you can always tell him that he's 'unarrested'."

Her shoulders sank. Clearly, it was a big bust for her.

"You're not supposed to do that," she said.

Edge smirked. "Tell you what, Hardy. Let us hear what you've gotta say. If it's any good, Ms Austin here will keep the joint and put you on probation. If you're just bullshittin' us, well, you'll have to take the ride, just for the aggravation."

"I won't git charged?"

"Well, not today. Speedy here has a whole year to sign a warrant on ya."

Hardy looked at them both and licked his lips. Clearly, he was conflicted. The information that he had he was sure would be helpful in the case. He didn't want to go to jail, but he didn't want to shoot his wad on such a menial charge.

He finally looked at them and nodded. "Okay. I was at the Blue Moon that night. I got there about nine. Sadie said if I'd go pick up the parkin' lot, she'd give me a couple'a dollars and a can'a Bud.

"So, I was outside pickin' up the trash when this car pulled into the parkin' lot and asked me where the high school was. I told'em I might know where it was, for the right price. See, I was tryin' to get some money from'em."

"Yeah, yeah. I got that. Go on."

"Well, one of'em raised a pistol and scratched his nose with it, you know, like rubbin' the barrel on the side; and then I knew I wadn't gettin' no money."

"What'd'ju tell'em?"

"I told'em how to get to South Mobile County High; how you go out to Highway 90 and turn right and then go two blocks and turn right again."

"What happened then?"

"They said, 'thank ya,' and left."

"What kinda car were they in?"

"It was a tan one; a Chevy, I think. It looked new."

"Are you sure it was a Chevy?"

Like all drunks, if you questioned their memory, doubt began to set in. He blinked twice.

"I, I think so. I mean, it could'a been a Chevy."

"What about the men?"

"The driver, the one with the pistol, he was blond and about average sized. The other one was a real big guy with a bald head. He looked like he could really hurt somebody."

"Could you see what they were wearing?"

"No. It was too dark. I just remember that pistol; and how big that dude was."

"What kinda pistol was it?"

"It was a automatic; like the one my cousin's got."

"Was there anybody else in the car?"

He paused. "Yeah, come to think of it, there was a woman in the back seat."

"How did you know it was a woman?"

He thought a second. "'Cause I heard her cough, and it was kinda high pitched, you know, like a woman."

"Did you get a look at her?"

"No. It was too dark."

"And how big was the dude in the passenger seat?"

"He was big. Like a football player."

74

Chapter 10

After getting contact information from Hardy Eubanks –
information that may or may not have been accurate – and
confirming that he truly was related to a deputy sheriff, Austin
reluctantly took the handcuffs off of him and let him go.
Hardy was last seen hot footing it west bound toward the Old
Pascagoula Road intersection, and a convenience store.
Austin's face said that she thought what she was doing was
wrong.

"I don't like lettin' him go. I had him dead to rights
on that joint. And besides, he was a lotta trouble to catch."

"Well, sometimes you gotta let the minnows go so's
you can catch the marlins. Just go downtown and impound
the grass, and when we need him, we can get a warrant and
serve it; heck, sign the warrant today if you want. But for now,
we got things to do."

She smirked. "This better work out."

"Hey, you're a deputy sheriff. If you want to arrest
him, go get him and do it." He motioned down the road. "But
if you have any desire to solve this murder case, I'm just sayin'
it might work out better for us, in the long run, to do it later."
He paused. "Trust me."

She smirked. "Famous last words."

They got in the car and started downtown toward
Edge's office. It was nearing four o'clock, and he didn't want
to work into the night against a five hundred dollar retainer.
He turned to Austin.

"There's a couple of things I want you to do before
we meet again."

On Highway 90, she pulled over and took out her notepad. "Shoot."

"Call Narcotics, and see if you can get a line on a dealer in Mobile Terrace. I don't know his name, but everybody calls him 'Mule Head.' If they've had him, they should have an address on'im. We'll pay him a visit.

"Also, call North Mobile County High, or maybe John Zachary, he's a Resource Officer at the school system, and see if you can get the names of the linemen on the football team; specifically, the tackles. I just need names, nothing else for right now.

"And after you've done that, call the Highway Patrol and see if they've got anything on that gun waving case that the truckers reported last month."

"You think that's a promising lead?"

"Well, it's a base, and it has to be touched . . . Speedy."

She looked at him disgustedly. "Is that how it's going to be from now on?"

He smiled. "I never saw a woman run that fast for any reason. You looked like you had a motor in your ass."

"I was the Connecticut state record holder for women in the two hundred, for three years. I can move when I need to."

"Well, let's hope you don't need to, very often." He paused. "Oh, and one more thing. When you get home, lay off the sauce."

She stared at him but said nothing. It had been her practice to have something to calm her nerves whenever she got home from work. Not doing so would be an aberration.

"I mean it. I don't work with drunks."

"I can handle it."

The next morning, Austin begged off work in deference to a case at the James Strickland Youth Center. Edge told her to call him when she was finished.

Since he was alone for the morning, Edge decided to do something he should have done initially: visit the parents of Carla Morgan. He hadn't done it partly because he didn't want to deal with another grieving family; and partly because if the information that Timmy Hankins had given him was true, and the girl was as far out of Ty Harbin's league as she was thought to be, Morgan's family would have little to offer concerning her death. They needed to be talked to for proprietary reasons, and not much else.

Edge found the address of Kenneth and Helen Morgan, a route and box on Celeste Road, in the street directory, and was at the gate of their three hundred acre estate at nine that morning. He pushed the intercom button attached to a brick pillar outside the entrance and waited. The residence was up a large hill eight hundred or so meters away.

"Yes," said a female voice over the scratchy speaker.

"My name's Edge. I'm a private detective. Could I talk to you?"

"Oh. A private detective? Oh, well, let me get my husband."

In ten minutes, Kenneth Morgan, a middle aged man with a white mane and beard, and a thin build, pulled up to the gate in a four wheeled, all-terrain vehicle. He got off and stood behind the driveway gate facing Edge and his Impala. Edge got out of the car and walked up.

"You Kenneth Morgan?"

"Yes. You're Mr. Edge. Otha Harbin called me and told me he'd hired someone to look into the case." He paused. "Frankly, I'm content to let T.T. Lawrence handle things. I've known him for years."

"That's fine. But, do you mind talking to me?"

"Do you have credentials? A state license or something?"

Edge produced his reserve deputy's badge in a leather case and showed it to Morgan.

"Oh. You're a reserve deputy?"

"Well, this week. I've been knighted by the Sheriff."

77

The left corner of his mouth went up slightly in the beginnings of a smile. "Okay. I just wanted to make sure you're who you say you are. You can understand."

"I understand."

"Follow me."

Morgan used a remote control to open the gate then got on the four-wheeler; after which Edge followed him in the Impala the nearly three quarters of a mile to the residence. It was a red brick, three-story mansion with a three car garage on the north side.

Edge was ushered past what because of its size and appointments could only be called a vestibule and into a parlor on the south side of the bottom floor. He rested in a brocade upholstered club chair, and Morgan took a seat on the couch opposite him. They were joined by Morgan's wife, a thin, blonde woman in her forties, with a patrician nose and perfect make up, who sat on the couch next to her husband.

"I hope you'll forgive the suspicion, Mr. Edge, but we value our privacy," Morgan said.

"Makes me wonder how Tyrone Harbin somehow made it past that gate."

Morgan spoke up. "Well, it wasn't our idea." His tone was dismissive.

Helen Morgan spoke. "Mr. Edge, Carla is our only child . . . and she's adopted, so I suppose you could accuse us of being overindulgent with her. She met Ty at school and, well, I guess you can't account for a young girl's taste." She paused. "I, for one, couldn't tell her no."

"I understand."

"I told her that there wasn't much of a future with that kid," Morgan said. "But she said she loved him, and she . . . well."

"How did they meet?"

Helen Morgan spoke. "They had a class together at North Mobile; World History, I think. She was a freshman, and he was about to graduate. Carla said that they were put in groups to work on some project together, something about the Peloponnesian War, and she said she felt sorry for him. He seemed to be lost. Can you imagine?"

Edge nodded. "Don't take any offense, but your daughter strikes me as a candidate for a private school education. Was that an option?"

Morgan spoke. "It was, but Carla wouldn't hear of it. She wanted to be around 'regular' people, she said. She said that she liked the diversity of the environment up there." He paused and looked away. "I should have put my foot down."

Helen Morgan dismissed him with a frown. "Anyway, she was always like that, bringing home stray cats and dogs. I guess it was because she was adopted herself." She choked back a sob. "She had a huge heart."

"So, Harbin graduated. Did they see each other after he finished school?"

"Well, we wouldn't let her date until she was sixteen," Morgan said. "I think she'd run into him at the movies or something, but they really didn't start seeing each other until last summer. He got that job at some factory in Chickasaw and was making a little money, so he could afford to do things with her, socially. He told me he intended to join the Marine Corps." He paused. "Now, I've got nothing against the service, but, come on. Look around you. Our daughter was used to much more."

Edge nodded again. Morgan's pretentiousness irked him.

"What did she want to do with herself?"

"She talked about being a lawyer. That's what I do, and, she's got the mind for it. I intended to send her to the University in Tuscaloosa, and I was hoping that when she went away she'd just grow out of him."

"You see, Mr. Edge," Helen Morgan said, "They had plans to marry after Ty got back from basic training. If she really wanted to do it, well, I guess we'd've . . ."

Morgan spoke up. "We'd've done everything in our power to stop her from going through with it."

79

Edge nodded again. "Not to be indelicate, but were they intimate? I mean could she have been pregnant?"

Morgan looked at his wife. She was resolute.

"Absolutely, not," she said. "I would have known it if they were, well, you know. We talked about that, and she knew of the dangers, the risks, the diseases, and of course, pregnancy and all. I'm sure it hadn't gone that far."

Edge was certain that it had, but he didn't belabor the point. If they wanted to live in fantasyland, well, at this late date, what was the harm?

"Tell me about that night. What time did she leave the house?"

Morgan spoke. "He came to pick her up about five thirty or so. They said they were going to dinner and then to the football game in Grand Bay; it was the first one of the year."

"Carla wanted to be a part of everything her senior year," Helen Morgan interjected.

"They said that after the game they'd probably stop off at the Dairy Dream, down in Grand Bay. Harbin said he knew the place and that it had homemade, watermelon ice cream. Carla was anxious to try it."

Edge had heard of it. It was on Highway 90 in Grand Bay, not far from the state line. So was the Red Shed a liquor store just over the line in Mississippi that sold 40's and enthusiastically served the young people from Alabama who ventured forth across the border to take advantage of Mississippi's more liberal drinking laws.

"What time did you expect them back?"

"Well," he said, "no later than eleven thirty; that was her curfew, and she had some function to attend early Saturday morning."

"It was a sorority car wash in Saraland," Helen Morgan said.

Edge took out his pad and pen. "Okay, well, that leaves only one more question." He paused and looked at them both. "Who would want her dead?"

80

Morgan shook his head. "I don't know. I've racked my brain trying to see it from that angle, but I'm sure they weren't after *her*. Tyrone Harbin was the target. She just happened to be in the way."

Helen Morgan said: "Oh," as if the idea had never occurred to her.

Edge nodded. "Is there anybody you can think of that didn't want to see that relationship go forward?"

"Well, there was me," Morgan said. "But I didn't kill my own daughter."

Edge thought it unusual that Kenneth Morgan might perceive himself as a suspect. He pressed on.

"How about another kid at school? I heard there was a football player that was sweet on her."

Helen Morgan spoke. "Oh, you mean Russ? Well, yes, he did come around a couple of times."

"Do you know his last name?"

"Russ Moore. He plays tackle on the football team. He has a scholarship offer to Auburn," Morgan said.

"I think they went out one time, to a party, last summer, but," Helen Morgan shook her head. "Carla wasn't interested in him. She told me so. She loved Ty."

"Did you ever get the impression that this Moore character might not wanna take 'no' for an answer?"

Morgan pursed his lips and shook his head. "Not that I could tell. He called up here a couple'a times, and I talked to him. He was always polite."

"I heard he was huge?"

"He's big, now. I think about three hundred pounds; and it's all muscle, too. He had an acne problem, though."

Edge looked at Helen Morgan. "How about other girls? Anyone seem jealous for some reason? Wealth? Status? Men?"

"You don't think a girl would, would kill her, do you?"

"Not herself, no. But it wouldn't be out of the question for a female to have it done." He paused. "You know kids."

She shook her head. "I can't think of anyone. You see, Mr. Edge, Carla was beautiful, but not really in a classical sense. She kept herself well, but her beauty was more, from within, I guess you'd say."

Edge nodded. "How about drugs or alcohol. Everybody's got a secret life."

Morgan looked back at his wife. "If it was there, we couldn't see it. She was always clear headed and clear eyed."

There was silence for several seconds. Then Kenneth Morgan spoke.

"I take it you've done police work in the past, Mr. Edge?"

"I was in the French Foreign Legion," he lied. "But I've got an association with a detective at the Metro Sheriff's Department. I guess you could say we're pooling our resources."

"You seem to know your business."

"I'm a hard worker, and I've studied a lot."

Morgan nodded his head and appeared to be thinking. He had something in mind.

"Mr. Edge, if you find out who killed my daughter, I'll pay you five thousand dollars."

Edge was taken a little aback by the proposal, but he didn't rush to it.

"You understand for ethical reasons, Otha Harbin will have to hear about your offer."

"Yes, yes, certainly. But there's no doubt in my mind, if you find his son's killer, you'll find my daughter's." He paused. "Consider it a reward."

"That's a very generous reward."

"This means a lot to me and my wife."

Edge nodded while thinking that was another odd thing to say. He prepared to rise.

"By the way, Mr. Morgan, what kind of law do you practice?"

"Criminal defense."

"Guess you meet a lot of shady characters in that line."

"More than God ever intended any one person to meet."

"Any of them come to mind as someone who might, ah . . .?"

He shook his head. "No. And, don't think I haven't thought of it. But, no. No one comes to mind."

"Pity."

Chapter 11

Edge spent the rest of the afternoon in his office trying to digest all that he had learned thus far. There was a lot to think about.

First, it was becoming clear that Tyrone Harbin was the target of this murder. Carla Morgan was, for lack of a better term, collateral damage. Harbin just had too many opportunities to come in contact with the seamier side of life, and if the witnesses Edge had spoken to could be believed, Harbin had made those contacts. Morgan was too young to have made a lot of serious enemies.

Second, it was also apparent that the murders were not a random street crime, or a crime of passion or rage. There were two weapons, therefore two shooters, and a conspiracy; and conspiracies always take planning. And, if there's planning, there's also a motive that has real substance. He had eliminated passion or 'love' and that only left revenge and pecuniary gain.

The three best suspects at that time were: 'Mule Head' the drug supplier; Russ Moore, the 'roided up' football

83

player; and the revenge motive associated with this long lost hunting accident that Hankins had mentioned. He and Austin had not yet delved into that aspect of the case.

Edge was nearly asleep at his desk at three that afternoon when Austin called. He rubbed his face hard and picked up the receiver.

"You finished with court?" he said yawning.

"Yeah. I made those calls and got that information."

"Who is 'Mule Head'?"

"His name is Willie Rae Stanton. He lives on Fifth Street in Mobile Terrace." She provided the address. "He's been up once for VAUCSA (Violation of the Alabama Uniform Controlled Substances Act), otherwise, just some petty stuff."

"How old is he?"

"Looks like, thirty five."

"Any crimes of violence?"

"Not that I can see."

"What did Narcotics say?"

"They said 'watch your back'."

"Meet me at WestPoint Hardware in thirty minutes."

WestPoint Hardware was a community institution in the area of The Boulevard and Cody Road. It had been there for years, and the owner was a heavy contributor to the Sheriff's political machine; therefore, seeing a deputy's vehicle at the business was not unusual. There were two patrol cars on site when Edge pulled up.

He parked on the west side of the parking lot near a convenience store and was waiting when Austin drove up ten minutes later. They parked door to door, and Edge handed her a copy of a map of 'the Terrace.' He'd marked an 'x' at the place of Stanton's address.

"Do you think we should get some help?" Austin said.

"We're just going there to talk, Speedy. This is not a bust. I went by the place. It's more of a broken down shack, really. My guess is he smokes up his profit just as fast as he can make it, or he doesn't actually do enough business to get out of his mama's house. Either way, I think we can keep him from gettin' the drop on us." He paused. "If it makes you feel better, put on a vest."

"I don't have one."

"Oh. Well, is there anyone you want me to call when you get plugged? Pat, maybe?"

She snorted. "Let's go."

Mobile Terrace was about a four square mile neighborhood of houses, and what one could charitably called hovels, laid out in a grid bounded by Cody Road to the east, and Old Shell Road to the south. The inhabitants were mostly low income and drugs were known to have been sold out of some of the homes in the area.

They stopped their cars one lot north of Stanton's house, a weather beaten shack with a three foot high porch and a yard full of trees. At the front door, they took places on opposite sides, and Austin readied her badge.

"Why don't you keep that in your pocket on this one. Let me see what we can get without showing our hand."

Edge knocked, and a tall skinny man with an Afro that had not been picked in a week answered the door. He was wearing boxers and a t shirt. The smell of greens wafted out the front door.

"Yeah."

"You Willie Rae?" Edge said.

He noticed that Stanton's right hand was hidden behind his leg. Edge slipped his hand to the small of his back and around the butt of his forty-five.

"Who wants ta know?"

"Friends of Ty Harbin."

"Ty? Who dat?"

"You know who. We just wanna talk." Edge paused. "I gotta proposition for ya."

"Uh, okay, uh, hold on. I hear the phone."

He closed the door in their faces. Edge heard no phone, but he did hear running feet heading for the backdoor.

"He's bookin'."

They jumped off the porch and ran around the side of the house just in time to see Stanton making it past the dog's house and through the back yards of his neighbors. Edge could see the revolver in his hand.

Austin set out after him. She was five yards in head of Edge when he called out to her.

"Wait! Let him go."

She continued running, so Edge continued following. It was late afternoon, but they could still see clearly the way to negotiate the obstacles – old tires, swing sets, clotheslines, and assorted trash. Stanton was on Seventh Street before Austin could catch him. They heard a door slam as they rounded the corner of an only slightly better-looking house than Stanton's.

Edge caught up to her and took her by the arm. "Didn't you hear me say stop?"

"Yeah, but I thought I could catch him."

Edge shook his head. "Did you see the gun he was carrying? You were running into an ambush. We're lucky he went into a house. If we'd cornered him, it could've been bad." He took a deep breath. "Besides, what were you gonna do with him if you caught him? It's not against the law to jog."

She smirked. "You think we'd'a done better with my badge?"

He frowned. "We'll never know, but I'm tryin' to keep you alive. From now on, listen to me. The same thing happened over in Chad in seventy-two. A couple'a guys chased a man through a village and never came out." It was a made up scenario; but it could've happened.

She said nothing.

"Let's go back to the house. You can show your badge then, if you want."

Back at the front door of Stanton's home, Edge knocked again. This time a woman answered. She was old and tired, and her faded dress hung to the floor.

"You Ms Stanton?" Edge said.

"Yes, suh."

"Ma'am, my name is Edge, and this is Ms Austin from the Metro Sheriff's Department." He paused. "Wonder why Willie Rae took off runnin' like that?"

"I don't know. He kinda mixed up. Sometimes he do thangs that be kinda crazy. What'ch'all want wid'im?"

"We want to talk to him about a white boy he knows from up north, Tyrone Harbin. You met him?"

"The only Tyrone I know stay in Orange Grove housin' project, and he black. I don't know no white boy Tyrone."

"Okay, well, take Ms Austin's card and give it to Willie Rae. Tell him we're tryin' to find out who killed Tyrone. Tell him it'll be worth some money to him to help us out."

She took Austin's business card and looked at it. "I'll sho give it to'im, but, you know, he don't spend too much time hangin' 'round wi' de white boys."

"We heard the two was in business together."

"I sho don't see how dat could be."

"Just ask him to call us."

"I sho will."

Off the porch and in the street Edge stopped. It was just beginning to get dark.

"Did you get any more of the information I asked about?"

"Yeah. All of it."

When they got to the cars, Austin retrieved her notebook. She flipped pages and studied her neat handwriting.

"The troopers say that the truck belonged to Treetop Transport outta New Orleans. They said they put a look out on it, but nobody ever spotted it, and none of the truckers wanted to do anything about it anyway, so they just let it slide."

"What about the football player?"

"Well, I found Zachary. He gave me a list with six names."

"Was one of them Russ, or Russell Moore?"

She looked surprised. "Yeah, how'd you know?"

"I'm a detective."

She tore out the information and gave him the paper. "What did you do today?"

"I visited Carla Morgan's family."

She snorted. "That's a visit I would've like to have made."

"Believe me it was no party." He paused. "But, come to think of it, you might've been of some help there. They're rich. You'd've fit right in."

Chapter 12

On Monday, Austin called and said she was once again stuck at court. Edge put his feet up on his desk, shut his eyes, and thought. He thought about the case, he thought about Harbin and Morgan, and he thought about his partner. A bad feeling began to creep over him.

Twenty minutes later he was at Austin's door. He knocked loudly then stood away from the peephole and waited.

"Who is it?" said a female voice on the inside.

"Maintenance. Gotta check the air conditioner filter."

Edge heard the dead bolt turn. The door opened slightly, and he put his foot across the threshold. Austin backed away. He stepped in and closed the door behind him.

She was wearing a t-shirt and plaid pajama bottoms. Her face was unmade, and her hair was disheveled. She stood with her hand on the back of a chair, nevertheless, she swayed noticeably. Edge stopped and looked at her.

"Wh, what are you doin' here?" she said.

"I could ask you the same question."

"Look, I . . ."

He shook his head in a mock display of disgust. "What a revolting development this is."

"I, I . . ."

"Don't even try to explain," he said. "I've heard'em all. You just need something to settle you down; to round out the corners so you don't feel so stressed; you haven't been able to sleep . . ."

She stared at him. There was a hint of sheepishness in her visage, as if she had been caught at something embarrassing. They stared at each other for several seconds. Then, suddenly, she squared her shoulders. Defiance replaced her shamefaced look.

"Well, don't you ever take a drink?"

"Not in the middle of a case."

She said nothing. "I can handle it."

"Bullshit. You ran out on me today."

"I can. I . . ."

"I ought'a call Randall and tell him." He snorted. "And after all the money your old man shelled out to getcha this gig."

Her shoulders slumped, and her face got desperate. By that it is meant that he her brows went up and her eyes got wide.

"Don't. Please. It'll mean my job."

"Give me one good reason."

She took a deep breath and exhaled. Then she stood up and once again squared her shoulders.

"Because, because, I can do it. I can hold it together."

Even as she spoke Edge could hear the slur in her words. He licked his lips.

"And," she said. "I'll call Daddy. He can, you know, make it worth your while."

Edge chuckled. "Your daddy's gonna pay me to keep you afloat in this thing?"

"He paid to get me on it." She paused and looked at him. "And . . . I'll certainly do whatever you think is necessary . . . personally."

She reached up and smoothed her hair, then fingered the hem of her t-shirt and licked her lips. It was a shameless come on from an attractive, yet drunk, woman. Edge was repulsed.

"I'd rather have the money."

She was taken aback; shocked even. It's probably the only time in her life she's ever been turned down, he thought.

It was his turn to breathe deeply and exhale. "You know what bothers me the most? Not that you're drinking; everybody's got flaws. Nope, it's that you lied to me." His face showed her his mock pain.

He saw her bottom lip quiver. She sniffed.

"I'm, I'm sorry."

"Don't be sorry. Clean up." He paused and pointed his finger right at her. "And, as long as we're working together, if you ever lie to me again, I'll slap the shit outta you."

He didn't know if she believed him or not. But she said nothing. She only swallowed and blinked. He turned and walked back out of the door, and he heard it slam behind him.

Back at his office, Edge called the public library. It was already noon.

"Yes, ma'am. I need some help. I'm trying to locate who owns a company called Treetop Transport, outta New Orleans. Do you have that capability?"

"I can call over to the license commissioner in that city; unless . . . you'd like to do it."

"If you'd make the call, I'd appreciate it."

"Please hold."

Edge held for ten minutes until the reference librarian from the Main branch on Government Street returned.

"Sir, apparently, Treetop Transport is a subsidiary of MapleHouse Syrups. They provide product transport, by eighteen wheeled trucks, for MapleHouse, to stores throughout the southeast."

"Interesting."

"Many of the large manufacturing companies have these associated companies to handle their ancillary services."

"Sure, sure. Well, thank you, ma'am."

Edge hung up and threw down his pencil. It was almost too much of a coincidence to believe that this clown in an eighteen wheeler, driving up and down the highway waving a gun on the same night as Tyrone Harbin was killed, could have been his coworker. He shook his head as he realized he might have to take a trip to New Orleans, his least favorite city. But, until then, there was another lead he wanted to take a look at.

The next morning, by prearrangement, Edge picked up Austin at her apartment and they headed north toward the tiny town of Grove Hill, Alabama, in Clarke County. Edge had it in his mind to either confirm or eliminate the hunting accident, if one truly occurred, as a motive for murder in this case.

"So, how are you feeling this morning?" Edge said as they turned on Highway 43.

She looked at him with disdain. "I'm good; rarin' to go."

He nodded. "Did you go to court the other day? The day before your 'incapacitation,' I mean?"

"I did." The look towards him was one of distaste.

"Well, you can understand my skepticism."

"He was guilty on all counts."

"What were the counts, by the way?"

"DUI, and, uh, DC (Disorderly Conduct); and Public Intox on the passenger in his car."

"Wow. You went to town on'em.

"They deserved it."

Edge didn't speak for a half mile. Then he said:

"You don't like drunks much, do ya?"

"What? No, I mean, they broke the law."

"But you like puttin' drunks in jail, don't'cha. I mean, those poor slobs you went to court on; that patsy from Dauphin Island that ate a face full'a cage; and even ole Hardy Eubanks. I had to practically beg you to let him go."

She said nothing and looked straight ahead as he piloted the car up US 43. He could tell by her demeanor that he'd touched a nerve.

"What is it?" he said, "You have a family member killed by a drunk driver? That's usually what drives officers to make drunks their own little crusade."

She smirked. "Yeah. Yeah, that's it."

He turned his head and looked at her. "Bullshit." He paused. "You know, this relationship ain't gonna work if we're not honest with each other."

Still, she said nothing.

"Son of a bitch. I never knew a female to be so quiet."

He thought about all the things that could cause her to police the way she did. He could come up with only one.

"Well," he said, "if it's not some tragedy that happened to your family, there's only one other explanation."

She turned and looked at him.

He hesitated before he spoke. His idea was to get at the truth, not to hurt her.

"You gotta real problem."

She took a deep breath and exhaled. He noticed it and knew that he had hit the nail on the head.

"You're a drunk . . . and you hate yourself for it; and every time you put one'a those DUI's in jail, you're just hatin' yourself a little more . . . you're tryin' to punish yourself. It's like you're puttin' your own self in jail."

He slipped a glance her direction and saw that her bottom lip was protruding slightly. He heard her sniff.

"Could we talk about something else?" she said.

He nodded. "Sure."

At exactly one o'clock they arrived at Grove Hill, a town of about eight hundred that was the county seat of rural Clarke County. They found the State Trooper/State Bureau of Investigation office, a single-story, brick building with marked trooper cars in the lot behind it, right off the four-lane, on the north side of the town. A sleepy-looking receptionist inspected their credentials, made one phone call, and ushered them back to a non-descript office in the rear of the building.

Edge stood at the threshold, with Austin behind him and to his right, until he had the attention of the man behind the desk. Then he took two steps into the room. The agent rose from behind his chair and smiled.

"Mr. Edge? Doug Banks. How are you?"

"I'm good, and yourself?"

Banks shook Edge's hand, and they both sat down. Austin took a seat next to Edge and produced a notebook and pen.

"Oh, I can't complain, I guess," Banks said. "It's just that I'm losin' my hair from all the stress. I get up in the mornin' and get in the shower, and then I look down and see a tub full'a hair." He paused and rubbed his crown. "I don't know how long you've been an investigator, but I've been in this business twelve years." He looked at Edge and smiled. "I'd like to know your secret. How'd you manage to keep them locks'a yours?"

"Good genes. And, I had the good sense to not spend any time in law enforcement." Edge nodded toward Austin. "Oh, this is Deputy Austin of the Metro Sheriff's Office in Mobile. She and I are getting on each other's nerves together." He paused. "And, as you can see, she's got all of her hair."

He nodded and smiled. "Ms Austin." She nodded in return but did not smile.

Banks was forty, portly, with dishwater-colored hair and green eyes. Wire rimmed glasses sat astride his thin nose.

His starched shirt and gray slacks were perfect, and his yellow tie hung down below his belt.

"Margene says you're a private investigator. You never spent any time in police work?"

"I was in the French Foreign Legion."

He raised his brows. "Oh, well, I wasn't so lucky." His eyes went up and he once again rubbed his scalp. "It'll all be gone soon. Then I'll mourn the loss and just move on. Luckily, I'm married. I'll tell my wife that baldness is a sign of virility, and she'll be none the wiser." He smiled at Austin. "It might even get me a few more fun Friday nights."

Edge smirked and looked at Austin while remembering her proposition on the day previous. "There's nothin' a good roll in the hay won't cure, is there? Even if you have to lie to get it."

Banks chuckled. "Nope."

Austin shot a glance toward Edge. "Well, I'm finding out that honesty in a relationship is, apparently, very important."

"Sometimes." Banks smiled. "But what she don't know won't hurt her." Banks cleared his throat. "Anyway, what can I do ya for?"

Edge began. "Do you remember a homicide about, oh, seven or eight years ago; maybe a huntin' accident, here in Clarke County? Would'a involved two teenaged boys from down in Mobile."

He leaned back in his chair and rubbed his hand across his mouth. "Let me see." He shut his eyes and thought. "Not off the top of my head. Let me check the book."

Banks reached around, took a bound volume off the short shelf behind his chair, and opened it about halfway. He set his glasses in front of his eyes.

"Let's seeeeeee," he said. "You got any names?"

"Victim would'a been a Terry Sawyer; the other party was, uh, Tyrone Harbin."

He ran his finger down a couple of names until he reached one three quarters of the way down the page. "Here it is. Says it was, 'accidental shooting.'" He looked up. "You got reason to believe otherwise?"

Edge shook my head. "Oh, no. Not at this time. What was the date on that incident?"

"Looks like December 11th, 1977. Not quite seven years ago."

"Any details?"

"Nope. Just says 'hunting accident.' Says here that Miller was the state's investigator. You want me to get'im?"

"Yeah, if he's in."

Banks picked up the telephone, dialed a three-numbered extension, and talked to Agent Tom Miller. In two minutes, a tall, muscular man in a starched, white shirt and red and blue striped tie entered the room.

"This is John Edge, Tom. He's a private detective from down in Mobile, and that's Ms Austin. She's a deputy from Mobile County." He paused and smiled. "I don't know if I quite understand their arrangement, but, you know, who cares."

Miller was thirty-five. He had blonde hair, an olive complexion, and a quick smile. He parked in a chair next to Edge.

"What can I do for you folks?"

"Is there anything you can tell me about a hunting accident that happened up here, about seven years ago; a couple'a teenagers?" Edge said.

"At the Piney Woods Camp, Tom," Banks said.

He squinted his eyes shut, the opened them. "Oh, yeah. I remember. Two young boys was out huntin', and it seems like one of'em was trying to run the deer down the creek bank. The other one got 'buck fever'; blew his head off with a 30-30 Marlin." He took his finger and pointed to the back of his own head indicating where the wound was. "Man, was it cold that day, or evenin', actually, when we finally got there."

"How about the families. Remember anything about how they took it?" Edge said.

"Well, sure. Everybody was bawlin'. And as I recall, the dead boy's daddy took it especially hard. He was cussin' and swearin' to beat the band; wanted the Harbin boy arrested. When I told him there didn't appear to be enough evidence, he lost it. Said he was gonna sue us all. I just counted that up to grief, you know. The other family didn't come to the scene. They was waitin' on us at the Sheriff's Office."

"Any problems with it? I mean, any reason to believe that it was intentional?"

Miller shook his head. "No. It was the Harbin boy's first time huntin'. The best I remember, he said they'd been out all day in a shootin' house, and they left out and started stalkin'. He said he thought he had somethin', and he just got overanxious. He didn't have a scope on his rifle and just let fly when he saw somethin' flash across his face. I did a little bit'a background down there at the high school where they both went, thinkin' maybe there was a girl or some dope behind it, but I never got anything. Turns out they was pretty good friends. Harbin was just a boy in the woods that didn't belong there."

"Did the Sawyer boy have on any hunter's orange."

"Nope. They was in a stand all day. You don't need it as long as you're in a shootin' house. I think he had a patch on his shoulder, but to see it in the brush," he shook his head. "no way."

"Was there a coroner's jury?"

"Sure was. Had it about a week later. Autopsy said that neither one was drinkin' and the wound was in the right place and from the right distance. It was ruled accidental; got no billed at Grand Jury, too."

"Did the Harbin boy testify?"

"Yep. Couldn't get through it without ballin', though."

Edge nodded. "I guess you both know the Harbin boy's dead."

Banks seemed shocked. "No shit? How?" he said. Miller was deadpan.

"He was the boy in the car that was killed out on I-10 a month ago; shot in the back of the head; a young girl was in the car with him."

"Son of a bitch," said Banks. "Any leads?"

Edge shook his head. "A few. I think the Sheriff's Office thinks it was drug related; you know, drugs/gangs." He looked over at Austin.

Banks looked at her also. "That what you're thinkin' Deputy? You hadn't said much."

Austin seemed to be caught off guard. "Well, uh," she swallowed, "I'm keepin' an open mind about it all." She paused and smiled slightly. "Besides, I told Mr. Edge I'd keep my mouth shut."

They all chuckled. Then Miller looked at Edge. "So you think his death might have somethin' to do with what happened seven years ago."

Edge raised his eyebrows. "I don't know. What do you guys think?"

Miller looked at Banks, then Edge. Then he spoke in a low tone.

"Well, I don't know who it was that killed Tyrone Harbin. But if Harbin had killed my boy, I wouldn't soon forget."

Chapter 13

On the way back to Mobile, they rode in silence. Edge pondered Tom Miller's words. He was right. Parents were not supposed to outlive their children, and when they did, there had to be someone to blame. Usually it was God. Edge started to think about how much grief it would take to drive a man to murder.

About halfway home Austin spoke. "Look. What'chu said before, on the way up here, I mean, about me having a problem. Well, that's not true. I mean, sure, I like a drink, but . . ."

He nodded. "Well, that opinion doesn't match what I saw at ten o'clock in the morning on a Tuesday. But, I understand. It was just the ramblings of an old man. Don't pay it no mind."

She shook her head. "I'm serious. I don't have a problem."

"Right. Forget I said anything."

Just outside of McIntosh, Alabama, Austin spoke again. "Where'd this hunting accident lead come from?"

"Oh, uh, Harbin's best friend. He told me about it." He paused. "What do you think?"

She shrugged. "Well, it's been nearly ten years. You think anybody would hold a grudge that long?"

"I'm askin' you."

She smirked. "Sounds kinda thin, to me."

"Maybe. When we get home, why don't'chu call your Daddy. Ask him how long it would take him to get over it if somebody killed you."

They were back in Mobile County at four. On the way into town Edge decided stop on Salco Road and see Tim Hankins. He found him lying on the couch watching the Early Show on channel 10. They knocked on the trailer door and Hankins hollered for them to 'come on in.'

"You busy, Timmy?" Edge said as he opened the front door.

"No."

"Can I buy you a sandwich?"

He jumped up off the couch. "Fuck, yeah."

Hankins reached for a shirt and shoes, and in a minute they were out the front door. Edge heard his mother holler as they were walking away:

"Bring me somethin'."

In the car, Edge introduced Austin. "Timmy, this is Ms Austin. She works for the Sheriff. You can talk in front'a her."

"Hey," he said eyeing her up and down. "Man, you sure are good lookin'."

Austin seemed slightly embarrassed. "Oh, uh, thanks."

Edge looked at her. "How about that. You got yourself a groupie."

Edge found an all you can eat buffet restaurant on Highway 43, in Saraland, about six miles from Creola, and the three took a corner booth, close to the steam tables. A waitress brought them all water, and Hankins an iced tea, and when the thin boy had filled a large plate, Edge began.

"Tell me more about this hunting accident."

"What'chu wanna know?"

"Did Ty tell anybody else what happened?"

"Not that I know of. I mean, he said he had to testify at some kinda coroner's thing up there, but far as I know, he never said anything to anybody else. See, me'n him was tight. That's why he talked to me."

"Where'd he tell you all this?"

"Up on Chickasabogue Creek one night. We was campin' out about a hundred yards from the park. Ty brought beer, and we drank a twelve pack. I guess he stole it from his daddy."

"Start at the beginning and tell me exactly what he said."

Between bites, Hankins talked. The conversation took twice as long as it should have, simply because he couldn't swallow fast enough. Austin took notes and sipped from her water glass. Occasionally, Hankins would close his eyes and look up while trying to remember a specific point.

"See, Terry's daddy owns some kinda business up in Chickasaw. I think it's a plumbin' company. Anyway, I guess he does alright with it. I mean it is his own business." He looked away. "Man, I'd sure like to have my own business someday."

"Talk," Edge said.

"Oh, yeah. Well, anyway, he's got this share in a huntin' camp in Clarke County, right outside'a Grove Hill. I know 'cause Terry was always braggin' about it. He said it was five hunert or thousand acres, or somethin'. So, he kept talkin' about what fun it was to hunt, and would Ty go with'im one weekend."

"How come he didn't ask you?"

"Shit, man." He looked at Austin. "Oh, 'scuse me, ma'am. I couldn't afford a bullet, much less a rifle. I'd'a had ta walk around in the woods in tennis shoes." He bit into a corn muffin. "In case you ain't noticed, we're kinda pore."

"I've met Ty's daddy. He don't look much better off."

"Well, I don't know about that, but I know I couldn't've afforded to go. 'Sides, they was friends, and I don't think Terry had'a a lotta other ones. I didn't know Terry so good myself." He forked up some peas. "I think Ty went up to the Goodwill and got some boots."

"Go on."

"Well, anyway, they made plans to go the week 'fore Christmas vacation when we was in tenth grade. I think Terry helped Ty get some cammies, and he might'a even loaned him a rifle. They talked about it for weeks. Best as I can remember, it was real cold that winter. I wouldn't'a wanted to go out in freezin' weather like that, anyway.

"Ty said the plan was for Terry's older brother to take'em up there on Friday after school, and they was gonna stay the night in the camp house. Then, the next mornin', Ty

said they went to the shootin' house. It's like a tree stand but .
. ."

"I know what a shootin' house is. What's his older brother's name?"

Hankins looked into the air. "Uhhhh, Jerry, I think."

"Terry and Jerry. Alright, go ahead."

"Okay, well, Ty said they sat in there all day from about five in the mornin' 'til two thirty or three that afternoon and didn't see shit. I mean there wadn't even a gopher. Ty said the stand was next to about a five acre field that had been cleared and that Old Man Sawyer had salted back before Thanksgivin'. But, I don't know, I guess the deer was just hidin' that day."

"He say what they talked about?"

"No, but it was prob'ly girls. That was all we talked about, back then; who had the nicest ass and the biggest tits," he looked at Austin, "Oh, uh, sorry. 'Scuse me, ma'am."

Austin said nothing.

"Anyway, it got late, and Ty said that Terry said they should get out and look around in the woods and see if they couldn't see somethin'. Terry told Ty that he could take the first shot since it was his first time huntin' and 'cause Terry was waitin' to get a shot at a ten pointer that he'd been tryin' to shoot for a couple'a years. Ty said he called him, 'Big Sam.'"

"Did Terry hunt a lot up there?"

"He went all the time."

"Alone?"

"I don't think he ever went alone. Either his brother or his daddy or his uncle usually went with'im." Hankins took a drink. "I think that's why Terry wanted Ty to go, 'cause the other ones was tired'a takin'im."

"Go on."

"Anyway, so Ty said they went over the field to a ridgeline that looked down on a creek, and Terry set Ty up behind a tree just over the ridge. It had a low hangin' limb so Ty could use it like a brace or somethin' to rest the gun on to hold it steady. Ty said Terry told him that he had heard somethin' in the brush, and he was gonna go down to the creek and walk along the bank and try to flush out whatever it was."

"Ty say how far he was from the creek?"

"He talked like it was thirty or forty yards." He paused. "Anyway, Ty said he waited and then something come runnin' by in front of him. He said he just pointed the gun at whatever it was and pulled the trigger. Then he said he hollered at Terry. After that he started down the hill, and he heard a groan, and he walked up on'im layin' by the side of the creek." He paused again. "That's when Ty started cryin'; while he was tellin' it, I mean. He just drank another beer and laid down."

"You ever talk to Terry's family about it?"

"I don't know them."

"Ever run into Terry's daddy or brother?"

"No. I ain't got no transportation into Chickasaw. If it wadn't for the neighbor lady that's a waitress in Mobile, I wouldn't be able to keep that little ole job I got." He paused and took a bite of cornbread. "But I heard for the longest his daddy was pissed."

"Who'd'ja hear that from?"

"Just kids at school."

"What about Terry's brother? How old is he?"

"I think he's about thirty. He was in his twenties back then."

Edge nodded and watched as Hankins continued to engorge himself. He wondered if the boy had eaten since the two of them had last gone out to breakfast. He reached and handed Hankins a menu.

"Here. Order somethin' to go . . . for your mama."

They dropped Hankins back at his trailer in Creola and then turned toward Mobile. Edge looked at Austin.

"How you feel about this lead, now?"

She exhaled loudly. "About the same. I guess I've never been one to hold a grudge, so, maybe, I don't see it in others."

"Well, that's a good virtue to have. Just remember it in case I get on your nerves."

Chapter 14

The next morning Edge was in his office trying to digest all that he had learned the day previous. It seemed to him that the hunting accident retribution angle was at least as viable a lead as any of the others, and it needed to be pursued. Nothing can dispel the grief of a parent who has lost a child, but revenge might come close. The only thing that bothered Edge was the fact that the Sawyers would be redressing a death that had happened seven years previous. That would certainly amount to a good healthy hate; an almost unbelievable amount of hate. Was it a hate born out of guilt? And, if so, guilt for what?

Edge decided that he and Austin would try to knock out some of these other leads first. After all, they were probably a lot hotter than a case of seven year old payback. Afterwards, they could take a longer look at the Sawyer family.

Austin met Edge at the General Jackson Hotel for lunch. The buffet there was frequented by attorneys and judges from the courthouse next door. Edge liked to see who was taking alcohol with their meal. He felt it was information somehow he might, in the future, be able to use.

"Can you put the word out to the city and county narcotics people," he said, "to have'em pick up Willie Rae Stanton? I feel sure he's probably got a warrant out on him, or he wouldn't't'ave run. We can talk to him better down at their office with paper hangin' over his head."

"Right," Austin said.

103

"Also, Treetop Transport belongs to the MapleHouse Syrup Company, where Ty Harbin worked," he said as he buttered a roll.

"Do we know who the driver was?"

"Not yet." He paused. "How about you making a couple'a calls to the PD over in New Orleans and get us some background on the company. Then if you think you can, call'em and find out the name of their driver who would have been in and out of Mobile on the night of August 31/September 1st; ask'em when they think he'll be through Mobile again. Maybe we can catch him at the truck stop, or up at Harbin's workplace. At least he'll be on our turf." He paused. "Just tell'em that the driver is a witness to this gun wavin' thing. They shouldn't be suspicious."

"Okay," she said laying down her pen. "I'll do that today."

Edge looked at the pen. "That what they teach you in that fancy college up there? How to take notes?"

"Well, yeah. That's the first thing they teach."

"What was your major?"

"Criminal Justice; well, Criminal Investigation. I've always wanted to be a detective. The first book I ever read was an *Encyclopedia Brown*."

"I'm sure I'd be impressed if I knew who Encyclopedia Brown was."

"He was a young boy whose father was the police chief in a small town. He solved crimes. It was a series for kids eight to twelve."

"Kinda like Nancy Drew?"

"Nancy Drew was a sissy. She had to have that guy helpin' her find out who did things."

Edge chuckled. "Right, right. Kinda like I'm helpin' you." He paused. "Well, kids get inspiration from all over, I guess."

"I guess." She paused. "Where'd you go to school?"

"The University of Djibouti." Edge smiled.

"Where's that?"

He'd been telling people that he had been a member of the Foreign Legion for so long that he was beginning to believe it himself. He'd have to get a new, more plausible cover story before too long.

"It's in Africa. Look," he said, quickly changing the subject, "why don't you make arrangements with Zachary for us to talk to Russell Moore, the football player, one morning, up at North Mobile County High. My guess is that he's got a pretty tight alibi for the time of the shooting – like bein' on the bus with the football team – but let's talk to him anyway." He paused. "By the way, the night you were out there, what did the coroner say about time of death?"

"He wanted to know when they were last seen alive – I didn't know that – and when they were found. That I did know. He said that the time of death was in between those times."

"That's what they always say." Edge paused. "If they can't nail it down any better than that, I just wish they'd keep their mouths shut." He looked away. "What about the detective's observations?"

Austin looked up at the ceiling with her eyes closed. "Well, both Will Eubanks and Rice said they were cold. Neither noted any animal activity."

"What about rigor?"

"Oh, yeah. Both said that rigor was in the joints, but it could be broken." She made a face. "I didn't touch'em."

"Alright. Well, suppose Hardy Eubanks at the Blue Moon Lounge saw our killers, whoever they are. He said he got to the bar around nine thirty, and Sadie Huff put him to work pickin' up the lot. Let's say he was out there by ten. Then if whoever it was went to the ball game at South Mobile, and Harbin went to get ice cream afterwards, and then the two in the car followed Harbin from there to the interchange, I think we can guess that Harbin and the girl were dead by eleven; maybe, earlier." He paused and took a bite. "Do you know if anyone confirmed where they went after the game?"

"I didn't know they did."

"They were supposed to go to the Dairy Dream in Grand Bay and get some ice cream; but they prob'ly went to the Red Shed to get beer, instead."

Austin made a note on her pad. "I'll see if Eubanks and Rice checked that."

"I'm thinkin' that they may have been approached, or maybe even waylaid, at wherever it was that they stopped after the game; either at the bar or the drive in. Then they were followed, or they met the killers willingly at the on ramp. Either way, Harbin pulled over, and the killers got in." Edge paused. "I'm sure he knew them."

At that moment, it occurred to Edge that he didn't want Austin sharing that hunting accident lead with the S.O. and having them misplay it. In the far reaches of his consciousness he considered it their best lead, and he wanted to notify Randall and his people about it only at the last possible moment.

"Why don't you keep this hunting accident thing to yourself, for now. Let that be *our* lead." Edge pointed to the meat that came off the buffet table. "Pretty good mutton, hunh?"

"It is good. You come here often?"

"About once every couple'a weeks. Lamb is just about my favorite dish."

That afternoon, Austin called and made them an appointment, for the following morning, with Zachary and Russ Moore at the fieldhouse at North Mobile County High. Austin was nothing if not efficient, Edge thought.

They met at eight o'clock the next morning in a sparsely furnished coach's office ten steps from the football practice field.

John Zachary arrived first. He was short, with a hard build, short hair, and a flat nose. He could run fast, and his large calloused hands attested to his previous career a competitive martial arts fighter. Edge had worked with him once before and found him kind of goofy; by that it is meant that he had a short attention span, and he had trouble keeping his mouth closed; and when he did open it, he always had something wildly outlandish to say. Nevertheless, there wasn't anyone that Edge would rather have next to him in a fight.

Russell Moore was just as big as the Morgans had said he was. His six foot six inch frame carried three hundred solid pounds quite easily, making him appear as if he should skip college and go directly to the NFL. Edge wondered whether or not, if the young boy got mad, the three of them (Edge, Zachary, and Austin) could control him. The two investigators and Moore took seats at a table. Zachary leaned against the wall near the door and folded his arms.

"How ya doin', Russ?" Edge said trying to get on his good side.

"Good. The season's goin' good. We ain't lost yet."

Edge thought it sad how that Moore saw his life in terms of how his football season was progressing.

"By the way, how old are you?"

"Eighteen; just turned."

"That's great man. I hear you're on the books for Auburn next year."

"Yeah. I give'em a verbal commitment right 'fore the season. I can still change my mind 'fore signin' day, but, you know, I think I'll stick with'em. They run my style'a offense."

Edge cleared his throat. Austin had her pen poised. Zachary took out a pocket knife and started to clean his nails.

"Russ, tell me about Carla Morgan."

"Carla? Well, you know, she got shot."

"Yeah, I know. What about her? I heard that you had the sweets for her; that you guys were a thing."

"Well, no, I mean, yeah, we went out once or twice, but she was hung up on that dude she was with when she got shot. I mean, I think I could'a changed her mind, but, you know . . ."

"I can understand that. I mean, why would she want a scrawny lookin' boy like him when she could'a had a man like you; a guy with a future."

"I know, right?" He shrugged his shoulders.

"Tell me something. What was it about her that you liked so much?"

He frowned and looked embarrassed. His eyes darted to Austin and her chest.

"I don't know, you know. She looked good, she had a good body, I mean. And she was nice, too." He paused in embarrassment. "I mean, come on."

"I know, I know. Well, we just wanted to talk to you and see if you said anything to her on that Friday night that she was killed; or, if she said anything to you."

"That was the SoMoCo game, right?"

"Right."

"Yeah, I think I did talk to her at the fence right after the game." He smiled broadly. "We killed'em 42-6. I had twelve pancake blocks; graded out 97%. I'd'a got a hunert, 'cept for a holdin' call, that wadn't really a holdin' call. See, the end moved at the last minute, and I . . ."

"Right," Edge interrupted. "But what we want to know is what was it she told you at the fence? How'd that happen? You call her over? She call you, what?"

"Oh, right. Well, she just said she'd be at the car wash Saturday mornin', and I should bring my truck over there to get it washed. It's a nice truck. My daddy got it for me, right after I committed."

"What car wash?"

"Some sorority thing; you know, they wash your car for free, but you make a donation."

"Did you call her over to the fence?"

"Yeah, I saw her standin' there with that dork, and I said, hey, come here. She said they was goin' to the Red Shed and this Harbin' fella was gonna buy a few people some beer; 'cause, see, he was old enough. I told her that I had to ride the bus back to school, but could she meet me up there, at the school, I mean, at eleven. She said she'd think about it."

"That make you mad, her goin' with him; and then she's gotta '*think about*' meetin' you, I mean?"

"Well, yeah, a little. But, you know, I thought, you know, my day'll come."

"So you rode the bus back to campus."

"Yeah. We got to. Coach says he can't be responsible for our safety if we don't. He says he don't want us havin' no car wrecks. We got to, unless we ride with parents, and if we do, we gotta come tell'im beforehand, and he has to check our names off on a list."

Edge nodded. If he alibied, he was off the suspect list; unless they got word that he had contracted out the shooting. Frankly, he didn't look smart enough, Edge thought. What does he have to gain by killing Harbin? Or the girl? Next year up at Auburn, he'd be swimming in girls.

"Look, Russ. I just wanna ask you one more thing, son. I look at you and I see a pretty big guy. I was wonderin', and Mr. Zachary here was wonderin' too, if you could pass a piss test. I mean, right now, today."

"What? What? Now, wait a minute."

"You take steroids, don't you."

Zachary stepped forward. "I can make you take the test, Russ. If you don't, you can't play."

"Wait, wait." Moore appeared on the verge of tears. "Wait, now. I take vitamins to help me digest my food. That's all it is."

"Relax, Russ," Edge said. "Me and Mr. Zachary just wanna know the name of your supplier. I think Mr. Zachary here might even forget about the piss test if you give him the name of whoever helps you with your 'vitamins.'"

Moore, who was clearly agitated, began to rise from his chair. Like a cornered animal, he could see his future slipping away.

"Sit down, Russ," Zachary said. "You ain't gonna do nothin'. Calm your ass down."

Moore pointed at Edge and looked at Zachary. His biceps were huge, and veins swelled on the underside of his forearms.

"He's tryin' to take my scholarship," Moore said pointing at Edge. "I can't . . ." His voice was two octaves above what it had been, and was much louder.

Zachary stood up straight. "Sit down and shut up, Russ. He's not doin' nothin'."

"I'll kick your ass," the boy said pointing at Edge.

Edge began to pick out places to kick and punch the Moore just to stave off an attack. He wasn't certain any of them would have any effect on the boy, but maybe he could keep him at bay. Then he looked at Austin. Her eyes were wide, and she had begun to back her chair away from the table.

"Calm down, Russ," Zachary said, confident in his ability to punch out Moore. "Sit down and give me the name."

Slowly, Moore returned to his chair. He took several deep breaths and tried to calm himself. His eyes darted from Edge to Austin, then to Zachary, and back again.

"It's Louis. Louis Anderton."

"How can I find him?"

"He works at the vet down in Grand Bay."

"How often do you get dosed?"

Moore sat, shoulders slumped. He was whipped.

"Once a week," he said.

"You know I'm gonna have to bust him," Zachary said.

"I know."

"You prob'ly got another supplier already, though, right?"

Moore said nothing, but a slight sparkle in his eye told Edge that Zachary's assumption was correct.

Chapter 15

The next day, Austin met Edge in his office for a strategy meeting. She looked tired and out of energy. He got up out of his chair and walked to the window, at the same time going past her as closely as possible. He inhaled deeply as he went by.

"So what's with you? You'n Pat keepin' late hours?"

"Please. Pat's in Connecticut."

"But you talk on the phone, right?"

"Sometimes."

"Visiting soon?"

"Maybe." She smiled.

He sat back down and looked her in the eye. "How much did you have this morning?"

She tensed noticeably. Her eyes got wide, and she said nothing.

"I can't work with a dishonest partner. I gotta know that I can trust you."

She swallowed hard. "Just one beer, early. I couldn't get to sleep, and I had something about four." She paused and looked away. "So, what happens now, you ditch me?"

"Should I?" He could see the redness in her eyes.

"Please, don't. I can stop, I promise I can. This is a big deal for me. If you bump me out, the Sheriff'll wanna to know why, and if he finds out . . . well . . ."

If she says one beer, that means it was at least two, maybe three, he thought. He could stick with her and encourage her to stay straight, or he could cut her loose. Frankly, he liked having her around; if for no other reason than she was a warm body in the room. And as it turns out, he thought, she *is* a quiet and humble drunk.

"No. But your driving days are done. From now on, I'm behind the wheel."

They sat in silence for what seemed like an eternity but what was really only two or three minutes. He cleared his throat.

"What's it gonna take to get you off the sauce for the duration of the case?"

She sat up straight and moved to the edge of her chair. "I can do it." She paused. "I'll pour it all out and just not buy any more."

Edge took a deep breath and looked off out the window. He didn't believe her, but . . .

"So, how about that Russ Moore, hunh. He got you a little unnerved, I could tell."

"No. I, I was ready."

"Ha, ha. If he'd'a gotten his hands on you, you'd be dead. Heck, I'd be dead. There was no way you'd'a gotten him off you."

"I could'a shot him."

"Yeah, right. When someone's got their hands around your throat, sometimes pullin' a piece is the farthest thing from your mind. Besides, he'd've attacked me before he would have you. The thing that saved you was the fact that he has a mother. A lotta violent men won't hurt a woman because of their mother. That is . . ."

"What?"

Edge turned back to the window and got a faraway look in his eyes "Unless his mother verbally and physically abused him. Then he'll kill every woman he can get his hands on."

Austin said nothing.

He returned from his short trance and snorted. "Okay. What's next? By the way, what kind of leads are Randall and his people working on over at the S.O.?"

"Well, they think that Harbin was into drugs pretty heavy. They're workin' it from that angle. They also think he might'a been tryin' to hook up with the Crips or the Bloods."

"They got all that from one roach in the ashtray?"

"That and the autopsy report. Harbin had marijuana and alcohol in his blood."

"What about the girl?"

"Just alcohol."

112

Edge smirked. "Oh, right." In his mind, Harbin's intoxication level was evidence of how or why Harbin had let the two killers into his car.

"Rice and Will Eubanks are also waiting for something called the, 'magic phone call.'"

Edge laughed out loud.

"Do you know what that is?"

"Yeah. I do."

She looked at him inquisitively. "Well?"

"Well, the long answer is this. There's a theory amongst older homicide investigators that if the community is responsible for committing crimes, it's also their responsibility to solve them. This theory purports that since the public is responsible for the crimes, they know more about solving them than the police do, since the police normally have little if any prior relationship with the perpetrators or the victims. The public knows who commits crimes, how they commit them, the tools they use, and how they get away with them.

"All that being said, it is therefore incumbent upon the community, that is, some member of it, to one day pick up the phone and call authorities and notify them of the identities of the perpetrators of a murder. Usually, the person who calls has some stake in its commission or its resolution and therefore knows, if not all, then at least a good many facts of the case.

"Sometimes it's a witness; sometimes, a spouse or family member; sometimes, it's a co-conspirator; sometimes, it's a jilted lover; sometimes, it's even a parent, though it's usually pretty hard for a mother to turn in her baby. Often, it's someone who just wants a reward for doing what they should do anyway – be a good citizen. But just about always, the call can normally lay out everything that a homicide detective needs in order to get a warrant and bring that perpetrator to justice."

He looked at her and smiled. "And, that contact, my dear, is what is known as the 'magic phone call.'"

"Come on."

113

"It happens; and more times than you might think. And, until science catches up with criminals, and forensic evidence can identify perpetrators without the help of live witnesses, there'll still be a need for, and a hope and a prayer from investigators for, the magic phone call."

"What's the short answer?"

"It's a lazy man's way to solve crime." Edge looked at her. "Learn something new every day."

"Yes, I guess so."

"Okay, so the Sheriff's Department will take care of the drug end. And they can wait by the telephone. Meanwhile, why don't you call Randall and give him Willie Rae Stanton's name and tell him that Stanton was a supplier for Harbin's small dope trade."

"I thought we were gonna talk to him? I want to get my hands on him, for runnin' from me."

"Oh, we still can. But let them have something. That way they'll think we're not holding out on'em." He paused and looked away. "In the meantime . . ."

In forty five minutes, Edge and Austin were in the home of Otha Harbin off Iroquois Street in Chickasaw, Alabama, a small hamlet of about five thousand that was contiguous to the north boundary of the city of Prichard, the most violent of all the bedroom communities in Mobile County.

They found the Harbin family home on the west side of the street a half block south of Myrtlewood Avenue. It was a brick cottage with a fenced front yard. Edge parked in the street.

A middle aged woman with a full figure, wearing a print house dress and thong sandals answered the door. Her hair was disheveled, but her lips were adorned with gloss, and her nails were painted. It appeared as if the two investigators had caught her in the middle of putting on her face. Edge was thinking it might be the first time she'd done so in a month. He hated to break her mood.

"Ms Harbin?" he said.

"Yes."

"My name's Edge, and this is Ms Austin from the Metro Sheriff's Department. We'd like to talk to you about your son."

Her shoulders slumped and what little animation there was in her face quickly vanished. She pursed her lips and nodded.

"Ya'll come on in." She turned aside in the doorway.

They entered a modest, yet relatively clean and well-kept home. Edge had not expected such. He and Austin took seats on a worn couch near the front window. Harbin sat down in a club chair that was just as worn.

"My husband ain't here. He's out pickin' up cans."

"He doesn't have a regular job?" Austin said.

"He works four days a week at the shipyard, doin' casual labor. It ain't much, but we git by."

Edge nodded. "I guess you know Mr. Harbin came to see me."

"He said he hired a private detective. I didn't really see how we could afford it, but . . ." She shrugged.

"Well, don't worry about that. The girl's daddy is helpin' out."

"Oh, well, good. I was shore sorry about her. I met her twice't. She seemed like a real nice girl."

"Ms Harbin, tell me about Ty. What kinda boy was he?"

She looked up and away, as if remembering better times; perhaps, the first time she held him, as a baby.

"Ty was a good boy. He was named after Tyrone Power. I was watchin' *Mississippi Gambler* on the late movie the night I went into labor. My boy was a hard worker, and he was goin' into the Marines. He was gonna marry that girl after he got outta basic training."

"Was that already set? Was he signed up?"

"Well, yeah. He said he was. And that was his plan."

"Did he work?"

115

"He did. He worked up at the syrup factory five nights a week."

"What did he do for them?"

"He worked on the loadin' dock, I think; helpin' to get the trucks loaded and on the road."

"Did he have any other jobs?"

"Not that I know of." She paused and looked at him, hard. "Oh, I know what ya'll are thinkin'. I told them other detectives, my boy don't use ner sell no dope. I don't think he hardly even drank. But I know he didn't mess with dope. And that goes for gangs, too. They come up here tryin' to say he was in some black gang. Shoot, there ain't no blacks in Chickasaw. How was he gonna get involved with a black gang."

"Yes, ma'am. Tell me about the night he went out."

"You mean when he . . .?"

"When he was killed, yes, ma'am."

"Well, he left about five or so to go pick up that girl. He said they was goin' out to eat in Mobile, and then they was gonna head down to the ball game in Grand Bay. I tried to make him supper 'fore he left, but he said he didn't want nothin', that him and the girl was gonna eat at a restaurant."

"Did he say what restaurant?"

She shook her head. "No. But, I didn't ask."

"Did you hear from him again?"

She shook her head.

"Was your husband home?"

"Naw. I, I don't know where he was."

Edge nodded, but the lack of knowledge of her husband's whereabouts on this important night told him that there was probably physical abuse or alcoholism in the home.

"Did you talk to anyone that night?"

"Well, let me see. Nobody's as't me that, yet. Uh, I got one call from Mavis up the street askin' if he she could catch a ride with me to the grocery store on Saturday mornin'; and there was a call from one'a the ladies at the church where

116

I go sometimes seein' if I could bring a dish for dinner on Sunday." She paused. "And there was one other call."

"From who?"

"From some boy, said he worked at the plant. Wanted to know where Ty was."

"He say who he was?"

"I thank he said his name was Allen, or Alvin, or somethin'."

"Did you tell him?"

"Well, yeah, I told him he took his little girlfriend to the ball game in Grand Bay."

Edge nodded again. "What time was that?"

"Oh, eight thirty, I guess. I was still up, but the news wadn't on yet."

Edge looked at Austin. "Make a note of that."

She nodded reading his mind. "What's your phone number, Ms Harbin?"

Annie Harbin recited a 457 exchange. Her eyes got wide, and she looked away, as she just that second realized that she might very well have talked to her son's killer, and led them to him.

"What time did you say that call came in?"

"Oh, uh, about eight thirty or nine, I guess; no later, but maybe a little before."

Edge took a deep breath and exhaled. "Just one more question." He paused. "Tell me about the hunting accident."

Annie Harbin's eyes widened. Edge looked at Austin. She was alert and ready with her pen.

"Oh. Well, I don't know. That's been so long ago."

"Yes, you do. What happened?"

She paused and looked away. "Well, there was this boy at school, Terry. Terry Sawyer. His daddy runs a business in Chickasaw and has some huntin' property upstate. Ty come home one day sayin' that he wanted to go huntin' with Terry. He said Terry would git him a gun and ever'thang else that he needed; 'cept the license. Ty's daddy got him a license. His daddy thought it'd be alright. So . . . I said okay." She paused.

117

"All I know is that Ty accidental shot that boy up there, in the woods. I don't know how it happened. Ty wouldn't never talk about it."

"Did Ty get charged with anything?"

"No. He had to go up to Grove Hill and testify at the Coroner's thang, the inquest, I thank they call it. But nothin' ever come of it." She paused. "It was a sad thang. Ty was only fifteen. He kinda changed after that."

"How so?"

"Well, he was a lot more quiet, and kinda distant, you know. He was just gittin' a little more open when . . ."

"Did you ever have any contact with Terry's family?"

She shook her head. "They was at the Sheriff's Office in Grove Hill when we got up there that night, but I didn't talk to'em. I do know the boy's daddy was real upset, and real loud. We could hear him in the other room, talkin' about how he wanted Ty arrested. Ty didn't mean to shoot'im. It was a accident."

"You're right, ma'am. That's all it was."

In the car, Austin looked at Edge. "You think it's time to tell the detectives about this hunting accident?"

"Noooo. It happened seven years ago. I don't know that there's anything to it," he lied. "I just don't want the Sheriff's Office to hear about it yet."

"You don't have a lotta confidence in them, do you?"

"I know your boss." He smiled. "Go ahead and get a subpoena for those phone records. They'll probably come back to a booth somewhere, but with any luck it'll be one outside the front door of wherever our killer lives. They'll take a while to get, so start tomorrow."

She nodded.

"And, for now, let's just keep this lead under out hats, okay?"

"Whatever you say," she said with resignation in her voice.

Chapter 16

The next day, Austin called and said that she had to be in court again.

"Do I need to check on you?" he said.

"You can find me at the courthouse. It's a marijuana case; courtroom 4200." Her tone was one of disgust.

He said nothing. Then he took a deep breath.

"I'll find something to keep me busy, and I'll catch up to you later."

Edge sat in his office, perused the Examiner newspaper, and thought. The words of Tom Miller, ABI Agent, stuck in his head: 'If Harbin killed my boy, I wouldn't soon forget.'

Turning to the Metro Section, Edge found the police blotter. There was a robbery at the 7-11 at Azalea and Cottage Hill; a burglary at Naman's Food Store on Broad; and a forged prescription case at Ladas Pharmacy, also on South Broad Street.

Crime and its causes were never a large mystery to Edge. People wanted things, and they weren't patient or resourceful enough to get them by the normal means – work. Work is a very moral activity. They couldn't say 'no' to their desires, so they went out and got what they wanted the simplest way they knew how. They took what they wanted from someone else – stealing. That is an immoral activity. It was as old as mankind, the battle between the two.

His eyes continued down the page and stopped at a blurb about a shooting in the Happy Hills Housing project. He laid down the paper.

After a twenty minute walk, Edge was at the Police Department's Detective Division on Church Street. He found Victor Riley at his desk eating a Tums and smoking a cigar.

Riley was in his fifties with a round belly, a widows peak, and a red nose. His white shirt was wrinkled and his shoes were scuffed. Edge had worked with him on several other cases in the past two years, and the two peacefully coexisted.

"Hi, ho. Lieutenant."

"Edge. I thought I got rid of you for a while."

"You mean that thing up in Tangerine? That went to bed two weeks ago. I'm onto something else."

"Well, what are you doing here?"

"I wanted to ask you about a murder that happened last night."

"The one in Happy Hills?"

"That's the one. Something in the paper made me think it was gang related."

"Like what?"

"Well, a drive by shooting in a minority neighborhood; rapid fire weapons; a recovered stolen vehicle."

Riley leaned back in his chair and smirked. "Keep all that to yourself. The city's tryin' to keep a lid on the fact that some'a the gangs from out west have been tryin' to make inroads here; while they're on their way to Florida, that is."

"Mum's the word."

"So, what about it?"

"You got anybody in custody?"

"Yeah, one kid." He moved papers around on his desk. "Alphonse Pendleton. They call him 'Freedom'."

"Ironic."

"Yeah."

"Can I talk to him?"

"You mean about this case?"

"No. About something else."

"What?"

"Come on, Vic. It has nothing to do with your thing. It's just about the state of gangs in the southeast. I'm doing a paper for school."

Riley smirked. "A paper for school? Shit, I didn't know you could write." He paused. "Edge, don't make a big deal outta this."

"I won't. But, really, don't you think the people in the 'hood already know that west coast gangs are here?"

"Oh, that's not the people we're worried about. It's the big money types out in West Mobile who don't need to know."

"My lips are sealed."

He smirked again. "Okay. But I don't think he'll talk to you. He lawyered up on us."

"He'll talk to me."

Twenty minutes later, Edge was at the visitor's room at the county jail underneath the courthouse. He signed in and was seated and waiting when Alphonse Pendleton walked through the door. Pendleton took a seat, also. He was rail thin, the color of chocolate, and angry. Green tattoos – one, a small teardrop at the outside corner of his left eye – were barely visible in contrast to his dark skin.

He was in the visitor's room because he was curious. He was new in town and did not know anyone in Mobile. That fact that someone wanted to talk to him was more than his sense of inquisitiveness could stand.

"Hey, Alphonse. How ya, doin?"

"Who is you, man?" His tone was confrontational.

"My name's Edge. I'm a PI."

"What'chu want?"

"I just wanna talk."

"'Bout what?"

"Tyrone Harbin?"

"Who?"

"Ty Harbin."

"I ain't never heard a no Tyrone Harbin." He said the words with a sneer in his voice.

"Are you sure? 'Cause it'd really help me if you did."

He thought for a minute. "So, what I git if I know'im?"

"Few dollars in your account."

"Well, yeah, come to thank of it, I do know'im. White dude, right?"

"Yeah. White dude. What do you know about him?"

"What'chu wanna know?"

"Are you local?"

"Naw, man. I'm from Compton."

"You're a long way from home. What'chu doin' here?'"

"Come to see my cousin. He stay here."

Edge nodded. "How long you been in town?"

"Two days."

"You ever been to Chickasaw?"

"Chickensaw?"

"Chickasaw."

"Oh, uh, yeah. I been dere. Now, where's my money."

"You're pretty high up in the gangs, aren't you, Alphonse?"

"I don't know nothin' 'bout no gangs." He paused, folded his arms, and looked away. "Who is you man?"

Edge exhaled deeply and disgustedly. "Just a guy tryin to make a livin' the right way – the moral way."

After lunch, Edge got in the Impala and drove north. He found Sawyer Plumbing on Highway 43, just north of the City Hall Building in Chickasaw. After that, he located a space in the shopping center parking lot next door and set up on the building, just to see what he could see.

It was a cinder block structure that appeared, with offices, showroom, parking lot, and warehouse, to be about four thousand square feet – large for a mom and pop business. In the rear, the warehouse was made of aluminum and painted light blue. The parking area was chain link fence-enclosed and adjacent to the north side of the building. Two marked trucks sat within, as did a half a dozen personal vehicles.

Edge got out binoculars and used them to identify and copy down all the license plates in the yard, even those for the commercial trucks. He didn't know what he was looking for, but he was sure that he could use the information in the future.

One of the personal vehicles was an 80's model, red Camaro. It had mag wheels, t-tops, and it looked well cared for. Another vehicle was a gold Cadillac Sedan de Ville.

Surveillance wasn't Edge's strong suit. He'd rather be somewhere talking to someone; but in this case, it was necessary, and right then he couldn't think of a ruse to get himself inside the business in order to have a look around.

At noon, two people exited a side door of the business that opened into the fenced parking area. One of the two was a male with a dishwater blond mullet, wearing jeans and a light blue company shirt. He got into the Camaro, started the engine, and left through the open gate.

The other was an older man; with a head full of gray hair and a pot belly. He wore a white shirt and jeans, and he walked like a man who had been riding a horse for too long; by that it is meant that he was severely bowlegged. The older man got into the Cadillac.

Edge started his engine and decided to follow the Camaro. The sports car drove out onto US 43 and headed north, toward Saraland. Edge's Impala caught him quickly and stayed within a quarter mile of the vehicle until it turned into the parking lot of a rundown apartment complex on the east side of 43, not far from the Saraland City Limit sign. Edge stopped at a convenience store nearby and used binoculars to note that the young man entered unit five. He waited.

In ten minutes, the blond exited the apartment and got back into the Camaro, after which Edge followed him on into Saraland. The Camaro a stopped at the Pizza Shack, and the driver went inside.

Edge decided he'd had enough, broke off the surveillance and started back toward Mobile. There was no reason to do anything else until he knew more about who the players were in the little drama of the family that couldn't forgive.

Shortly after lunch, Edge met Austin at his office. Edge got out a list that he'd been working on since that morning.

"I need you to check some tag numbers."

"Hold on." She got out her notepad. "Okay, go ahead."

Edge read out eight numbers. Two were for the commercial vehicles, and six for the private ones in the lot at Sawyer Plumbing.

"Okay, what's this about?"

"These are people who work for Terry Sawyer's family."

"So you *do* think there's something to this, this, getting even."

"I don't know yet. But it's a lead and it has to be checked." He paused. "You may not believe this, but we're gonna put this thing together. I'm sure of it." He paused. "And I'm never sure of anything."

Edge and Austin pulled up at the loading dock of the MapleHouse Incorporated manufacturing plant on Telegraph Road in Chickasaw, a quarter mile north of the Prichard City Limits sign, around three that same afternoon. There appeared to be little if any activity at the docks.

They ascended the concrete steps on the north end and found the supervisor's office on the left. A white man with brown hair, wearing a white shirt and white socks, sat behind the desk with his feet up, his arms folded, and his eyes shut.

Edge stood in the threshold and knocked on the open wooden door. Ten seconds worth of pounding finally roused the man. He sat upright, wiped his face with both hands, and tried not to look surprised to see his two visitors. He gestured for them to enter, while yawning obnoxiously.

"Yes, sir. Can I help you?"

"My name's Edge, and this is Ms Austin from the Metro Sheriff's Office." She displayed her badge. "I'm an Inquiry Agent working on Ty Harbin's murder case."

"That somethin' like a PI?"

"Something like. You gotta minute?"

He yawned again. "Sure. Sit down."

Edge and Austin took seats in wooden chairs across from a man who appeared as if he'd sampled a little too much product over the years.

"My name's Peacock. I run the loadin' dock.

"Mr. Peacock, what kind of employee was Ty?"

"Oh, he was okay. You know, now, that he just worked for us casually. He wadn't no full time employee."

"He just worked on call?"

"Right. We called him in when we knew there was gonna be trucks to load and unload."

"You gotta pretty big crew here?"

"Oh, six or eight with the same status as him, guys we call when we need'em; and four full time, if you don't count the drivers."

"Did Ty get along with everybody?"

"Yeah, well, for the most part. See, I'm not here after five, so I don't know what goes on in the evenin'. Another supervisor is around here then. He's supposed to write things up on an incident sheet whenever anything goes wrong, and he never put anything on there about Ty. But during the day, he never had any trouble with any'a the other guys."

"Ty have any other kinda problems?"

"How do you mean?"

"Did he ever come to work drunk? Fail a urine test? Anything like that?"

"Well, we don't piss test the casual laborers, so I don't know about that. As far as drunk, he never let on like he was drunk. I'd'a sent him home if I found he was drinkin'. I

125

mean, we got forklifts and such back here, and he can't be usin'em if he's had a few."

Edge snuck a peek at Austin whose head was down. She seemed oblivious to the man's remarks about drunkenness on the job.

"Tell me about the truckers, this Treetop Transport. I understand they haul all your merchandise."

"Yeah. The home office is located in New Orleans and they gotta half dozen plants throughout the southeast. Treetop is a subsidiary of MapleHouse and they do all the haulin' of product for us; mostly to food stores in this part of the country."

"What about the drivers? Any of'em have a hard on for Ty?"

Peacock shook his head slowly. "Not that I know of. They've got some screwy types drivin' them trucks, now, and if one of'em flew off the handle about somethin' while they were here, it wouldn't surprise me. But as far as anything Ty or anybody else did to piss'em off," he shook his head again, "I don't know about nothin' like that."

Edge nodded. "Well, okay. How about this? Who do you think is the screwiest of all the drivers?"

Peacock smirked. He wanted to help, and there were a couple of the drivers that he really despised and wished the company would get rid of – one in particular.

He looked from side to side. "Well, you didn't hear this from me, but the guy at the top'a the list is probably Dwight Trueblood." He looked from side to side again. "But you didn't hear that from me."

"I understand there was an incident involving one of your truckers about a month ago. Can you tell me about it?"

Peacock, no doubt schooled on whether or not to admit wrongdoings committed by any employees, was cagey. He looked sideways at Edge and raised a brow.

"Like what?"

"Well, apparently one'a the Treetop people was drivin' down the interstate waving a gun at other drivers;

126

maybe took a shot at one or two. You hear anything about that?"

"Ha. Really? No, I ain't heard it; but like I say, it wouldn't surprise me. Some'a them boys are kinda crazy."

"Think it could be this Trueblood character?"

Peacock pursed his lips. "Don't know. But . . ." He raised his brows again, and cocked his head.

Edge nodded. "I understand." He paused. "Say, did Ty ever talk about joinin' the Marines? Maybe gettin' outta here?"

Peacock shrugged. "Not that I remember; but, hey, that wouldn't be unusual. The young people we got workin' for us ain't what you'd call career minded about this place. Most of'em are workin' their way onto somethin' else anyhow."

Edge couldn't think of anything else to ask, so he said, thank you, nodded to Austin and the two rose from their chairs.

"I was sorry to hear about Ty," Peacock said as he rose from his chair also. "He was a pretty good ole boy. Not too awful bright, but he didn't bother nobody."

"Apparently he bothered somebody."

In the car, Austin thumbed through her notes. "I thought Ty Harbin worked full time for these guys."

"That's what he told everybody."

"Well, casual labor isn't full time."

"I know it." Edge paused. "I wonder what else he was lying about."

It took thirty minutes to get to the US Marine Recruiting station on South Sage Avenue in Mobile. Edge parked in front of a short strip shopping center that housed the recruiting offices for all four branches of service, as well as the Alabama Army National Guard, and he and Austin walked in the unlocked front door.

A lance corporal, whose name tag identified him as Stryker, was seated at the first desk on the left. No other

Marines were in the room. He was a tall man with a buzz cut and a perfect uniform that bore only a good conduct ribbon and an 'EXPERT' marksman badge. He rose quickly and stood at attention.

"Good afternoon. How you folks doin'?"

"Good, Lance Corporal. My name's Edge and this . . ."

He smiled broadly and put up his hand in the 'stop' gesture. "Don't tell me. Let me guess. You wanna put your daughter here in the Marines. Well, sir, that there is a fine idea."

Edge looked at Austin and smiled. "You know, a hitch in the service just might do her some good."

"Now, wait a minute," she said, her brows raised.

"But," Edge continued, "maybe some other time. This is Deputy Austin of the Metro Sheriff's Office." She displayed her badge. "Is the station commander available?"

Stryker, if he was embarrassed by his mistake, didn't show it. He eyed Austin up and down with interest before jerking his head toward the back of the room.

"Well, the Lieutenant was here, but he stepped out. Is there something I can help you with?"

Edge spoke. "We're on a case and, well, we were just wondering, really, if you guys are working a recruit named Tyrone Harbin?"

Stryker sat back down and leaned forward on the desk. Edge and Austin took seats across from him, and Austin took out her pad. The Marine steepled his hands.

"You two are on a case?"

Edge nodded. "Yeah." He paused. "You know this kid?"

"Well, he came by a couple'a times to talk. He wanted to know what the pay was, how long before he'd have to report, where he'd do his Basic, that sort of thing."

"Things go any farther?"

"Well, I'm not supposed to talk about it."

128

Edge looked at him, hard. "You do know the boy's dead, right?"

Stryker looked stunned. "No. I didn't."

"He was murdered about a month ago."

He leaned back in his chair. "Son of a bitch." He paused. "How?"

"He was shot out on I-10, with his girlfriend. It was in the papers." He paused. "So, you can see how that what was going on in every aspect of his life could be important."

"You think his death had somethin' to do with him joining the Marines?"

"Don't think so. But . . ." Edge didn't wait for him to start spouting off about privacy. "Did he take the ASVAB?"

"Yeah; didn't score too well, though. I think he placed highest in Mechanical Ability."

"What happened after that?"

"Well, I was gonna get him set up for a physical and a piss test, up at the MEPS (Military Entrance Processing Station), in Montgomery, but he said, 'well, hey, I need a little time to prepare.' So, I figured he was usin', and I just told him we couldn't take him."

"Just like that?"

"Oh, yeah. We gotta lotta guys wantin' to enlist, what with the economy the way it is. Right now, we can afford to be selective. I told him to come back later. They tell us not to just cut somebody off, but to tell'em to come back some other time when maybe times are a little better, or they're a little more serious about it."

Edge nodded. "How'd he take it when you shut him down?"

"Well, he wadn't real happy, but he did seem a little relieved; like he wadn't too anxious to join."

"The few, the proud."

"Well, not Ty Hardin, I don't think."

Chapter 17

The next morning, Edge picked up Austin at the Sheriff's Office in Theodore, and they were at the Allied Truck stop in Grand Bay by eight AM.

Austin had called the home office of Treetop Transport the afternoon previous, spoke to a secretary, and learned that their driver, Dwight Trueblood, would be passing through Alabama on his way to Mobile to pick up a load of syrup and would then be leaving out on his way back west, to Biloxi, Mississippi, to deliver it. The people at Treetop said that according to his credit card receipts, he usually stopped at the truck stop in Grand Bay to fuel up and eat, and would probably do so again.

Austin said that Treetop had learned of the allegations against one of their drivers, considered Trueblood a likely suspect, and were more than anxious to help. From what they said, it seemed to her that Trueblood was not their favorite employee.

Edge found a parking spot in the southwest corner of the lot near the scales, and they set up to wait. He had called Peacock at MapleHouse and found out about when he was due. The timing indicated that Trueblood and his truck would hit the truck stop around ten that morning.

While they waited, there was nothing to do but make conversation, so Austin started in early.

"You from around here?" she said.

"I'm from Compton." He smiled.

"Really? California?"

"No. I was just joking. I had a fella yesterday tell me he was from Compton. It sounded like a good place to be from."

"Oh."

"I'm originally from Oklahoma."

"Yeah?"

"I owned a ranch out there. Folks called me Curly. I dated a blonde haired girl, named Shirley. We eventually got married, after I rescued her from a crazed and obsessed hired hand, who wanted her for himself and intended to do her harm if he didn't get her."

"You got married?"

"Sure did. Oh, what a beautiful morning that was. We rode to the church in a yellow surrey with fringe on top."

She looked at him hard. "Shut up."

Edge smiled. "Had you goin' there, didn't I."

"Come on. I told you about me?"

"Not much. Just that you're from Connecticut and that you got a squeeze named 'Pat' – who may or may not be a man."

She paused and looked out the car window thoughtfully. "I don't tell people I'm a lesbian because down here, they might not understand."

"Hey, up in Connecticut they might not understand either. Believe me, when it comes to homosexuality, prejudices are what you'd call omni-regional."

"Well, up there we keep private things private. Down here, everybody seems to want to know your business."

"Well, you wanna know my business."

"Just to pass the time."

"Just the same, you still wanna know it." He paused. "But you're probably right about the privacy thing bein' more pronounced up there. Down here, family is pretty important. They all want to know about who your mama and daddy are and where you come from. And, there's a reason for it."

"What's that?"

"Security."

"Security?"

"Sure. Money, property, even safety." He paused. "It helps people make good matches in marriage; it keeps 'em outta trouble."

"I never thought'a that." She paused. "Pat and I are gonna get married one day."

"Married?"

"Sure. It'll happen."

Edge chuckled. "Well, something may happen, but it won't be marriage. In case you haven't noticed, you don't really fit the definition."

"The definition can be changed."

"Hey, you just don't go around changin' definitions. There's got to be a committee; and Webster and Oxford, they both gotta agree. It's not that easy."

She said nothing.

"Besides. What do you wanna get married for? You'd be better off signin' a contract, or somethin'. What do they call'em? Civil unions?"

She looked straight ahead in thought. For her it was the same thing every time she brought up the subject with someone. People were always telling her why it wouldn't, or shouldn't happen.

"But, we love each other."

"Hey, I love my favorite pair'a boots, but I don't wanna marry'em." He paused. "So, you love her, but if one day you find that you don't, as a lot of couples are want to do, and you decide you don't want to live together anymore, you can just dissolve the contract." He paused again. "Marriage is for people who want kids and a house, and a dog. If you want kids, you get married. And from your choice of a profession, and your partner, I'd say kids aren't high on your priority list."

Neither spoke for several minutes. Then Austin said:

"You ever been married?"

He shook his head. "Nope."

"Why not?"

"Because a woman once told me that I didn't have the face for it. She said I wasn't 'capable' of being a husband."

Austin looked at his scarred visage, close-set eyes, and drooping brows, and wondered.

"What did she mean?"

"She meant that I've seen and done too much for a woman to think she could ever trust me."

132

"Where have you been? And what have you done?"

Edge looked at her and smiled. "I was in the French Foreign Legion."

"No, really."

"Okay, okay. I and my family were marooned on the coast of Africa by mutineers. My mother died when I was an infant and a gorilla killed my father. I was adopted by the troop, the oldest female began to nurse me, and I was raised in the jungle. I lived with them for eighteen years, eating what they ate, swinging from trees as they did, and learning their peculiar screeching noises, until an English merchant corporation came to the area to mine for diamonds. A woman with the group, Lady Greystoke, found me and adopted me . . ."

"Okay, okay, that's enough," Austin chuckled. "I think I've heard this story before, too, *Tarzan*. If you don't want to tell me about yourself, fine."

He smiled at her. She wasn't a bad sort, he thought. She just had some screwy ideas about interpersonal relationships, as well as a problem with alcohol. But, she was young.

They both amused themselves with the newspaper until a green, Mack brand, semi-tractor pulled onto the lot from off the highway shortly after nine. The truck was pulling a silver aluminum trailer that bore the markings of Treetop Transport and was making its way toward the scales. Edge saw the vehicle and got Austin's attention.

"Let's see if he'll park here on the lot and go inside. If he does, we can waylay him when he gets outta the cab." He paused. "I'd sure like to get a look at the inside of that truck."

"But, we don't a have a search warrant."

"Right," Edge said dismissively.

The truck drove slowly onto the scales, after which the operator provided the driver with a print out of its weight. Then the semi rounded the curve and made its way to the east side of the lot.

Edge started the engine and drove up right behind the trailer. "When he parks, we'll pull up next to him."

They followed the vehicle to a location on the southeast corner. The truck came to a stop next to a Campbell 66 Express transport truck that reminded fellow travelers that he was, "humpin' to please.' Edge smiled at the slogan and pointed it out to Austin.

They parked in the open space next to the passenger door and were around the front end, and with Trueblood, just as he was climbing out of the cab.

Edge spoke. "You Dwight Trueblood?"

"Who's askin'?"

The man was short, but with bowlegs, thick arms, and a pot belly. His hair was firey red, and his eyes were green. Just the sort who'd lose his temper, Edge thought.

Austin threw up her badge. "Sheriff's deputy. Show me some ID."

"What's this all about?" Trueblood took a step back and raised his arms.

"Just show us the ID," Austin said.

He reached around for a leather wallet on a chain in his back pocket and pulled out a Louisiana driver's license. Austin looked at the card.

"Look, Trueblood. It's nothing, really, we just want to take a look at your gun," Austin said.

"My, my gun?"

"Yeah. You've got a gun in there, right? All truckers do."

"Yeah, but I gotta permit and everything. It's all legal."

"Well, sure it is, Dwight," Edge said. "We just need to see it. See, we got witnesses that say you was wavin' it around out on I-10, on a Friday night about a month ago."

"Well, now that ain't right. I hadn't done nothin' like that. That's just pure bullshit."

Austin was writing down the information off his driver's license, and Trueblood was watching.

"We'd like to look at your gun, Dwight," Edge said. "Just tell me where it is, and I'll climb in and get it."

Edge put his hand on the railing next the door and lifted himself up.

"Wait a minute, mister," Trueblood said. "Just who are you?"

"My name's Edge. I'm with her."

"Well, just get your ass down off my truck."
Trueblood put his hand on Edge's right arm.

Edge stepped off the shiny steel step and made a large circle with that limb. He took hold of Trueblood's own arm and in a second it was bent back in a painful 'come along' hold.

"Don't put your hands on me, Dwight."

"Owwww."

Two seconds later Austin, who had looked up from her notes and saw the altercation between the two, stopped.

"Did you hear that?" she said.

"What?"

"That bumping noise."

All three stood motionless. Then Edge heard it. It was a bump as if someone was kicking or banging their head on the side of the sleeper portion of the cab. Edge let go of Trueblood and looked at his face. The red haired man was in a complete panic.

"Watch him," Edge said as he raised himself back up on the steps of the truck and opened the door.

He pulled himself into the driver's seat and quickly noticed the forty-five in a holster on the passenger side. Then he looked over his right shoulder and pulled back the curtain of the sleeper.

When he did, he found himself staring into the wide eyes and bruised face of a brown haired female whose mouth was duct taped shut, and whose hands and feet were handcuffed. A dirty blanket covered most of the woman's nude body.

Edge slid out of the driver's seat, down the steps, and was on Trueblood like a shot. He punched him, hard, right in the nose and then backhanded him across the right cheek. As the red haired man was reeling, Edge kicked him in the groin and watched him fall, backwards, onto the asphalt. Austin was stunned. Edge turned toward her and gestured with his thumb over his toward the cab.

"You better take a look in there."

Austin went up the steps into the truck and quickly made a u-turn. Her face was flushed.

When Trueblood was upright again, Edge hit him, this time in the jaw. He fell to the ground, out cold. Austin intervened and handcuffed the man's hands behind his back.

"Don't hit him anymore." she said.

"I'll stop when I wanna stop."

"Well, yeah, but . . ."

"Don't go soft on me."

"The Lieutenant'll be here in a few minutes. He'll need to be up and around." She paused. "Don't kill him."

Edge reached down and raised Trueblood to his feet. He slapped him four times on the face, and the red haired man began squint and moan. Edge took him around the front of the tractor and leaned him over the hood of the Impala.

"Now, you just wait right here you son of a bitch."

Edge looked all around. When he saw no one, he slugged Trueblood one more time, right in the gut making sure that he placed his punch in Trueblood's short rib on his left side. The trucker sat down, hard, on the parking lot and gasped for breath.

Two hours later, Edge and Austin were still in the parking lot answering questions about how they'd come to find the young woman in the cab of Dwight Trueblood's truck. She had been spirited off in an ambulance to Springdale Hospital, and detectives from the Metro Sheriff's Department, as well as troopers from the Highway Patrol, were awaiting agents from the FBI to arrive and take charge of the case.

Before she left the scene, the woman told Austin that she was a waitress at a truck stop outside of Baton Rouge, Louisiana, and that she had been held captive for three days. She said that Trueblood had raped her several times, but other than that, some bruising, and the psychological trauma, she was unhurt.

When Nathan Randall arrived, he talked to Austin first, then to Edge.

"What made you go up into the truck?"

"We heard somebody kickin' the sleeper door."

"Austin said you were lookin' for a gun on this Harbin thing."

"Well, now I'm not gonna lie. I was lookin' for a way to get up in there and look around. The bumpin' just gave me a reason."

"It could'a been a dog."

"But it wasn't." He paused. "It's a good bust, Lieutenant. Austin did a good job."

He nodded. "I know, I know." He looked around. "So, how'd Trueblood get that bloody nose?"

"He ran into the car door."

"Right."

"Don't make this about me, Randall. This guy's a bastard, and he deserved what he got." He paused. "Doesn't what he did make you just a little angry?"

He nodded slowly. "Yeah. Yeah, it does."

Chapter 18

The next morning, Austin was finished with what she was doing by ten, namely reports and debriefing at the main Sheriff's Office, after which she called Edge.

"Anything else on ole Dwight?" he said.

"Yeah. The FBI says that they're working another case involving a woman found at a truck stop on Highway 59, near I-10, in Baldwin County, who'd been kidnapped and held the same way. She described our man to a tea."

"Men with red hair should never commit crimes." He paused. "I bet there's a few others around. Funny, he didn't kill anyone, though."

"Please, let's be thankful he didn't."

"Right." He paused. "Did you send his pistol off to firearms examiner?"

"I did that yesterday afternoon. They'll have an opinion in a couple of days. Anyway, I'm done for now. What can we do on the Harbin thing?"

"I'll pick you up. Let's go north."

At eleven thirty they were in the shopping center parking lot next to Sawyer Plumbing. The Camaro was inside the fence, as was the Cadillac and an old Chevy Apache 10 pickup.

"You run those numbers like I told ya?"

She opened a padfolio that she held in her lap. "Yeah. The Cadillac belongs to Walter Sawyer with a Saraland address. The commercial vehicles belong to the company, and the Camaro . . ."

"That's the one I want."

"Darrell Henry."

"Good. Let's try to talk to him."

"We might have to wait all day."

"Nope. He goes to lunch at noon. We can follow him and try to make our play then."

Austin nodded. They sat back and no one spoke for several minutes. The sights that she had seen the day previous had clearly given Austin pause. She was still in a bit of daze.

"How do you feel about yesterday?" she said.

"What you do mean?"

"I mean, you know, a kidnapper/rapist; that beat up girl. Didn't that affect you at all?"

He looked at her. "Look. I've seen much worse. I know how people treat people. In fact, I've about had a bellyful of it." He paused. "If I fell a little too hard on Trueblood, well, it's because he deserved it, and he sure as shit won't get punished at the courthouse." He paused. "How 'bout you? Did you have to get something to help you sleep last night?"

She looked at him. He was clearly fishing.

"If I say, yes . . . what'll you say?"

"I say whatever gets you through the night." He paused. "Just don't let it affect your work."

"I told you, I'm under control."

He nodded. "It's okay. Everybody needs something to take the edge off."

"What do you use?"

"Whatever I can find."

He looked toward the building and noticed when a few drops of rain began to fall upon the windshield of the Impala. He hit the mist wipe once to clean off the glass.

It was twenty minutes later when Darrell Henry – or the man they believed to be Darrell Henry – walked out the front door of the plumbing business and started down the sidewalk toward the fenced parking area. Edge cranked the Impala and waited.

Henry, who was wearing dark blue coveralls, entered the lot, got in the Camaro, and left traveling north on Highway 43. Edge had a hunch about where he was going. A young man with a healthy appetite would be looking for the same buffet lunch he had eaten the other day. The two were made for each other. Henry stopped at the Pizza Shack on Highway 43 in Saraland, parked and walked inside. Edge and Austin parked and waited.

"Well, what do you say?" Edge said. "Do you feel like a bite?"

"I can't stand pizza."

He looked at her. "Well, I know it's not the filet mignon you're used to, but . . ."

139

Edge got out of the car, and Austin did the same. "Just follow my lead." Inside he waved at the waitress.

"We're meeting someone," he said.

They walked to the corner booth in the rear where Henry was seated. The name 'Darrell' was stitched in cursive writing over his right hand shirt pocket and it confirmed his identification. Edge slid in next to him, and Austin got in on the other side.

"Hey, what's goin' on?" Henry said as he moved away, toward the window.

He was thirty with a pock marked face and a bulbous nose. He appeared to be, even at his young age, a beginning alcoholic.

"Darrell, my name's Edge, and this Deputy Austin from the Metro Sheriff's Department." Austin held up her badge. "We need to talk to you for a minute. Then you can get back to your lunch."

"About what?" Henry's voice was indignant. "I ain't done nothin'."

"Nobody said you did, Darrell. We just want to talk a little about the plumbing business."

"Like what?"

"Like, how long you been working for Mr. Sawyer?"

He looked at them, and when he decided they weren't going to leave, he exhaled deeply and said: "'Bout two years."

"You know anything about the family?"

"What'cha mean?"

"I mean it's a family-owned business, right? Who all works there, from the family, I mean?"

"Well, there's Mr. Sawyer, Walter; Josh, he's Walter's brother; and Ms Sawyer, uh, Alice, comes in ever' so often to keep the books. And, me, I work there, but I ain't no kin to'em."

"What about Jerry Sawyer; he work there, too? Sometimes?"

Henry shook his head. "No. He used to, but he moved away. He lives in Tampa, I think."

140

"He in the plumbing business down there?"

He shook his head again. "Nunh, unh. I think he works in a club; Holly's Place, or somethin' like that."

"What's he do there? Bartender?"

"I think he's a bouncer."

Edge jerked his head over his shoulder back south. "I bet you do most of the work down there, don't'cha."

He looked down at the table. "I do my share."

"I bet you don't get paid much, either."

Henry said nothing as he rubbed his hands over the vinyl tablecloth. Edge looked straight into his eyes, but it looked as if he was nowhere near gaining Henry's trust.

"What's he like to work for? Old Man Sawyer, I mean."

Henry paused. You could see it weighing in his mind whether or not to say something bad about his boss. Edge spoke instead.

"I get it. Pretty tough, hunh? Long hours for not much money? I bet he comes down hard on ya when you make a mistake, right?"

"He don't like mistakes." He paused. "Look, what's this all about?"

Austin spoke up. "Have you got a record, Darrell?"

He looked at her. "Just little stuff, like DUI, an' fightin'. No felonies."

Austin requested his birth date, and he supplied it. She took out a pad and wrote the information down.

Edge had to think fast. If he asked him point blank about the murder, the first thing Henry would do is run back and tell Walter. If he didn't ask him about it, he'd still run back and tell Walter they'd talked to him. Edge had to think up a story to keep from letting Walter know they were onto him about Ty Harbin's murder, and still keep Henry quiet; at least until they knew more.

"You say Alice comes in and keeps books? She pay you in cash?" Edge said.

Henry shook his head. "No. I get a check."

"They take out social security, taxes, and all that?"

"Yeah. I said, what's this all about?" His voice went up.

"Well, we heard that Walter was payin' his people in cash, under the table, you know? Tryin' to pull one over on the government. Maybe he ain't payin' all the income tax he's supposed to. You see any of that goin' on?"

He paused. "Well, maybe they give me a bonus in cash ever' now and then, when I do a really good job, but I always claim it." He looked away. "If Walter's got a dodge, I don't know about it. I don't know nothin' about tryin' to cheat no government." He shook his head. "I don't wanna be involved in none'a that."

Edge leaned forward with his elbow on the table. "Okay, Darrell, Detective Austin here is gonna leave you her phone number. You call her when you see somethin' suspicious. If you do, the IRS might have a little something extra for you come tax time." He paused. "Oh, and mum's the word."

Henry looked at them suspiciously. Then he looked at Austin's card. He nodded slowly as Austin and Edge rose from the booth and turned to walk off.

Outside in the car, Austin was perplexed. "You wanna tell me what that was all about?"

"Yeah. Let's go up the street and park."

In front of the Saraland City Hall, Edge stopped. He put the car in park and waited. Austin looked around.

"We gotta find a way into the Sawyer family. Darrell Henry, not bein' family, is the obvious weak link. If we can get him talkin' to us, then we can pick up some pieces that might help us." He paused. "We already found out that Jerry Sawyer's in Tampa workin' at a club down there."

"You think he's involved in the murder?"

"Maybe, maybe not. But working where he works, it's a cinch that he knows a lotta shady characters that are capable of it."

"You're pretty hot on this revenge angle aren't you."

"You gotta better story to work?"

She stopped and thought. "Well, I was just thinkin'. Ty Harbin and Carla go to the ball game. Then they leave and go who knows where, but they end up at the Interstate on ramp. They're either forced to stop, or they pull over willingly. My guess is they stopped 'cause they saw who it was. I mean, it's hard to force a car off the road without one of'em wrecking. So, they knew whoever it was that killed'em."

"And, who's that?"

"Well, it could be anybody."

"So, we just need to find out everybody that Harbin was acquainted with."

"We need to start a list."

Edge looked straight ahead and smiled. "Okay. You keep that list. I've got one of my own. One where everybody on it has a motive for murder."

She said nothing.

"And the whole Sawyer family, they're all on it."

"What about Darrell Henry?'

"I don't think Darrell's involved. I mean, he don't want nothin' to do with a tax dodge, for Pete's sake, so my guess is that he's on probation for somethin'; and I didn't get the feeling he'd spring for a murder, not even for his boss.

"That just leaves Walter Sawyer; his brother, Josh; and this other son, 'Jerry.' I've got Jerry in my sights. He's family, and he knows a lotta shady people." He paused. "Why don't you get us a rundown on Jerry Sawyer – criminal history, driver's license, whatever. We can find out if he really is in Tampa and maybe take a trip down there."

Austin didn't speak.

"What?"

She shrugged and raised her brows. "I think, this is another lead, and it needs to be run down," she said, biting her lip.

Chapter 19

The next Monday, Austin called Edge at his office. She sounded disappointed.

"What have you got?" he said.

"I couldn't find a DL for Jerry Sawyer here or in Florida. There's no arrest record and no traffic tickets."

"There's gotta be. Henry should know his name." He stopped. "Run it Jerome Sawyer and try it with some alternate spellings. Try it with J E R E, or G E R E, or G E R R Y Sawyer. Try it with Jerry as a middle name. Just keep digging."

She sounded re-energized when she said: "Right. I'll call you back."

Edge sat at his desk with his feet up and his eyes closed. Every other lead, to this point, had not panned out, or was otherwise flimsy. He had in mind that Hardy Eubanks, the bum from the Blue Moon lounge had probably talked to the killers, whoever they were. It didn't eliminate anyone, but it didn't point strongly to anyone either. Unless his alibi didn't pan out, it still could have been Russ Moore in the front seat of the car that Eubanks saw in the parking lot of the lounge.

But, operating on the chance that the Sawyer family was involved, Edge began to think of how the murder could have been committed.

Jerry Sawyer had family in the area, so he could easily have stayed with them when he came to town. He would also have access to weapons and other logistical items that he would need in order to get the job done.

The evidence indicated that there were two shooters involved; two weapons; two males in the car that Eubanks saw. Edge didn't really believe that a woman had committed this crime.

Who else was it Darrell Henry said worked for Old Man Sawyer? He thought. Uncle Josh? Could he be involved? He's family. He's beholden to the old man.

His involvement was at that time unknown, but there might have to be more than family ties to get him involved in murder. Blood was thick, but was it thirty years, or even death penalty thick?

Edge continued to think. Assuming it was Jerry Sawyer that did the shooting, and he came from Tampa with his own accomplice, there had to be evidence of transportation, weapons, lodging, and gasoline purchases – *if* it was Sawyer. He struggled to keep from getting tunnel vision.

Edge picked up his ringing phone. Austin was on the other end. Before she could speak, he said:

"Look, check on this Josh or Joshua Sawyer, also. See if he's got a sheet," he said.

"Sure. But, look, I got something on Jere Sawyer."

Edge picked up a pen. "Go ahead."

"Born in '57, he's got a DL in Florida. His name's spelled J E R E. He's been busted a half dozen times here and two more down there; three for marijuana possession, and once for assault."

It suddenly occurred to Edge that Sawyer might also be a supplier of marijuana to Harbin's weed business.

"Okay, good. You got an address on him?"

"In Tampa. His Mobile address is at his daddy's."

"Okay. Just call me if there's anything on Uncle Josh."

"Right."

Edge hung up and considered what he had learned. With each passing minute he was becoming more and more convinced that the Sawyers were a part of this case.

An hour later Edge was at the Dairy Dream Drive In on Highway 90 in Grand Bay, about a quarter mile west of the Grand Bay-Wilmer Road intersection, on the south side. It was a small, wood frame building painted white with an overhang in front, to shield the walk up trade from the elements when they approached the sliding glass windows.

The parking area, large enough to accommodate fifteen or twenty vehicles, was paved with gravel. Three large oaks populated the lot.

At one of the windows, a full figured woman with rosy cheeks, wearing a hairnet, pulled back the sliding glass. Edge ordered a single scoop vanilla.

"You the owner?" he said as he licked the white cream from the top of the cone.

"Sure am. Louise Fletcher."

"My name's Edge. I'm working with the Sheriff's Office to try to find out who killed those two kids up on the highway."

"I heard about that. That was a shame."

"Were you working that Friday night?"

She nodded. "I was. I work ever' Friday and Saturday night in football season. Me and another girl, Pansy, we run the place."

"Any chance you'd remember seein' those two here after the ball game? They, uh, they ordered the watermelon ice cream."

"Are you kiddin'? There musta' been two hunert kids out here that night. It's always busy after a home game. There ain't no way'a knowin' whether or not they come up out here."

"How 'bout Pansy? She here?"

She shook her head. "Pansy ain't but sixteen. She's in school. But, I don't think she'd'a seen'em. She mostly works the back makin' the dishes. I handle the front, gettin' the drinks and takin' the money."

Edge pulled out a business card. "Would you ask her? Give her my card and ask her to call me."

"I will, but like I said, she ain't gonna remember."

"When does she work again?"

"This comin' Friday." She paused and turned to a schedule tacked on the wall. "Tigers vs Davidson."

146

It took only fifteen minutes to make it down to the Red Shed Lounge on Highway 90, about fifteen feet into the state of Mississippi. It was a wooden building with a Coca Cola sign out front, painted red and weathered by too many storms.

Edge entered the dark interior and let his eyes adjust. The counter was straight ahead, illuminated by a Pabst Blue Ribbon sign. Several chairs and tables were broadcast about the room and there was a juke box in the corner. The place appeared deserted. Edge walked toward the light.

A man with hair that was in the process of transitioning from red to gray rose from under the counter and smiled.

"What can I do for ya?"

"My name's Edge. I'm looking for the owner."

"That'd be me. John Shedrick."

"How about a little bit'a Jack, and a whole lotta Coke."

"Comin' up."

The man began his work. Edge thought of something, and smiled; smiled at the irony.

"They call you Red?"

"They used to. Now, I'm just the old man."

Shedrick poured cola into a more than generous portion of whiskey and put the glass on the counter. Edge laid down two dollars and took a sip.

"Man, that hits the spot."

Shedrick started wiping up the counter. "What can I do for ya?"

"Just some information."

"I'll try."

"Did you read about the two kids murdered up on the highway in Grand Bay, about a month ago?"

The old man nodded. "Yeah. I heard about it. You the law?"

"Private."

"I was wonderin' when somebody was gonna come down here and ask me about it."

147

Edge took another sip. "I take it you know something."

"Not me. One'a my girls. And, no, don't ask me which one 'cause I ain't tellin' ya who it is."

"One'a your employees?"

"Yeah."

"Okay. Go ahead."

"Well, that night, prob'ly about eleven or so, a couple'a kids that looked like the ones whose picture was in the paper come over here after the football game. There was a little bit of a crowd here that night, but she remembered'em 'cause'a what happened."

"Which was?"

"My girl said that the tall, skinny boy talked with a shorter, blond haired man out in the back parkin' lot. Then the tall, skinny boy got in his car, and the blond got in his, and they drove off together on 90 back toward Grand Bay."

Edge looked around at the walls, walls that had no windows.

"How'd she see all this?"

"Oh, she was outside havin' a smoke break. She likes to go outside instead of in the back'a the buildin' 'cause'a the fresh air. It was kinda cool like, for September, I mean."

"Did it look like they were arguing?"

"No. That was the thing. She said they was smilin' and laughin'. She just said it looked like that they was up to somethin'; said they had their heads together, pointin' and gesturin', like they was makin' plans. You know, 'you go here, I'll go there,' that kinda thing. But they was both smilin' in the end."

"What about the girl?"

"She just sat in the front seat. The two boys talked, back around at the trunk."

"What time was this?"

"Oh, prob'ly around eleven or a little after. When the kids come over from the ball game, they don't usually break up 'til twelve or one."

Edge nodded and took his last sip. "She say what the car looked like?"

"Said the tall, skinny boy's car was blue; she don't remember what color the other one was."

Edge nodded and looked around. "Say, what is this place? A bar? A lounge? A general store?"

Shedrick looked him dead in the eye. "We are engaged in the operation of the business for which we were created," he said parroting the words on his incorporation papers. "We fulfill a public need."

Edge nodded. "Oh. You sell beer. Got it."

Chapter 20

When Edge got back to the city, Austin was waiting for him at his office. She followed him in the door.

"I got the low down on Joshua Sawyer."

"And?"

"Not even a traffic ticket."

"Interesting. Well, we can rule him out for now. What about Willie Rae Stanton? Have your folks picked him up yet?"

"Not yet. But they're looking for him."

"Okay. Just get'em to call us when they have'im." He paused as he put his feet on his desk. "I'm thinkin' it may be time to have a chat with Randall."

"About the Sawyer lead?"

"Yeah. The way I see it, we're gonna have to take at least one trip down there, and if Randall wants to keep himself inside the loop, he's gonna have to let you go. That, unfortunately for him, is gonna cost the Sheriff a little money."

149

She paused to think. "If I have to, I'll take vacation time and pay for it myself."

Edge laughed. "Don't say that too loud. You could be broke pretty soon."

They met Nathan Randall in his office near the Records Section, off the main hall at the Metro Sheriff's Office. At three o'clock in the afternoon, the place was deserted.

Randall was behind a small desk. He didn't look happy.

"What do you want, Edge?"

"We, that is, me and Ms Austin, here, have got a lead. We wanted to run it by you."

Randall looked up at Austin then at Edge. "Go ahead."

"Tyrone Harbin killed a teenaged boy in a hunting accident seven years ago. The SBI worked the case. We think the dead boy's family might still be taking it a little too hard."

Randall said nothing.

"The kid's family is the Sawyers up in Chickasaw; the Sawyers of Sawyer Plumbing. The oldest son is in Tampa, Florida."

Randall looked at Austin. "How do you feel about this?"

"Well, I think, it's, uh, it's a viable lead. And it ought to be run down."

"You wanna go to Tampa," Randall said.

"If need be," Austin said.

Randall rubbed his face. "You know the Sawyers are big supporters of the Sheriff; have been for years."

"That doesn't mean anything to me," Edge said.

"Well, it does to Ms Austin." He paused. "What do you really have at this time?"

"You mean, evidence-wise?" Edge pursed his lips. "Nothing. Just a motive."

Randall rubbed his face again. He looked at Austin.

"Okay. I'll give you one trip to Florida – by car. If you don't have anything else by then, move on. I don't want you harassing a businessman for no reason."

He turned to Edge. "And, as for you, I can't control what you do, but all I'm saying is don't get her in a trick bag. She doesn't deserve it. And you've gotta license to worry about."

Edge's license had been threatened numerous times. He had a good lawyer and good insurance. He wasn't worried.

"Fine."

"I mean it."

"I said, fine."

That evening, Edge visited the Harbin residence on Iroquois Street in Chickasaw. He found the couple seated in front of the television in the living room; just two souls weary in their grief, she in her house dress, him in his dirty jeans with flat, bare feet.

"Come on in, Mr. Edge. Good to see ya," Otha Harbin said.

Edge nodded to Annie Harbin. "How ya'll, tonight?"

"We're gettin' by, I guess." he said. "You have a seat."

Edge took the same seat he did the other day when he spoke with Annie Harbin. He rubbed his face.

"I ain't told nobody about you workin' for me," Otha said.

"That's good. That's good."

"'Cause I don't want the Sheriff to be crawlin' all up on you about this thang."

"That's good."

"Have you found out anything yet?" Annie Harbin said.

Edge swallowed. He didn't want to spill it about the Sawyers, but he had to give them something, especially if he was going to ask them to fork over additional money.

151

"Well, I've been able to eliminate about three people. The Metro Sheriff's Department is looking for a man named Willie Stanton that they have reason to believe has information about the case. I've been able to almost eliminate a wanna-be boyfriend who was hung up on Carla Morgan, as well as a trucker who used to run loads at the syrup factory where he worked. I talked to Ty's best friend, and I've talked to his boss."

The Harbins stared at him with questioning eyes.

"And, I wanted to let you know that you need to prepare yourself for some things that are gonna be said about your boy."

"What thangs?" Annie Harbin said. They both leaned forward in their chairs.

"Well, for one, the Metro Sheriff's Department has reason to believe that while Ty didn't use dope . . . he did sell it; at least on a small scale."

Otha Harbin sat back in his chair. "I don't believe it."

"I didn't say it was true, only that you might hear it."

"My boy didn't use ner sell no dope. He was goin' into the Marines." His tone was animated.

"Well, that's another thing. I checked with the Marines. They talked to Ty, and he took their written test, but, when it come time to take the piss test, he left and didn't come back." Edge paused. "Did you ever see any enlistment papers?"

The Harbins exchanged surprised looks. "Well, no," Annie said.

"He didn't sign up, and, until he got all of the marijuana out of his system, I'm assuming he wasn't going to."

"Well, he was goin' to," Otha said.

"That may be. But he hadn't yet. And if he hadn't, there was no reason for him not to use, if he wanted to."

"I still don't believe it."

"I understand."

"What else?" Annie said.

"The night he was killed, Ty and his girlfriend were down at the Red Shed in Grand Bay, drinkin'." He paused. "Oh, he prob'ly took her to the ice cream parlor first, though I haven't confirmed it yet, but afterward . . ."

Both were silent. Apparently, to them, it was one thing to take a drink. That could be tolerated. It was quite another, however, to use or sell drugs.

"We think that's where he made contact with whoever killed him," Edge said.

"You know who that is yet?"

"No, but I've got a pretty good description. If I can get a name, I think the people we've got that saw them can identify them."

"Them? There was two?"

"I'm almost certain of it."

They were silent again.

"Which brings me to what else it is I had to tell you." He paused. "Carla's daddy has put up a five thousand dollar reward in the case."

"Well, that's good, right? Maybe it'll shake somethin' loose," Annie said.

"No. The reward is for me, if I find the killer of his daughter."

The Harbins said nothing.

"Do you have any objections?"

His brow was furrowed. "Well, no, I don't guess. I mean, if you find out who killed her, you'll find out who killed him, right?"

"Presumably. But, I was working for you. Now I'd be working for both of you; only with him, it's on commission."

Harbin said nothing for a minute. Then, "I got no objections."

"The second thing is: Do you still have any of that two grand left?"

"Yeah. Well, some."

"I'm gonna need some money for a trip to Tampa, Florida."

Harbin said nothing.

"There's a good suspect down there, and I need to locate and talk to him."

Harbin exhaled. "Okay. I can give ya five hunert more." He rose from his chair and reached for his wallet. "I, I'm about . . . broke."

"I don't think you'll be disappointed."

Chapter 21

The next morning, Edge made a preliminary call to the Police Department in Tampa. He wanted to talk to someone in the Homicide Bureau and get the low down on this, 'Holly's Place.' He also wanted to get a feeling about whether or not the police down there could be trusted and counted on to help if they were needed. As a rule, police departments were suspicious of private investigators.

Lieutenant Aldo Suarez answered the phone. Edge put the call on speaker just as Austin walked into the office.

"Suarez, my name is John Edge. I'm a deputy sheriff reserve working with the Metro Sheriff's Department here in Mobile County on a double murder case. Detective Amy Austin is listening on the speaker."

"How are you folks doing?"

His voice was heavily accented, and Edge thought about how his heritage probably made him very valuable to his department.

"Fine, fine. Look, we've got reason to believe that a couple of the players in our murder case live in Tampa – or at least in the Metro area down there. One of them works at a place called 'Holly's Place.' What can you tell me about it?"

"Well, first of all, there isn't a Holly's Place. It could be, The Hollywood Palace. It's a titty bar over on the Dale Mabry Highway, just south of the stadium. What do you need to know?"

"What kinda joint is it?"

"It's a pretty clean place; that is, we don't have too much trouble there. I can only remember one shooting in the past two or three years, and that one was domestic related."

"Nothing hinky about it at all?"

"Well . . . there are rumors that at one time the place was mobbed up, but it's changed hands a couple of times since then. I don't think they're involved now."

"You know anybody that works there?" Austin said.

"Yes, as a matter of fact. I've got an informant inside."

"Don't tell me. A dancer, right?"

Suarez chuckled. "You guessed it."

Edge paused. "Look, you ever run across a guy by the name of Jere Sawyer?" He spelled the first name. "He's supposed to work there; maybe a bouncer, possibly a bartender."

Suarez was silent. "No. Doesn't ring a bell."

"Well, let me ask you this. Who's the baddest guy there? Working there, I mean; somebody that everybody's afraid of."

He paused again. "According to my girl, it'd have to be John Evans. She says all the girls are afraid of him. She heard he killed a man in Alaska when he was in the military, back in the seventies."

"He a bouncer?"

"Yeah."

"Any truth to this murder rumor?"

"Well, I don't know. You know, a lotta guys start this kind'a shit just so they don't have to fight every night. They start a buzz and people stay in line a little better."

"What's this guy look like," Austin said.

"He's a big white guy; short hair. Seems like she said that he had been to wrestling school."

"Steroids?" I said.

"Don't they all?" Suarez said.

"I guess so." Edge nodded to Austin. "You got anything?" She shook her head.

"Okay, Mr. Suarez, we're looking at a short trip down there within the week. When we get there, we'll fill you in and let you know what we're gonna be up to. That okay?"

"Sure. I'll probably hand you off to one of my people, though."

"That's fine."

They said their goodbyes, and when Edge hung up, he looked at Austin.

"So, what do you think?"

"Not enough to tell . . . yet." She paused. "Oh, by the way, I asked Daddy."

"Asked Daddy, what?"

"What you said: that if somebody killed me, would he forget."

Edge smiled. "Oh, yeah? What'd he say?"

"Not in a million years."

In two days, Edge and Austin were in Tampa, Florida, driving into the parking lot of the Tierra Verde Hotel, on Hillsborough Avenue, two blocks east of the Airport. They had been on the road since five AM and Edge, who was behind the wheel of the County car, was worn out.

He'd had to fight Austin for the right to drive, but having a reserve deputy status, and what with her problem, he had insisted. Reluctantly, she'd handed over the keys.

"Tell me again why I'm not gettin' off a plane right now?" Edge said.

"'Cause the Lieutenant told me that this was a 'chickenshit' lead – his words, not mine – and because we'll need a car to use while we're here."

"Right." He paused. "We'll see."

They checked into the hotel shortly before eight. After a late supper, they met in the lounge for a strategy session.

Austin took a swallow of club soda and leaned back on her side of the booth. Edge drank iced tea.

"Well, what's our first move?" she said.

"Tomorrow morning, we'll hit the Police Department and try to make contact with Suarez and see what he's found out so far. With any luck, maybe he'll have talked to his informant about Sawyer and this John Evans character; and, with even more luck, he won't have tipped them off that we're coming, and they won't have skipped town."

"Would he?"

"It's been known to happen."

"Then?"

"Then, we try to get a look at Sawyer, Evans, and their situation, and see what we can dig up. You game?"

She took a deep breath and exhaled. "Sure."

Edge looked right at her. "You okay?"

"Yeah, yeah, sure." She paused. "Just a little nervous. I mean, two weeks ago I'm ridin' around in a patrol car, and today I'm workin' on a capital murder case. It's, it's a little overwhelming."

"Think you need something to round off the corners a little?"

She looked down at her glass of water. "Well, yeah, most of the time." She paused. "I don't know . . ."

He looked at her, hard. "Well, don't freak out on me. I need you; especially, now."

"I'll hold it together."

"Okay." He looked away. "Alright, back to what we were talking about. There's one thing I need to warn you about." He paused. "At some point, we may have to turn this from a police investigation to a private investigation." He paused again. "Do you get my drift?"

"No."

He looked away. "Things might not all be black and white. Things may turn a little gray."

"We may have to bend the law."

"I didn't say that."

She took another sip and smiled. "Right."

"It means that when we get back to Mobile, don't go runnin' off your mouth about every little thing that you see or hear down here; especially, about what you see me do. You'll have to trust me that I've got my reasons for doing the things I do." He paused and looked at her. "Understand?"

She nodded slowly. "Yeah. I can keep a secret. What happens in Tampa stays in Tampa."

"Right. I'm counting on you."

She smirked.

"Aw, don't worry," he said. "What's the worst that could happen?"

"Oh, I could get, I don't know, fired – or *killed*," she said.

Edge looked at her, stone faced. "Well, you were about to get fired anyway, weren't you?" He paused. "And, I promise, if you buy it, you'll die with a smile on your face, doin' what you love to do."

The next morning, they found the Police Department downtown, at the corner of Franklin and Madison Streets. It was a ten story, blue steel building across from City Hall. The Homicide Bureau was located on the fifth floor, below the administrative offices. Edge called ahead, so Suarez was waiting for them when they got off the elevator.

"Good morning. I trust you had a good trip," he said smiling.

"It was long." Edge said. Austin didn't speak as she walked down the hall, two steps behind the men.

Suarez, a short and stocky man, with coal black hair and a swarthy complexion, led them into his corner office. Edge noted that he carried no sidearm, and he walked with a noticeable limp.

"Looks like you're IOD (injured on duty)." Edge said.

Suarez raised his brows in question until he saw that Edge was looking at his leg.

"Oh, this? I had a car accident two days ago – light duty for three weeks." He smiled and rubbed his right hip. "Stupid, really. I was tryin' to answer the radio and just ran through a red light." He shook his head. "It cost me."

They settled into chairs across from his desk, and Austin took out her notebook. Suarez grunted down into a large leather piece behind his desk and squinted his eyes in pain.

"Now," he said, "what is this case all about?"

Edge cleared his throat. "There was a double homicide in Mobile County on the last Friday in August – the 31st; a twenty-two year old male and his seventeen year old girlfriend were head shot sittin' in their car on the interstate on ramp in Grand Bay, Alabama, about ten or twelve miles west of Mobile. The boy's daddy hired me privately to look into it. Detective Austin here is spyin' for the Metro Sheriff's Department so that I don't get any credit when I put the case together." Edge smiled.

Suarez raised his brows again.

"I know it's a bit unorthodox, but they wanna make sure that even if I get the money, the Sheriff gets the glory."

"I see." He nodded. "So, what's your angle?"

"Well, this Jere Sawyer that I told you about, had a brother that was killed in a hunting accident seven years ago – shot by our male murder victim. We're tryin' to find out if maybe Sawyer came back to town and killed our victim – or had him killed – in retaliation."

"And the girl?"

"Wrong place, wrong time."

"I take it the S.O. doesn't think much of this theory," he said nodding toward Austin.

"Well, uh, they've got some other leads that they're pursuing; some pretty good ones, in fact." She paused and looked at Edge. "This one seems a little off the wall, to me, but it does have its merits."

Edge smiled. "I'm bettin' my gut against theirs."

He nodded. "So, how do you want to handle it?"

Edge took a deep breath. "Here's what I was thinking. You fill me in with as much background as you can, here, this morning. Austin and I'll take a trip over to this, this, uh, Hollywood Palace, this afternoon and tonight – incognito, of course – and kind'a get the lay of the land; then maybe tomorrow we'll get up with you, or your man, and try to talk to some folks. How's that?"

He nodded again. "I put in a call to my informant at the club, but she hasn't responded yet. I'll give her a day and try again."

"Any way that I could maybe talk to her?"

He smiled. "She's a little skittish. But," he paused and smiled, "if it's your *destiny*, I think you two'll find each other."

Edge nodded and smiled slightly. He turned to Austin. "Sure."

"In the meantime, I'll tell Detective Hawking to supply you with what we can, information-wise." He rose from his desk and extended his hand. "If you have any problems, let me know."

Edge and Austin stood also. They shook hands, after which Suarez used the phone to call Detective Stephen Hawking. Hawking walked into the office and introduced himself.

"I know, I know," he said smiling. "I'm not a genius, but I've been told I'm very above average." He shook Edge's hand and looked approvingly at Austin.

Hawking had that Florida look about him: tall and blonde, with a dark tan. He had a muscular build, and when he smiled his teeth were blinding.

"Step over here to my desk and let's see what you need."

They walked from the corner office into a large squad room with about ten or fifteen cubicles, and Hawking led them to the far corner near the window.

He pulled up an extra chair, and Edge gave Austin the seat closest to him. Hawking smiled at her and turned toward a writing pad.

"How can I help you folks?" he said.

Austin supplied him with the two names, Sawyer and John Evans. Hawking made two phone calls: one to the public service commission and the other to the motor vehicles bureau, and in short order, he was reciting information as Austin jotted it down.

". . . and John Evans' address is 4500 Hillsborough Avenue, apartment 4." He supplied a phone number also. Then he paused and looked Austin in the eye. "Now, if I could just get your number."

Austin glared at him. Edge chuckled. She clearly had never had this much of the wrong kind of attention – as little as it was – paid to her. Edge sat back and enjoyed the show.

"You ever get up to Alabama?" she said.

"Every chance I get."

"Well, how often is that?"

"Is it a date?"

"You aren't there yet." She looked down at her pad. "I'll think about it."

"Ohhh, hard to get. I like it." He looked at Edge and winked.

They continued the banter for another five minutes, him pursuing and her running away. Edge decided to step in and put a halt to it.

"I hate to break this up," he looked at Austin, "but we've got a little work to do."

She smirked. "Sure."

Chapter 22

After lunch at one of the local chains, Edge and Austin easily found The Hollywood Palace Lounge in a mixed use neighborhood on the Mabry Highway. It was painted green with a pink and white neon sign on top, and it appeared to be a converted fast food restaurant that had been additionalized with two new wings. The sign out front advertised drink specials from six to nine PM, as well as a lunch buffet. The parking lot was about one third full.

The building sat next to a car lot, and across the street from a convenience store and a small park. A community of two and three bedroom homes was situated one block to the south, near, surprisingly, an Episcopal church. Edge parked in the rear lot and got out his binoculars.

"This looks like a pretty seedy place," Austin said.

"How can you tell?"

"Well, look at it. It just looks dirty."

"You can't tell from the outside."

"How can you tell then?"

"You gotta go inside and look at the women when they take their shirts off." He smiled. "If their breasts are saggin', it's low class and maybe on the decline. If they're not, that means the women are younger, the tips are better, and the place is on the way up."

She snorted. "Oh, please. That's not true."

"No, really. I've done some research."

"You can't tell anything about a club by the sag of the women's breasts."

"Well, you tell me, then. I didn't realize you were such an authority."

She took a deep breath. "Well, all of these places are pretty sad as it is. The women that dance are by and large undereducated and pretty much overwhelmed with life. They've made the decision that the only thing that they have to offer the world is a display of their sex. Most have no dance training, so there's not an artistic component. They've just learned to move in time to the music, and they're counting on the libidos of the young men, or the hopelessly pathetic older men, for their livelihoods. They're prone to drug use, body mutilation, prostitution, and ultimately, HIV."

"Sounds like you've thought this through. What was it you said about the men?"

"Well, I said they were pathetic. The young boys are just looking for arousal. They've got it in their minds that somehow an attractive young woman wants to have sex with them. And the older men have nothing to look forward to anymore. They're just lookin' for that last erection before the testosterone is all gone."

Edge smiled. "That sounds like a paper you wrote in college; up at dear ole John Jay."

She raised her brows. "Sociology 301."

"You pass?"

"A+."

"You've got a gift."

Neither of them spoke for five minutes. Edge scanned the lot. His eyes fell on a red Ford F-250, backed in, three spaces away.

"Get me the tag number for Sawyer's vehicle."

She produced her notebook and read him off the Florida plate number. Edge slipped out of the car and compared the number given to them by Hawking to the number displayed on the truck. They matched.

Back inside the car, he picked up the binoculars. "What kind of car did he say was Evans'?"

Austin scanned her notes. "Oh, ah, a Chevy Blazer."

Edge made a scan of the parking lot and could not locate anything matching Evans' vehicle. He made a quick decision.

"Looks like Sawyer's inside. Let's go." He started the car.

"Where to?"

"His house."

On the way to Sawyer's residence, they passed a strip shopping center that featured a sandwich deli. Edge made note of it.

They found the Sawyer residence off Westshore Boulevard, in a cul de sac about a quarter mile east of Old Tampa Bay. The rear of the lot backed up to that same shopping center he had seen earlier, the two being separated by about a hundred and twenty-five yard wide vacant lot.

Sawyer's residence was what was commonly known as a 'cracker box' house, white with green shutters and a flat roof; one of a type of homes built in the fifties that was thought better able to withstand hurricanes. There were no vehicles in the driveway. Edge made the circle slowly and stopped the car at the corner.

"Okay, here's one of those times when our investigation has to go from police to private." He put the car in park and reached for the door handle.

"Where are you going?" she said.

"I'm gonna take a look around. You take the car and find that shopping center up there. Park and wait for me. I'll be back in fifteen or twenty minutes."

"But . . ."

"Don't argue. If anybody asks, you're waitin' on me to bring sandwiches."

"But . . ."

He was out the door and walking toward Sawyer's home before she could speak. He looked over his shoulder and saw her slide over behind the wheel, then make the turn back onto Westshore Boulevard.

A minute later, Edge marched up to the front door of the house. He knocked twice and rang the bell. No one answered, he heard no movement, and he heard no animals. Edge looked three directions and then walked to the rear of the structure.

At the back door, he tried the knob. It moved, but there was a deadbolt above it. Edge looked around again, and then produced a pick and a tension wrench, and in thirty seconds he was inside the house. He went immediately to the front door and flipped the dead bolt, thereby assuring himself a second exit if he needed it.

The interior was not as he anticipated. He expected disheveled and dirty, but what he found was tidy, in order, and clean; especially the kitchen. It appeared to him as if a woman lived there also. Was Sawyer married, or at least living with someone? He had to assume so, which meant she could appear at the house at any moment.

Edge didn't know what he was looking for, but he figured he'd know if he saw it. A quick scan of the living room revealed nothing incriminating. There was a color television in the corner and one potted plant to go along with a three piece naugehyde set. Edge walked down a short hall and found what served as the master bedroom.

The queen-sized bed was unmade, but there were no clothes on the floor. He stepped over to the dresser and looked closely at the articles on top. Ah, ha, he thought. There is a woman. In front of the large mirror he saw lipstick, perfume, and nail polish.

This was good because having a female who was apparently intimate with one of the killers possibly gave him one more inroad to information. Two conspirators might possibly keep a secret, but with three consociates – one of whom was a woman – it would be impossible hold anything in.

Carefully, Edge slid open the closet door. There, in the corner was a sawed off shotgun. Edge picked it up by the checkered foregrip and quickly copied down the serial number and make. He debated taking it, but decided against walking down the street with a shotgun in his hand, for all the neighbors to see and thereafter inform the police. He was an information broker, not a burglar.

165

Edge looked further. There was one marijuana stalk in a red clay pot, sitting on a large plate, under a lamp in the far corner behind some coats. It was about three feet high and rooted in black soil.

Near a window, over next to the bed, Edge hit paydirt. There was a brown leather valise standing open. Edge looked down, inside it, and saw nothing; however, attached to the handle he found an airline luggage ticket. He reached and yanked it free, and slid it into his pocket. He didn't look closely at it right then, but he did notice one word: Pensacola.

Edge scanned the master bath (clean) and saw more feminine products in the medicine cabinet. There was a picture of a cat in a frame on the wall above the toilet tank.

Walking back down the hall, he looked into a half bath to his left (not as clean) and a second bedroom (also, not so clean) as he went. When he set foot in the living space he was startled by the door of a car being slammed. He looked out the window and saw a female walking forward, through the car porch, and toward the rear of the home. She was young, attractive, and blonde. She wore jeans and a pullover shirt, and carried a brown purse and a grocery bag. Since she was on her way to the back, Edge assumed she lived there.

In two steps, Edge was out the front door, just as he heard a key slide into the dead bolt at the back. He didn't remember pulling the front door closed behind him, but he was around the front of the house, to the side yard, and then into the backyard in seconds.

It was over a hundred yards to the shopping center. He stopped twice to hide behind a couple of oaks that were in his path, but he covered the distance to the back side of the shopping center in four minutes.

Blending into the foot traffic on the front side, he stopped in front of a shoe store to survey the scene and locate Austin's vehicle. He stepped into the shop and pretended to inspect the men's loafers near the front window.

Austin was parked just about as far from the stores as she could get. Edge's eyes found her car, but he was shocked to see a motorcycle cop standing at the driver's window chatting her up.

He thought fast. Remembering their cover story, he looked and found the small sandwich shop three doors from the end of the building. Edge went inside, ordered two ham and cheese sandwiches and two bottled drinks. It took the woman behind the counter ten minutes to prepare the food. Edge paid her and walked out the door. In short order he was at the passenger door of the county-issue Ford with a brown paper sack and the drinks.

"Whew," he said as he looked at the cop. "I thought she'd never finish with my order. That lard ass woman took forever." He smiled broadly.

"Hey, Johnny," Austin said nervously. "This is Officer Harvey."

Harvey nodded. "Hello, sir. Are you related to this lady?"

"Ha, ha. Take my wife, please." Edge smiled again. He looked at Austin. "Have you gotten yourself another ticket, baby? I told you to be careful." He looked at Harvey. "She can't drive worth shit."

Austin frowned. "No. This officer was just checking on me to see if I was broke down. We were just talkin'. I told him you was gettin' food."

Edge smiled again. "Well, officer, if you could talk some sense into her, I'd appreciate it. There's fifteen rows of parkin' 'tween here and the sandwich shop, and she picks the space farthest from the building; made my ass walk a quarter mile to get up here."

Harvey smirked. "A little exercise never hurt anybody."

"Well, when you're right you're right," he said patting his flat stomach.

Austin frowned again. She turned to the policeman.

"Well, Dennis, we gotta be goin'. I've gotta get my husband to his psychiatrist's appointment and pick up the pills for his," she raised her brows, pointed to her temple, and whispered, "his schizophrenia." Then she spoke normally. "And if we're late, he loses time on his hour. Thanks for lookin' in on me."

Harvey nodded, put on his helmet, and took a seat astride his Harley Davidson. Edge opened the passenger door and got in next to Austin. The officer left driving east, away from the shopping center.

"Start the car and get outta here," Edge said.

"What happened?"

"Just drive." Edge looked over shoulder toward Sawyer's house. "You think he bought it?"

"I think so. I don't even think he noticed the police radio."

"You didn't tell him you were a cop did you?"

"No. He just asked me if I was broke down. I told him I was waitin' for you to get back with food." She paused. "Then he asked me for my phone number."

Edge threw his head back and laughed. "Well, hey. This is fantastic. You beginning to notice a trend here?"

"What are you talking about?"

"First Hawking, now this cop; maybe you ought'a give men a second look."

"Oh, please."

Back at the hotel, they repaired to the lounge. Austin said she needed something to calm herself. She ordered whiskey neat and told Edge that he couldn't stop her. Edge got a screwdriver with no vodka.

He looked at her askance. "Steady."

"Okay, okay. What happened at the house?"

"I can't tell you that. But, I can show you this."

He pulled the airline luggage tag out of his pocket and showed it to her. She looked at it carefully.

"It's dated for the first, the Saturday when we found the bodies," she said.

"Right. That's how they got outta town. They probably flew from Tampa to Pensacola, and then they drove to Mobile and left the morning after the murder." He leaned back in his seat. "You ever drafted a subpoena douces tecom before?"

She looked at him. "What, for records?"

"That should be all you need."

"But, we can't use this in court?"

"You won't have to. Just say that you have reason to believe, and then ask for records from the airline. If you have to, tell'em you've got a confidential informant who's been reliable in the past. Me."

She looked at the tag, apparently deep in thought.

"He's also got a sawed off shotgun in the closet. Here's the information; make, serial number, all that."

"Really?"

"In the master bedroom closet."

"Why hasn't he gotten rid of it?"

"I'm not sayin' it's the murder weapon. We couldn't prove that anyway. But, it's a trophy. He has it around to show his daddy; to say, 'Look, daddy, look, how much I love you. Look, how much better a son I am than Terry ever was. Love me more.'"

She looked at the numbers. "So, how can we get it?"

"We can't. Not without burning me."

"So, we just let him keep it?"

"For now." He paused. "Relax. We've got motive, and now we've got opportunity. When you've got those two, the means don't matter so much. They can get a gun anywhere."

Austin took one sip of the whiskey, wiped her mouth with a napkin, then pushed the glass away. She looked longingly at it, then said:

"Get rid of this – before I drink the rest of it."

Edge nodded. He picked up the glass and slugged the contents in one gulp. He squinted hard and blew out a breath.

"There. Danger's gone."

She smirked. "Thanks."

Chapter 23

They both tried napping for the rest of the afternoon in preparation for another visit to The Hollywood Palace. Edge couldn't sleep.

At four, he called Hawking and asked him if he could get in touch with the Narcotics Bureau to find out if Jere Sawyer was on their radar. Ten minutes later, Hawking called back and confirmed that he was. In fact, there were two state agents who might have information about him. Hawking said he could have the agents at his office the next morning.

Austin knocked on Edge's door at eight that evening and was admitted by voice. She was dressed in slacks and an obviously expensive print blouse.

"Look at you, all gussied up," Edge said.

"What?"

"It's an old southern expression." He paused in thought. "Oh, right. This place is like a candy store to you, what with all the dancers and all." He paused again. "Don't get in there and fall in love or anything."

"Screw you."

"I don't want to have to tell Pat, or whatever her name is, that I corrupted you." He checked his .45 and slipped it into the holster on his belt at the small of his back, underneath his safari vest.

She stared at him. "It's Wendy. I just tell people it's Pat to keep 'em guessing."

"Well, I feel honored. It sounds like we've passed a milestone in our relationship. You trust me."

"Don't get too comfortable. It's just that I don't mistrust you."

He snorted. "My mother used to tell me the same thing. Usually, it was right after I broke a lamp or something."

Thirty minutes later they were in the parking lot of The Hollywood Palace. As he was getting out of the car, Austin held out her arm.

"Wait. What's the plan?"

"The plan? Well, I'm gonna try to make contact with Destiny. Maybe she can give us some background about Sawyer and Evans. You, in the meantime, are gonna enjoy the show." He reached into a grip bag in the backseat and pulled out a stun gun. "You know how to use one'a these?"

She pulled the trigger twice and watched as electricity jumped from one pole to the other. "Sure."

"Okay. If for some reason, and I can't think of a possible scenario where it would, things were to break bad, use this to get yourself, or me, or both of us, out of a jam." He looked at her. "Just hide your badge and keep your eyes open. You got your piece?"

"On my ankle." She smirked. "I don't have a good feeling about this, at all."

He smiled. "What could go wrong? I'm gonna get a seat, tell the waitress I wanna get a lap dance from Destiny, and slip the girl a fifty for whatever she can tell me. We oughta be outta there in thirty minutes."

"Sounds too easy."

He smirked. "You're right. Be prepared to shoot it out."

At the door, Edge paid a thin white man wearing a polyester print shirt that was open to the navel a five-dollar cover charge for each of them. His blow-dried hair and pencil-thin mustache made him look as if he should have been running the door at Studio 54.

Inside, Edge found a small table near the main stage where a Hispanic-looking woman was moving slowly around a pole. Austin took up a position at the bar. The crowd was well below 'packed', and Edge didn't think he'd have any trouble getting Destiny's attention.

A blonde waitress in a short skirt took his order and returned five minutes later with a virgin screwdriver. Edge took a sip and laid a five on her tray.

"Has Destiny been out yet? She's my favorite."

The woman leaned over and spoke in his ear. "She should be next. I saw her in the doorway a second ago."

"Thanks." Edge smiled broadly.

As he sat and waited, Edge kept his head on a swivel, looking for the bouncers, or other evidence of Sawyer and Evans. The DJ's amplified voice caught his attention.

"And, now, gentleman, coming to the main stage, the lovely, Destiny," he said in a very theatrical-sounding baritone.

Edge turned and watched as a petite young woman with long brown hair walked quickly to the end of the stage and begin dancing around the shiny, golden pole – an obvious phallic symbol. The music was *Jump*, by the Pointer Sisters, and while the young woman did seem somewhat animated, her eyes still bore that heavy-lidded look of drug use.

She was about two minutes into her routine when Edge stood up, took a five from his pocket, and walked up to the lip of the stage. The young woman walked over, bent down, and smiled. Edge put the bill into the waistband of her g-string, near her left hip, then nodded his head, and pointed, toward the private rooms against the far wall. She nodded also and resumed her show.

Ten minutes later, Edge was sitting in a small, raised alcove, on a brown, leather loveseat of questionable cleanliness, in what was called the 'Gold Room,' and Destiny was adjusting her clothing, preparing to dance. He waved his hand at her.

"Sit down and rest your feet." He extracted a fifty from a gold plated money clip that he took from his right front pants pocket and handed it to her. "How much conversation will this get me?"

She took the money, and her eyes widened. Then she plopped down on the couch next to him.

"Oh, two songs, I guess," she said as she put the bill into her brassiere. Destiny worked on a piece of chewing gum as she spoke. Her voice was high and breathy. "They don't like for us to sit for too long."

It was a large amount of money, but Edge was prepared to spend more if he had to; even buy one of those overpriced bottles of champagne.

"You wanna drink?" he said.

"No, thanks. I . . . ."

Edge knew what she was trying to say. He could tell that she was just a little wasted already and with any more liquor she might not be able to stay upright and dance. When she was settled, Edge spoke.

"So, you and I have a mutual friend."

She looked at him, her blue eyes suddenly more alert. "You from Alabama?"

He nodded.

"Oh. Yeah, he said you'd be coming by; said you were workin' on a murder case."

He nodded again. "So, how well do you know John Evans?"

"Big John?" She smirked and shrugged. "Well enough, I guess. He hangs around the dressin' room talkin' to the girls. I don't like him; he smells bad."

"He ever talk about killing anyone? Like a hit, maybe?"

She shrugged again. "Not in so many words. Every now and then he'll take a couple days off and say he's got to go, *do a job*. I just thought it was about movin' some dope or somethin'."

"You ever see him with a gun?"

She shook her head. "I never saw one, but the other girls say he carries one."

"How about Jere?"

"Jere? Oh, well, yeah. Uh, about a month ago, Jere said he had to go back home and take care of some, *family business*. That what you're talking about?"

173

"Could be. Did Big John go with him?"

"I don't know. I don't think so. They may not have been gone at the same time. Billie'd know."

"Billie?"

"Billie Hitchcock. She kinda dates John. I can call Suarez if I find out."

The first song was ending. "Is Big John here tonight?"

She looked toward the stage. "Yeah. He stays in the back with the girls mostly, but he's not supposed to. He comes out and checks the room every now and then."

"What about Jere?"

"I haven't seen him. I think he worked the day shift."

"Who's Jere's old lady?"

"Oh, uh, that's Tammy. I don't think they're married. I think they just live together."

"What's Jere look like?"

"Uh, he's got blond hair and blue eyes. He's not too tall and kinda slim."

"How about John?"

"Oh, he's big, like a football player big; and bald. He used to have brown hair, but he shaved it all off. Be careful with him. One time, I saw him pick up a guy over his head and throw him across the room."

Edge nodded again. "Is Tammy here tonight?"

"I ain't seen her. She usually works when Jere does."

"Okay," Edge said. He nodded toward her chest. "Is that enough?"

She touched her bosom and nodded. "Yeah. Thanks." Then she rose and walked toward the stage.

Edge waited two minutes then walked out of the 'Gold Room' and down the steps also. He looked over toward Austin who had her arms crossed and wore a disgusted look. Edge shrugged and raised his brows as he took his place at the same small table near the stage.

An obnoxiously buxom black woman was dancing, and Edge began scanning the room once more. He had yet to

174

see Sawyer, or Evans. The blonde waitress from earlier came and took away his glass.

"You want somethin' else?" she said.

Edge shook his head. "Not right now."

About halfway through the black dancer's set, Edge spotted a large bald man in the corner looking through a curtained doorway next to the far end of the stage. His eyes were set close together, and he had a Fu Manchu mustache.

He looked around the room, and his eyes soon fell on Edge. Edge could see the frown settling on his face. So much for a confidential informant, he thought. Destiny must have walked right up to Evans and told him who he was. Never trust a drunk to keep her mouth shut.

Evans came through the door and walked directly to Edge's table. He stood and spoke with a voice that sounded as if he needed to clear his throat.

"You're gonna have to leave, pal," he said.

"What for? I ain't done nothin'."

"The lady says you was botherin' her."

"What lady?"

"The one you was talkin' to, up there." He nodded toward the Gold Room.

Edge looked back at the alcove, then at Evans. He didn't want to make a scene, but he didn't want to leave either.

"Get lost," he said as he turned his eyes back to the stage.

Evans was immediately incensed. "I said you gotta go." He reached and grabbed Edge's forearm.

Edge rose and made a large circle with his limb thereby breaking the big man's grip. He looked up at Austin who had come off her barstool and was moving toward them. Edge held up his hand in the 'stop' gesture.

Evans, believing that if he could get a handful of Edge he could control him, reached out again. This time he reached for his upper arm.

175

And this time Edge was ready. He kicked Evans in the groin, took two steps back and then gave him a flying front kick right under the chin. The big man fell backwards.

Edge stood over him. Austin had stopped her movement toward them. Edge looked her direction and saw the bartender, not a small man himself, come out from behind the bar with a baseball bat in his hand.

Nodding toward the door, Edge and Austin walked quickly that direction. They were moving at a trot when they hit the parking lot and made it to their car. The bartender was fifteen yards behind.

"Let's get outta here." Edge said.

He woke the car's engine and dropped it in gear just as Austin fell into the passenger seat. The bartender took a swipe at the hood but missed, and the force of his failure made him fall on the ground just in time to hear tires scratching and see gravel flying. They were out of the lot and safely on the Dale Mabry Highway in seconds. Austin looked over her shoulder and took deep breaths trying to calm herself.

"What happened in there?" she said.

"He put his hands on me," Edge said while looking over his shoulder for pursuers. "I had to get him off. He could'a killed me; and I think Big John has had experience"

"What did you say to make him mad?"

"Nothing. Destiny, the chick I talked with up in the room up there, tipped him, and he tried to throw me out."

"What did she have to say?"

"Not much, yet. If we get anything else from her, we'll probably have to get it from Suarez first." He paused. "She did say that Sawyer told everybody had he had to leave town to go home to take care of some 'family business.'"

Chapter 24

The next morning, Edge called the Police Department. He was trying to get Hawking, but Suarez intercepted the call.

"Edge, what the fuck happened last night?"

"What do you mean?"

"At the club. John Evans has a broken jaw. He wants to file a police report."

"Well, he started it." He paused. "Does he know who I am?"

"No. But he says we do."

"Look, just call him a liar, take his report, and send him on his way. I'll go over to his place and smooth everything out a little later this morning."

Edge could imagine Suarez shaking his head on the other end of the line.

"No, no. Don't do that."

"Yeah. I wanna talk to him anyway. That's what I was tryin' to do last night."

"What about your partner?"

"She didn't touch him."

There was silence on the other end of the line. Edge heard Suarez exhaling loudly.

"Look, Hawking has gotta man here to talk to you. He's Bitterman, with the state police."

"Yeah, okay. Tell him we'll meet him in the lobby of your building in thirty minutes.

"I'll tell him." He paused. "Oh, and Tina, uh, Destiny, says tell you that Billie Hitchcock's real name is Elizabeth Banks, in case you wanted to know."

"Thanks." Edge wrote down the name.

"Hey, Edge. After you leave, we gotta live here. So, calm down a little. Okay?"

"You're as safe as kittens, Aldo. We got it handled."

"Just tone it down."

177

In thirty minutes, Edge and Austin sat down with Agent Bitterman of the State Department of Law Enforcement at the snack shop in the lobby of the Police Building. He was a husky man with shoulder length black hair and a thick brown mustache. Edge made him a police officer immediately. He was just in too good a physical condition to do any undercover work.

"John Edge," he said by way of introduction. "This is Amy Austin." They took seats at a booth with orange plastic benches.

"Jack Bitterman."

"You have some information for us?" Austin said as she took out her pad.

Bitterman smiled at her and leaned forward. "Yeah, you guys are workin' on a murder case involving Jere Sawyer?"

"Right."

"Well, we been workin' The Palace for about two months on a dope tip. Suarez got an informant in there, and she put us onto the bartender; said he was movin' weed."

Edge spoke up. "Yeah. Watch out for Suarez's girl. I think she's a double agent," he said.

"Right. We'll be careful. She don't know us." He paused. "Anyway, me and my partner, we got to talkin' with Jere, oh, sometime, back in July, and he said he could move us some dope. We asked him how much, but he'd never say, so we just thought he was talkin' out his ass."

Edge said nothing. Austin wrote.

"Anyway, we were talkin' to him about dates when he could lay hands on some product, and we mentioned the first weekend in September as a possible. Well, Sawyer says no, that he's gotta go back home and take care of some business right around that time. My partner, asked him about what, and he said his younger brother had been murdered about six or seven years ago, and he was gonna go home and make it right with the boy that did it." He paused. "Was Sawyer's brother murdered?"

178

"No. Well, killed in a huntin' accident."

"Oh. So, anyway, we asked him why now? And he said 'cause it's been enough time and there wouldn't be nobody lookin' his way; meanin' he wouldn't be a suspect. He said that, besides, the kid sold weed his self and the law would be lookin' for suspects in that direction."

Edge looked at Austin. Her eyes were big as she wrote furiously. They had a lot of circumstantial evidence, Edge thought, but this was the first time they had anything that remotely resembled a confession, albeit before the fact.

"How close are you guys to a case?" Edge said.

"Not far. We got the bartender for holdin', and one other bouncer at the club for transportin'. We're just tryin' to get as much as we can."

"Will Sawyer be a part of it?"

"Yeah. He brought us a joint one night and said that it was a sample of what we could have from him; said he grew it outta town, that it was some kinda new exotic breed'a plant; some kinda hybrid. It wadn't a very good grade'a weed."

"Are you gonna search his house?"

"Yeah. We already got the warrant. We're just waitin' to serve it when we know he's gonna have somethin' there for us to get."

"Okay, good." Edge paused. "Don't ask me how I know this, but he's got a sawed off shotgun in his bedroom closet, right next to one marijuana stalk under a hot lamp. Make sure you take it and hang onto it."

Bitterman smiled. "Sure. How do you know that?"

"I have x-ray vision. Just make sure when you pick up that gun that you give it to Suarez at the PD. He'll know how to get in touch with Austin here."

Bitterman smiled at Austin. "Sure, sure. We'll probably hit it in a couple'a days." He paused. "I hope this helps."

"Oh, it does. It does," Austin said smiling.

"So. Amy, was it? How long *you* gonna be in town?"

On the way to John Evans address, Edge looked at Austin. He smiled broadly.

"Man, you got yourself a great career as a straight woman if you want it."

"Screw you."

He smiled. "That could be arranged; but it looks like I'll have to get in line." He looked at the road ahead. "Come on. You're gettin' offers left and right. You're a good lookin' woman. Have you ever tried men? I mean how long you been, you know, like you are?"

She looked straight ahead. He could see that he was hitting on something sensitive.

"Since my daddy left. I don't know, I . . ."

He didn't speak.

"After that, every time I looked at a boy, I . . ."

"You don't have to tell me."

"I know, but I want to. When my mother and father separated, I was just so mad." She paused. "That's when I started drinkin'; seems as if I was depressed all the time. I ate, too; gained about fifty pounds. Every time I looked at a boy, I couldn't see anything except my father's face. Then, when I got to college, I just, well, you know, experimented."

"Sounds like you just got a toe in the water. You could get out if you want to."

"I don't know. Wendy's been nice. It's . . ."

"You get any therapy?"

"A little. When Daddy found out, I mean, when I'd come to visit, he'd send me to a guy, in Mobile."

"Did it help?"

"A little. I know why I drink. I just can't stop. But, I *was* able to lose all the weight."

Edge, feeling like a father confessor, nodded but said nothing else and drove on in silence.

They found Evans' address, a modern, sprawling apartment community near Tampa Bay, and parked in front of his building at ten minutes to ten. Edge knocked hard.

"Just follow my lead."

"Come in," said a voice from inside. It was muffled but they were able to make it out.

"Did he just say what I think he said?" Edge said.

"Sounded like he said, 'come in.'"

"Let's go."

Edge opened the door and the two walked inside. Evans was seated in a recliner with his legs up. He looked up and saw Edge, and picked up a large revolver that sat on a table next to the chair.

"Wait a minute, John." Edge reached for his .45, and in a second it was in his hand and pointed at Evans. He held his other arm out in a stop sign. "Just wait a minute. I'm here to apologize." Austin moved behind Edge and produced her own weapon.

"Mim gomma ki' you," he said through wired jaws.

"Just calm down. You invited us in, remember. I just want to say I'm sorry and see if you need anything."

They stepped to the middle of the great room, Edge with his weapon at the ready, Austin with hers by her side. It was a sixteen by twenty space that was sparsely furnished but otherwise clean. A television and stereo were prominent.

"Oo are you?"

"I'm Larry Fine, and this is my wife, Lisa, Lisa Fine."

"Gut out." He waved his gun toward the door.

"Just wait a minute, now," Edge said pleadingly. "I'm sorry for that little dust up last night, but I wadn't messin' with your girl."

"So?"

"So, why don't you just lay that gun down and everybody can relax."

Evans looked at the revolver, turned it over in his hand, then laid it back down on the table. Edge reholstered his .45.

"What I was askin' about last night before you went all apeshit on me was about Jere Sawyer. I gotta buddy back in Alabama that says that Jere stole his car from'im a few weeks ago."

"So?"

He looked over at Austin. "So, we was just tryin' to help our friend get his car back. He says Jere took it from him."

"Youse detetives?" he said in his mush mouthed way.

"No, no. We're just helpin' a friend. His ride was stolen back in September, the first weekend."

"In Tampa?"

"Yeah. My buddy was here in town visitin' his girlfriend, see, and he spent some time at the club. He says Jere rousted him, kinda like what you tried to do with me, and when he got ready to leave, his keys was gone and so was his truck."

"Fust weeken in Sephtembuh?"

"Right."

"He wush outta town."

"How do you know?"

"I wush wi him."

"Where'd he go?"

"Fransh (France). Now geddowa here 'fore I callsh the copsh."

"Well, okay, okay, sure, John. I guess my buddy got some bad information. We'll go, and, really, I'm sorry, dude."

They backed out the door before anything else was said. Edge had the information that he wanted.

In the parking lot, Austin slid into the passenger seat.

"What did we get outta that?" she said.

"Well, John admits that they were both out of Tampa, and were with each other at the time of the murder. They can't use that, 'I was alone in the apartment,' defense."

Austin exhaled loudly. "Don't you think we should share any of this with Randall?"

"Are you kidding? I've got five grand ridin' on this thing. Besides, we really don't need him yet."

"Well, he is my boss."

"Don't worry about it. After we hand this thing over to him with a bow on it, you're liable to be at least a captain.

182

Heck, you'll be tellin' Randall what to do." He paused. "Say, I never asked you, but how much real juice do you have at that department down there?"

"Not much. My Daddy gave the Sheriff some money; well, you know about that. And, I think he made another donation when I got hired. I think it helped, but I don't know how much."

"Well, if this thing comes through, I predict you'll be in the pink for the rest'a your career." He paused. "Yes, sir, first, sergeant; then, Lieutenant; then, who knows."

They pulled over to a booth, and Edge got on the phone. Hawking answered on the third ring.

"Can you check and see if Evans has a pistol permit?" Edge said.

"Sure. You need to know the make and serial number?"

"If you got it, yeah. Also, I'd like to get mugshots of Sawyer and Evans if you've got'em. Driver's license photos if you don't."

"Well, I know we've got one of Evans. I checked it. Sawyer might be too new in town. Anything else?"

"And, how about an Elizabeth Banks, alias Billie Hitchcock? We've got a witness in Alabama that might be able to put her in the car at the time of the crime."

"Will do."

"We're about to head outta town. You wanna talk to Austin?"

There was silence on the other end of the line. "No, my wife might not like it too much. I'll just look her up when I come to Alabama. I'm assuming I'll be up there for some kinda trial, if, or when, it happens."

Edge chuckled. "Right. Okay, I'll tell her you said, so long."

"Thanks."

Back in the car, Edge filled Austin in on what she could expect through the mail in the next few days. He also told her:

"If that Hawking comes to town, stay away from him."

"Why?"

"Well, let's just say we don't want another homicide on our hands."

"He's married."

"Right."

"And you wonder why I only hang around with girls."

"Na. You'll be back. It's like a drug. You can't say no."

Chapter 25

After driving through the night, they were back in Mobile by three in the morning. Edge took the next day off and tried to rest. He made plans to meet Austin at the courthouse, in the Youth Aid Division office, the day after.

That day was Friday. Edge was at the office at ten. He called Austin at home. When she answered, he could tell something was wrong. Her speech was slurred and at times non-sensical.

"What are you doing?"

"What? Oh, uh, nothin'. I, I . . . It's time to go for a, uh, to do a, you know."

"I'm coming over."

He was at her door in twenty minutes. On the way over, he speculated on what was the matter with Austin. There could be only one thing.

She opened the door wearing a man's shirt and nothing else. She had an empty gin bottle in her hand, and her face was stained with tears. Mucus drained from her nose. Edge walked inside, closed the door behind him, and stood in front of her with arms akimbo.

184

"What's wrong with you?"

She shrugged her shoulders and started crying. The bottle fell from her hand, and she ran forward and threw her arms around Edge's neck. He wrapped his arms around her waist, and they stood in silence as she sobbed softly into his shirt front.

They were that way for several minutes. Edge felt the warmth of her and gently stroked her hair. Music, Frank Sinatra, played on the stereo. It was an atmosphere that at any other time might have evoked another outcome; but not on this day.

Edge took her by the shoulders and held her out in front of him. He used his handkerchief to wipe her face and blow her nose. Then he walked her to the couch and sat her down. He settled himself next to her.

Neither of them spoke for several minutes. She took his handkerchief, blew her own nose, and looked at him.

"I guess I look like shit."

"You've looked better." He paused. "What happened?"

"I, I don't know. I got up this morning, and it, it just hit me, all of a sudden. I, I . . ."

"What?"

"I'm so confused. I want my Daddy." She started crying again.

He pursed his lips. "Well, from what I've seen, he's as close as your phone. Why don't you call him?"

"He, he doesn't want me. He hates me."

"Bullshit. That's the liquor talkin'. He doesn't hate you."

"Yes, he does. I'm the reason he and Mother split up."

"No, you're not. Every kid thinks that, but it's never true. You were a good kid. You got good grades, you got a good job; you're accomplishing something in life. I'm sure he's very proud of you."

She shook her head. "No, he's not. He won't take my calls anymore; he's, he's getting married again," she said through her sobs.

"How do you know?"

"Mother called this morning and told me."

"So, he's gettin' married again. So what. You're still his baby girl."

"But, don't you see, we won't be a family again."

Edge said nothing for a minute. He smirked and took a deep breath.

"So, get your own family. Get married, have some kids. Give up the cops. It's no life for you anyway." He paused. "Look, start at the beginning. Tell me what happened this morning."

She sniffed twice. "Mother called to tell me about Daddy; that he was gettin' married. She was crying, and she said, that was it, that was the end of our family."

He knew what was happening. Austin's mother was playing an emotional game on her. She was upset, so she had to call and get Austin outta sorts also; because misery loves company. It seemed to him like such a trifling matter. But he knew that with women it was all about family; that was the most important thing in their lives. He said nothing.

"So, Mother was crying, and so, I started crying, too, and I, I just took something to calm me down." She nodded toward the gin bottle. "Well, you know . . ."

"Yeah, I know. How much'd you have?"

She looked toward the bottle. "I, not much. Just a little." She looked down and away, and sniffed. "There was only about this much in the bottle." She held two fingers about an inch apart.

"Well, look," he said, "is there somebody you want me to call?"

"No. There's nobody."

He nodded. "Well, okay. Is there anything that I can do for you?"

She shook her head while blowing her nose.

186

"Well, then. I'm leaving." He rose and turned for the door.

"Wha, why?"

He stopped and turned back toward her. "Look. Get yourself some help. I'm no doctor. If you're this emotionally fragile, I can't do anything for you."

"Well, wh, what about the case?"

"What about it? I'll take it from here."

She stood and walked to him, taking his arm. There was desperation in her voice when she spoke.

"You can't . . . you can't."

He looked at her, hard. "Look, if you can't keep it together any better than this, I can't use you." He paused. "Now, let go of my arm."

"No! I, I've got to stay on this case . . . it's all I've got left."

"Oh, grow up. Your mother ran a game on you, and now you're trying to run one on me. Well, forget it."

"Please."

Edge didn't know what to do. She was of no help to him in her condition. But he did have a deal with Randall and the Sheriff's Office.

He looked at her and exhaled loudly. "Pull yourself together. I'll be back to get you at five o'clock," he said. "If you're still drunk then, it's over, and I go to the Sheriff."

Then he turned and walked out of the door.

That afternoon, Edge picked up Austin on the sidewalk in front of her apartment looking well dressed, clean, and reasonably put together. She got into the front seat of the Impala and belted herself in.

"You sober?" he said.

She looked at him and nodded.

"You're not talking, so I'm going to assume you're still at least a little bit under the influence, but you're sober enough to know you can't show it to anyone." He paused.

"So, you just ride along. Keep your mouth shut, and don't speak unless you're spoken to."

She looked at him angrily but said nothing. They rode in silence down Airport Boulevard then onto Government Street. Finally, Edge spoke:

"Where to?"

She cleared her throat. "The basement of the courthouse. I gotta friend in Youth Aid that lets me come down here to write reports on the typewriter. I've been keeping a journal about our case. It's locked up down there."

"Has anyone else seen it?"

"No."

"Good."

They turned off Church Street into the courthouse tunnel twenty minutes later. Edge parked in front of the ID section door, and Austin used a key to enter the Youth Aid squad room.

It was a thirty by fifteen space with cubicles for five officers and a desk for a supervisor over in the corner. It being after five on a Friday, the place was deserted. Austin sat down at a desk in the corner, and Edge drew up a chair.

"Okay. Get out your pad and pen and let's start putting together what we have, and what else we need."

She pulled out a legal pad. "Are all homicide investigations this exhausting?"

"You don't know the half of it. Usually they're worse. You tired?"

"Yeah."

"Well, what hope is there for me? I'm fifteen years older than you are." He paused. "Just take some vitamins and butch it up. You can make it."

She looked at him with disgust as she readied her pen.

"Okay, first is motive. Notify the SBI, Doug Banks at the Grove Hill post. He can get you a copy of his file. That and Agent Miller should be all we need, but take down Otha Harbin, also. He can testify as to Old Man Sawyer and how

188

mad he was seven years ago. You'll need to get a statement from him.

"Second, is opportunity. Use that luggage tag to get a warrant for the flight information from whatever airline it was that they used to get to Tampa. There shouldn't be more than one or two over there. Call'em first, and ask if they have the information, and then tell'em you'll get'em them a subpoena. Start on that now 'cause it may take a while. It'll have to go through their legal department." He paused. "Do the same thing with the rent-a-car companies over there. I think we're lookin' for a tan Chevy, but don't mention that. Just throw around Sawyer's and Evans' name, and Elizabeth Banks, too; oh, and somebody named Tammy. If you need some help drafting the paperwork, call the DA's office. Have you got someone over there you can work with?"

She nodded and continued writing.

"By the way, did you send for the phone records for Harbin's house for that Friday night?"

"I've already done that."

"Good. Now, when you get photos of Evans, Sawyer, and Hitchcock, take'em next door to ID and get three photo lineups. We're gonna need'em to show'em to Hardy Eubanks; maybe even at a motel here in town."

"You don't think they stayed with Walter Sawyer?"

Edge shook his head. "My thinking is that the old man wants to stay as far away from this as possible; to keep his fingerprints completely off everything. His part in it was to gripe and complain for seven years and tell son Jere that wadn't it a shame about how his brother was murdered and nothing was ever done about it; and wouldn't it sure right a wrong if somebody in the family would step up, get some balls, and kill the Harbin boy to even up the score." He paused. "The old man's job was to egg him into it, and maybe supply some money. Nothing else."

She looked at him and marveled at his mental machinations. Even in her mildly-intoxicated state, she admired his grasp of human nature and his understanding of the criminal mind.

"Third, is the means. Now, as far as the guns, they couldn't take'em on the plane unless they smuggled'em in their luggage, so the ones we've seen and heard about already are prob'ly not what was used in the crime; unless they mailed'em back to Tampa, which is a possibility. But my guess is that their guns are in the drink somewhere between here and Baldwin County. We may never know where, and they probably couldn't tell us if they wanted to. We'll just have to live with not having them.

"By the way, ask Randall about that rifle shell that you said you saw on the front seat the morning you responded out there to Grand Bay. If that spent cartridge was same caliber that Harbin used to kill Sawyer seven years ago – a thirty caliber – that would be a pretty powerful piece of evidence."

She nodded as she wrote. "I'll ask him."

He looked at her. "Can you think of anything else?"

She said nothing but closed her eyes.

"Now," he said. "What do we have left to do?" He looked up. "One, we have to talk to Old Man Sawyer."

"What?" Her tone was incredulous.

"Yeah. You wanna go?"

"Sure."

"If you don't, I'll go by myself."

"No. I'll go."

"Two, we need to hunt up Hardy Eubanks and show him the photos in our line up. I'm thinking his liquor addled brain won't admit to recognizing anyone, so leave all of that out of your journal, and any report that you might write. We don't want to give the defense anything exculpatory." He paused. "By the way, did you sign a warrant on him?"

"No yet."

"Well, wait 'til after we show him the pictures so we can be sure that he's not picked up. No sense in getting on his bad side."

She nodded her head.

He looked at her and smiled. "Relax. Pretty soon we'll have this case made and you can celebrate all you want."

She looked at him, hard. "You were a real ass to me this morning."

"I was. What about it?"

Chapter 26

Three days later, Edge and Austin, photo line ups in hand, started checking motels looking for where Sawyer, Evans, and possibly Hitchcock might have stayed either before or after the murders of Ty Harbin and Carla Morgan. There were several in the Tillman's Corner area, right outside the city limits of Mobile, one in Theodore, Alabama; and one in tiny Irvington, Alabama, an unincorporated community on Highway 90, five or so miles east of Grand Bay.

Tillman's Corner was a bust, as was the Commons Motel on Highway 90 in Theodore. But when they made it to the Racetrack Motel in Irvington, they hit paydirt.

'The Track,' as it was called, was a twenty room fleabag with a bacteria trap called a swimming pool out front. It was located on the south side of US 90, not far from the half mile long, dirt, stock car race track dubbed, somewhat grandiloquently, the Irvington International Speedway. There was a convenience store just down the road, with a chicken restaurant attached, for the dining pleasure of the motel tenants.

A white woman wearing a print dress, behind the glass at the front desk, admitted that she was working the nights of August 30[th,] 31st and September 1st, but she denied ever having seen the principles in the lineups that Austin showed her. Edge assumed she was lying.

"I don't 'member nobody like that."

"It would'a been two men and a woman," he said. "One of the men would'a had a bald head and possibly a mustache. He's huge. You can't miss him."

"Sorry." She looked at them askance. "You two with the police?"

Austin produced her star and the woman tensed. Edge continued.

"Can you check your book?"

The woman, who was about thirty-five but already had some gray streaks in her hair, thumbed pages in her record book for the time around the last of August, first of September. She came to the pages in question and ran her finger down the column.

"We gotta Mr. and Ms Hitchcock, and a Mr. Brown, in room 20 down on the end."

"What were they driving?"

"Says here, a tan Chevrolet; I mean, that's what they put down. I don't know nothin' 'bout cars. It could'a been a Rolls Royce for all I know."

"What about housekeeping? Is she here?"

"Yeah, but she's Mexican. She don't speak much good English." Edge wanted to tell that, 'neither do you.'

"I can talk to her," Austin said.

The desk clerk nodded her head, picked up the phone on the counter, and dialed a three digit number. She told whoever it was that answered to meet Edge and Austin in room 20.

They found a short, pudgy woman with black hair and a round face the color of chocolate milk waiting for them on the sidewalk out front. She looked afraid when Austin showed her badge.

"Habla englais?" Austin said.

"Si, un poco."

"Como se llama?"

"Maria. Maria Hernandez."

Austin held up her badge. "Maria, I'm not from Inmagracion. I just want to show you; fotografias." She produced the lineups. "Maria, do you know these people?"

She looked at the three lineups. Hernandez pointed to Evans and Hitchcock. She wasn't sure about Sawyer.

"Where did they stay? What room?"

"Si, si. Room 20. They stay room two, maybe three weeks ago. Room very dirty."

"Ask her if she saw anything suspicious in the room," Edge said.

"She doesn't know suspicious." She turned to Hernandez. "Did you see anything, uh, extrano in the room?"

"Si. Guns." She held out her hand like a pistol.

"When? Quando?"

"When they spill drink on floor. They call for me to clean. I see guns on the bed."

"Ask her what kind?"

"Long guns? Pistolas?"

"Si. Los pistolas, escopeta (shotgun)." She held her hands about two and half feet apart.

"Did the people say anything to you?"

"Si. They say clean up mess."

Edge looked at Austin. "Clean up the mess, hunh.' I only hope we can."

That afternoon, Austin used a pay phone near the Bonanza Lounge at US 90 and Azalea Road, in Mobile, and called Sawyer Plumbing. She asked for Walter Sawyer, but the young woman that answered said the he wasn't in, and they didn't expect him back for the rest of the day. Edge nodded at the information and turned the Impala north to Saraland.

"Are you sure this is a good idea?" Austin said.

"Well, if it's not, we'll know it pretty quick. I just feel like if there's a case to be made against the Old Man, we've got to talk to him and give him a chance to incriminate himself."

"You think he'll roll?"

"Oh, he won't roll. As a matter of fact, he'll say what he has to say to keep himself outta jail. And, he won't say anything if he thinks we've put this case together. But, we won't tell him that."

They found the Sawyer home on Celeste Road, five or six miles west of Interstate 65. It was a sprawling, three thousand square foot ranch, with a brick veneer and a carport in back. Oddly, it was not far from the Morgan property.

At the end of a concrete sidewalk, there were three large, white columns holding up the front porch. Walter Sawyer's Cadillac was in the driveway, as was a surprise: Jere Sawyer's pickup with Florida license plates.

A cool wind blew out of the north as they exited the car and walked up the pavement toward the front door. One of those black lawn jockeys sat about ten feet from the porch. The smiling figure spoke volumes about the man with whom they were about to speak.

Austin pushed the small white button on the door facing, and they heard a faint 'ding, dong' sound far back inside the home. It took nearly two minutes for someone to answer.

A podgy woman of fifty or so in a sweatshirt and jeans stood in the threshold and stared suspiciously at them. She was barefooted, and her gray hair and lined face said she had a few miles on her. She didn't smile.

"Who are you?" She said.

"Alice Sawyer?"

"Who's askin'?"

"My name is Edge, and this is Detective Austin. We're county investigators. Is Mr. Sawyer available?"

She stared at them and said nothing. Finally, she turned to walk away.

"Wait here," she said over her shoulder.

In another minute, the same short man with the distended abdomen that Edge had seen a week earlier waddled up to the portal dressed in a t-shirt and overalls. He, too, was barefooted.

"What can I do for you folks?" he said.

His voice was high and squeaky and had a rasp to it, and that, along with his yellow teeth, told a story of years of tobacco abuse.

"Could we talk to you for a couple'a minutes?"

"About what?"

Austin looked at Edge as if she too was wondering, what was the purpose of their visit.

"We'd like to talk to you about your son's case – that is, uh, Terry's death. In light of Ty Harbin's murder, we've reopened the case of your son's death to see if he might have been killed intentionally."

Austin's eyes widened. Sawyer's did also. Everyone was wondering where Edge was going with this. He jumped in with both feet.

"We think that Harbin's murder might have been to cover up the perpetrator's involvement in a conspiracy with Harbin to kill your son."

This is all a huge bucket of bullshit, Edge thought. But he could tell from the look on Sawyer's face that the old man was completely hooked.

"Well, it's about time that you guys wised up about my boy's case. Ty Harbin murdered him as sure as I'm standin' here, and all I can say is it's about time."

"Could we come in?"

Sawyer bladed himself in the doorway and then pointed to the living space off the foyer immediately to the right. Inside, the house smelled of mothballs and boiling vegetables.

Edge took a seat in one of two club chairs that flanked a small table in front of a large bay window. Austin took the other. Sawyer took a load off his stubby legs and plopped onto a brown leather recliner.

"Now," he said, "who was it that was in on killin' my boy."

Edge knew he had to throw him a bone, or he'd run them out pretty quickly. His mind raced.

"Well, first of all, we know Ty Harbin killed Terry. That fact is not in dispute. But lately, some information, information that I'm not at liberty to divulge, has come to light that makes us believe that there was another boy involved in the shooting; someone from the high school where they went."

Edge didn't want to name any names. If he did, he would surely be putting a target on that person's back. He spoke quickly before Sawyer could question him further.

"Tell me about your son, Mr. Sawyer," Edge said.

The old man took a deep breath and exhaled. Then he shook his head, and Edge could see his lower lip quiver.

"He was a good boy. He loved his mama, and he never give me a bit'a trouble." He paused. "He liked to hunt, 'cause I liked to hunt. I taught him how to track a deer, where to go to look for one, how to read sign. We spent a lotta time in them woods together. I . . ."

Edge could tell immediately what was bothering him the most. One word: guilt.

"What about school, or other sports, besides huntin'?"

"Oh, he played a little football, but he didn't love it as much as he did huntin'. He was just a good boy. He loved his mama, and . . . " This time he choked up

"And?"

"And, well, things'll all get right. Justice be done."

"I hope so."

"Now, who is it that you think was in on killin' that bastard and my son?"

"We can't say, right now, Mr. Saywer. Things are at a very sensitive stage." Edge cleared his throat, a sure sign of deception. "What we wanted to do was to ask you about your recollections of that time."

Sawyer sat back in the recliner and crossed his legs at the ankles. He interlaced his fingers on top of his massive belly and closed his eyes.

"Well, it was cold. My boy, Terry, had went huntin' with that piece'a shit; took him huntin' 'cause he ain't never been before, tryin' to do him a favor. They said that when my boy spotted a deer, he went down to the creek and tried to run it toward . . ." He couldn't say Harbin's name. "And that little maggot shot my boy for no reason. Hit him in the . . ." Sawyer choked up again.

"How did you find out?"

"My boy Jere was supposed to go up there and pick'em up in the afternoon. When he got there, he found that bastard back at the camp buildin'. . . He just left my boy in the woods, down by that creek."

Edge nodded. "I can see it still hurts. Did you ever hear of anyone at the high school having a grudge against Terry? Maybe somebody who could encourage or egg Harbin into shooting him?"

He shook his head. "My boy didn't have no enemies that I know of."

"Did Terry have any, well, shall we say, vices? Drugs, perhaps?"

"No. Absolutely not."

"How about a girl? Could Terry have been killed over a girl at the high school?" Edge was just killing time, fishing.

"How could he? He wadn't old enough to date, or drive, or go out. If he had a girlfriend, I don't know nothin' about it."

"Did you talk to anybody about Harbin bein' killed?"

Sawyer paused. "Well, why would I? I read about it in the newspaper like ever'body else. Didn't nobody say nothin' about it to me."

Edge nodded again. "What did the sheriff's deputies up in Clarke County say after the shooting?"

His eyes opened wide. "They tried to say that it was all a accident. But I know better. He shot my boy for no reason." He paused and leaned forward. His eyes narrowed, and his voice got low. "I hate that little son of a bitch, and I'm glad he's dead. And, if you tell me who the other bastard was that talked him into it, I'll pray for his death, too."

Chapter 27

It was another week before Austin got back a return on the subpoena from the phone company for the calls made to the Harbin phone on the night of the murder and from the payphone at the Blue Moon Lounge. The numbers from the Blue Moon were unremarkable. The number from Harbin's house was very remarkable.

They looked at them in Edge's office. He nodded toward the cross reference City Directory.

"Look up this number," he told Austin. He provided the exchange.

"It comes back to a Darrell Henry, in Chickasaw," she said. She looked up, wide eyed.

"You know who that is."

"Yeah. That's the guy we ambushed at the Pizza Shack."

"Right. It seems like he may know about a little something more than just tax evasion."

They were waiting at four o'clock outside the small apartment building on Highway 43 in Chickasaw when Darrell Henry pulled into the gravel parking lot and brought his Camaro to a stop.

Had Edge been alone, he would have strong armed Henry into the residence and forced the truth out of him, from the beginning. With Austin present, he couldn't afford to be so bold. They let Henry get inside and then walked up the steps to the door of number five, his second floor apartment.

Henry answered Edge's knock with his shoes off and a beer in his hand. He was surprised.

"Hey. What'chu guys want?"

"We need to talk to you, Darrell. Some new information has come to light," Edge said.

Edge, with Austin in tow, walked boldly past Henry into the apartment. The room was dark and warm.

"Wh, what are you talkin' about? I been keepin' my eyes open, and I ain't seen nothin' outta place, money wise." He looked around and picked up Austin's card off of a table by the door. "See, I still got'chur card. I was gonna call ya."

"Well, good, Darrell. Good. But we got somethin' else we wanna talk to you about."

Edge and Austin arranged themselves in a semicircle in front of Henry, one that pinned him into the corner near a closet.

"What?" His voice shook.

"I think you know. A phone call."

"A phone call?"

"That's right. One made from here on August 31 . . . by Jere Sawyer."

His eyes widened and his face went deathly pale. He began to fidget nervously.

"I don't know nothin'. I mean, what phone call?"

Edge held up his hand. "Shut up Darrell. You just make yourself guilty when you deny the obvious. Just tell us what happened."

"Okay, okay. But, can I just set my beer down first?"

Edge said nothing, and Henry turned away. When he turned back, his hand was empty, but it was a club heading for Edge's jaw. Edge threw up his right arm to block the blow, and his left fist buried itself deep into Henry's midriff. The pock marked man bent forward. Edge struck him again, this time with a knee to the nose. Blood issued from the wound, and Austin stepped back to keep from getting it on her clothes.

"Stand up straight, Darrell."

Edge lifted him up and hit him flush on the jaw. Henry was stunned, and Edge took the opportunity to push him toward a chair on the other side of the room. Henry sat down with a thud.

Edge walked over and stood over the semi-comatose young man. "Now, Darrell," he said, "we've fought the battle of wills, and you lost. Let's cut out the bullshit, and you tell me what I wanna know."

Henry shook his head and then wiped his nose on the sleeve of his blue work shirt. He looked at the blood then he looked up at Edge.

"Yeah, okay." He took a deep breath and exhaled. "Jere was here. He come over here about eight that night and said he needed to use the phone."

"Why'd he come here?"

"He said he needed to hook up with a boy in Chickasaw, and he said it was too far to drive up to his daddy's house."

"Why didn't he use a payphone?"

Henry snorted. "I don't know. Ask him."

"Don't be wise ass. Who'd he call?"

"He didn't say the boy's name; but I knew who it was."

"Who?"

"That Harbin kid."

"How'd'ju know?"

"'Cause, it ain't two days go by without the Old Man sayin' how much he hates Harbin and how that one day he's gonna get his." He paused. "When Jere come to town that weekend, them two had their heads together all day Thursday."

"Was Jere alone? When he came here, I mean."

"No. He had this big dude with him. He didn't come in."

"What'd he look like?"

"I couldn't see him real good. He was bald, though."

"What'd the car look like?"

"It was tan, I think. A Chevy."

"Why do you think he called the Harbin boy?"

"'Cause Jere said he was in town to take care of some family business and 'cause Walter is all the time talkin' about Harbin, only he don't call him Harbin. He calls him 'the maggot,' or 'asshole,' or 'that little son of a bitch.' Jere tol' me once that Walter said over and over how that somethin' oughta' be done about that maggot that killed his boy walkin' around free as a bird." He paused. "He said that it was like Walter didn't have no more sons."

"What else has Walter said?"

"Nothin'. Just that he misses his boy, Terry. See, I think he wanted Terry to get the business when he dies."

"Why not Jere?"

"'Cause Jere, well, Walter says he'd screw up a wet dream."

"Did you hear Jere's end of the conversation?"

"Yeah. He talked to somebody, told'em he was from the syrup plant; and then he said, 'well where did he go?' Then he hung up."

"You say anything to him?"

"No. He just said he was gonna have to go to Grand Bay."

"What were his exact words?"

Henry looked at Austin. Then he looked away.

"He said he was goin' night huntin' down in Grand Bay."

After Austin got Henry some ice for his nose, she and Edge told Henry they'd be in touch. Edge told him that he should just stick to his story that he didn't know why Sawyer came to his house and what the call was all about. He might still have to testify, but only to the fact that Sawyer made the call from here. Anything more and he could be considered an accessory.

In the car, on the way to the courthouse, Austin spoke:

"You ever hated anybody that much?"

"What are you talkin' about?"

"You know, as much as Walter Sawyer did Harbin."

Edge took a deep breath and exhaled loudly. He tried to remember a time when he hated anyone.

"I don't think so. My anger tends to come in short spurts. It's more like indignation; not so much hate. It comes and goes pretty quick."

"You been angry enough to kill?"

"What makes you ask that?"

"I don't know. I mean, you seem to get mad really fast. And you react so violently. I just thought . . ."

Edge thought back over his life; in the military, in police work; as a PI. What Austin didn't know wouldn't hurt her.

"A couple of people; but only in the line'a duty, so to speak. You know, in the Legion, when somebody shoots at you, you just gotta shoot back in self-defense." He paused. "How 'bout you?"

"Oh, no. I haven't killed anybody. I've only been a deputy for two years."

"No. I mean hated, held a grudge."

She shook her head. "Not like this. I tend to get angry in short bursts, like you. People say things about me; disparaging things about being a lesbian. It makes me mad for a minute, but I let it go pretty quick."

"Look, don't take it so hard about that orientation thing. I mean, folks don't mean nothin' by it. They just think it's a little odd." He paused. "They prob'ly look at you, the boys at least, and think, 'man, what a waste.'"

Chapter 28

The next day, Edge got a call from John Zachary, the school resource officer. He was calling from Grand Bay to say that he and the DEA were on their way to bust Louis Anderton for peddling steroids to the football players at North Mobile County High School, and did Edge want to come.

"Yeah. Yeah, I do, John. Can ya wait on me?"

"Meet us at the Vet's office in Grand Bay. You know where it is?"

"On Carmichael Road, off the Wilmer Highway?"

"Right. Not far from the interstate."

"I'll be there in twenty."

Edge pulled up in front of the small brick building and parked next to several government vehicles at ten that morning. The officers were already inside and searching the office. Edge found Zachary standing by the front door eating an apple.

"Did Russ Moore make a buy for ya?"

"Yeah. The DEA was waitin' with a search warrant when Russ come outta the door. They got the dope and hit the office straight away."

"You're not worried about his safety?"

"Nope. Big boy like Russ can take care'a his self."

Edge looked around at the federal investigators as they went about their business. Zachary finished the apple, opened the front door, and hurled it as far as he could toward a stand of trees to the south.

"By the way," Edge said. "Did you check Russ's alibi for the Harbin thing?"

Zachary nodded. "Yep. Coach said he was on the bus goin' back to the school. Says he remembers him 'cause he kept complainin' about a holdin' call that he got flagged for. Coach said he finally had to tell the boy that they won the game; that he should just shut up and let it go."

Edge nodded. He looked toward the inside of the building.

"Think any of this'll make a dent?" Edge said.

"Naw. Like Russ said, he's already got a new supplier. I bet there's half the football players in this county juiced up."

"I don't doubt that at all. So, did you get to talk to Anderton?"

"I didn't bother. But he's out in the car. You wanna say a word to him?"

"Yeah, if nobody objects."

"Hey, it was my information. We're golden."

Outside, in the backseat of a black fleet car, underneath a pecan tree, Edge leaned into the door and spoke to the handcuffed man. An agent who was standing next to the car eyed them suspiciously.

Anderton was in his twenties with brown hair over his ears, and a brown mustache. He was wearing blue scrubs and a sour look.

"Hey, Louis. My name's Edge. I'm a PI. Anything I can get for ya?"

"Yeah, outta these handcuffs and a hundred yard head start."

"Ha. Well, let's not get greedy." He paused. "You know a guy named Ty Harbin?"

Anderton didn't speak for a moment. "He's that boy that was killed up the hill last month, right?"

"Yeah."

"No. Never met him."

It was a telling statement. A lot of people have been killed who never met their killers.

"Louis, you know anything about that killin'? You know, about Ty and Carla Morgan?"

204

"Well, not directly. I heard from some folks down in Grand Bay that whoever it was that did it met him and her over at the Red Shed."

"Okay, well, I knew that."

"Well, I was there, too. I saw the two with a blond headed boy and an older dude, a big guy, talkin' out back'a the Shed."

"Think you could identify'em? A picture, I mean."

Anderton looked Edge right in the eye. "What's it worth to ya?"

"You lookin' to cut a deal?"

Anderton said nothing.

"Well, that'll be up to the feds. I'll do what I can, but, I can't promise ya nothin'. I mean, I prob'ly got less juice than anybody around here."

He looked away. "Well, I don't know if I can ID them fellas or not. My memory's kinda fuzzy."

Edge nodded. Everybody's got their price.

That afternoon, Edge got an urgent call from Austin to meet her at the Sheriff's Office downtown.

"What's up?"

"The guys from Narcotics are goin' on a raid."

"Where?"

"Mobile Terrace."

On Church Street, behind the Courthouse, Austin got in the car with Edge, and in twenty minutes they were on the west side of town near Stanton's mother's home on 5th Street. Edge parked down the street just as the SWAT van deposited six heavily armed and camouflaged deputies in front of the house. The men quickly surrounded the building.

Shortly afterward, they could hear some distinct yelling: ("Sheriff's Department! Search Warrant!"); then a loud thud: (one of the plainclothesmen using a battering ram to punch open the front door); and then a loud bang, (one of

205

those flash bang hand grenades). Three plainclothesmen wearing bulletproof vests swarmed inside.

"I hope they don't hurt that old lady." Austin said.

"Why not?" Edge said. "She deserves it. Her boy has been sellin' dope outta that house for years, and she's been lettin' him. If he took the money and used it to improve her life, you might could understand it. But they haven't done one thing to make their lives any better. I bet she smokes as much as he does." He paused. "It'd probably do her good to get smacked around a little."

Austin looked at him with distaste. "Please. She's an old woman. She's got no control over what he does."

"She's got more than you think."

In short order the plainclothes deputies exited the house with Willie Rae Stanton in handcuffs. He wore boxers and was barefooted, and looked as if he'd just awakened.

"Where are they gonna take him?"

"Downtown to the Narcotics office; right across the hall from Youth Aid."

"Is Randall gonna be there?"

"Yep. They're gonna try to put our case on him. Will Eubanks and Rice will be there too." She paused. "I think my colleagues are about to make a huge mistake."

The trip back downtown took thirty minutes in late afternoon traffic. The raid detail at the Stanton home stayed behind to go through the ramshackle house in Mobile Terrace looking for drugs and evidence of drug sales. Edge and Austin followed Will Eubanks, Randall and the others, with Willie Rae on board, downtown.

They watched as the sheriff's vehicles turned down into the tunnel underneath the courthouse while they parked on Church Street. Edge started to get out of the car. He stopped and looked at Austin.

"Wait," he said. "Are they gonna let us in?"

"Yeah. I think so."

"How about me?"

"I don't see why not. I mean, you and Randall have a deal, right?"

Edge nodded. "Let's go."

They both started down the tunnel, turned into the Narcotics hall, and Austin led the way through the unlocked door.

A hush fell over the room as everyone inside turned to look at them. Randall, Eubanks, Rice, two detectives from Narcotics, T.T. Lawrence; and Stanton, sitting, handcuffed to a chair.

"Ms Austin," Lawrence said. "You're here." He looked surprised.

"Yes, sir." She spoke nervously. "Mr. Edge and I uncovered this lead. So, we, uh, well, we just felt it would be, you know, right for us to be here."

I've got to hand it to her, Edge thought. She's got guts. That's what money'll do for you.

Lawrence looked down at her and smirked. Then he looked at Randall.

"Is that true? Did Ms Austin here hand you this lead?"

"Well, yes, Sheriff. But, Willie Stanton's somebody we've had our eye on from the beginning."

Stanton, glassy eyed and nodding, sat quietly in the chair, his right wrist handcuffed to the arm. He looked like anything but a double murderer.

Lawrence looked back at Austin. He snorted.

"Austin, you can stay." He nodded at Edge. "But we don't need him in here."

Edge smiled. "That's okay, T.T. I can see you don't need my help to screw this up."

He turned and walked back out the door and into the hall. There was a rush of air from out on the street that hit him in the face as he turned toward the mouth of the tunnel. Austin followed him into the hall.

"Wait a minute, Edge. Let me talk to him."

"No." Edge shook his head. "They don't need me. They've probably got enough dope cases to put Stanton away for a few years, and you know what I know about the murders. We both know who killed Harbin and the girl, and why. Just go in there, and don't let'em railroad him. If they try, it might screw up the case on the Sawyers. Give Randall what information he needs to convince him that we've got the right people. If they wanna slap Willie Rae around a little, that's okay. He deserves it. Just don't let'em give him anything to sign. He might cop to killing Harbin if they hit him hard enough. If you need to, show Randall your journal and just get him to hold off doing anything rash for a couple'a days. By then, we'll have the information from the airlines and the rent a car company, and that'll be all we need to go to the Sheriff, or the DA, or to somebody who'll listen to us and get Sawyer and Evans indicted."

"But . . ."

He chuckled. "Is that all you got from what I just said?"

Edge turned away and started walking up the ramp toward Church Street. Just at that moment, he had a very peaceful and satisfied feeling that he was about to be five grand richer.

Chapter 29

The next morning, the Mobile Examiner newspaper heralded the announcement that Willie Rae Stanton was being held on drug charges and that charges were pending in the case of the murders of Tyrone Harbin and Carla Morgan. The Sheriff praised the Narcotics Bureau and the Homicide Squad for the tireless work that they had put into the case, but he made no mention of the work of Edge and Austin.

That afternoon, Edge and Austin met at his office and afterwards headed west. They were looking for Hardy Eubanks to show him the lineup with photos of Sawyer and Evans.

On the way, Austin was chatty.

"This is really coming together isn't it."

"Apparently, you didn't read the morning paper."

"I did."

"The killer of Harbin and Morgan has already been arrested."

She shook her head. "I gave the Lieutenant what he needed to put the brakes on the Sheriff. What came out in the paper is a compromise. The Sheriff wanted to charge him, Randall said, wait."

"Well, thank heavens for compromises."

She smirked and looked ahead. "They're really not bad people you know."

"They're self-serving politicians; and don't you forget it."

They found Hardy Eubanks at the Daily Double. He was pretending to pick up trash in the parking lot when Edge stopped the Impala next to him. The rabbit was in his eyes, until Edge spoke.

"Calm down, Hardy. We just wanna talk."

Edge and Austin cornered him next to the front wheel well, and Austin produced the photos. Eubanks looked down at the pictures and looked away quickly.

"You see anyone you recognize, Hardy?"

His eyes got wide, and he forced himself to look back at the lineup. "I, I don't think so."

Edge smirked. "Really, Hardy? Really?"

He took a deep breath and exhaled. "I, I . . . I like livin' too much. I ain't no snitch."

Edge smiled and looked around at the Daily Double, the parking lot, Eubanks' old clothes, and his gin soaked face.

"Really, Hardy? Living? Really?"

In the car on the way to town, Edge looked at Austin and said:

"You can sign that Possession warrant on Hardy Eubanks now. Serve it as soon as you can." He paused. "I'll help you if you want."

The next evening, Edge met Austin at the Youth Aid Division office to go over the paperwork that the two of them had put together on the Harbin murder, and to see what they had left to do to make the case against the Sawyers.

"So, you got the papers from the Airline," he said.

"Yes. Here are the passenger manifests and copies of the tickets. Elizabeth Banks made the reservations under all their own names. That was stupid."

"Not really. They had to show ID to board."

She pulled out another paper. "And here is the rent a car contract, with Banks' credit card. It was for a Chevy Citation." She smiled. "I wonder how Evans got into a car that small?"

"He coiled. Just like the snake that he is."

Edge put his hands together, closed his eyes, and leaned back. "Okay. They fly out of Tampa to Pensacola. They drive to Alabama then they check into the motel in Irvington and spend Thursday night. The next day, we don't know what they do; lay low, maybe, until about eight or so, when they drive to Chickasaw, stop at Henry's, and call Harbin's house. Harbin's mama says he ain't there, he's gone to the ballgame. They leave Henry's house, drive to Grand Bay, and hook up with Harbin and Morgan at the Red Shed."

"How do they find them there?"

"I don't know exactly, but the unknown waitress and also Anderton the 'roid salesman both put them there talking with Harbin. They probably just followed the crowd." He paused. "Put it on your 'do list' to have Will Eubanks and Rice work up those two witnesses; when or if they ever take over the case."

"Right. Was this a contentious meeting, you think? At the bar, I mean."

"Not according to the waitress at the Red Shed. They were laughing and smiling. I'm thinkin' that Sawyer tells Harbin that he's got a line on some good, grade A weed from south Florida, and would Harbin like to move it for him here in Mobile. They leave the Red Shed 'cause there are too many people around. Sawyer tells Harbin he's on his way outta town, and he suggests that they stop at the on ramp at I-10, and he'll let him sample the product and give him the rundown on how the operation will work; how they're all gonna get rich.

"When they get to I-10, both cars pull over, and Evans and Sawyer get into the backseat, share a toke, do the deed, and get back in their own car."

"Who has the shotgun?"

"Evans uses the shotgun, and Sawyer the pistol."

"But Sawyer had the shotgun at his house, you said."

"He did. I'm thinking that he talked Evans into giving him his pistol because if a match can be made on the bullet, it'll come back to Evans' weapon. He probably told Evans that the shotgun couldn't be traced, so he should use it."

"He snookered him."

"You could call it that. Evans doesn't strike me as too bright." He paused. "Then again they could have thrown both guns into Mobile Bay when they went over the bridge back toward Pensacola, on their way home, and the weapons we've seen are what they managed to get with whatever old man Saywer paid'em."

"And then?"

"And then, Harbin's dead; Old Man Sawyer's happy; Jere Sawyer makes points with his father; nothing connects the shooting to the old man; and Evans keeps his mouth shut 'cause he goes up for capital murder if he talks. Banks, well, in my opinion, Banks probably is, or will be, an unsolved homicide for Suarez to worry about in the very near future." He paused. "What'd I forget?"

Austin thought. "Money."

"Right. I figure the old man financed everything, but I'm sure he probably did it all in cash. But, just to be on the safe side, you might think about getting a subpoena for his personal, as well as the business accounts, and take a look at'em. My guess is he's probably been planning this for years and everything was in a safe deposit box somewhere so he could dole it out when he needed to." He paused. "And, we need to locate Banks."

"How much do you think the old man paid?"

"For a slob like Evans? Oh, five grand. Banks got one or maybe fifteen hundred. Sawyer got only the undying affection of his dear old daddy." He paused again. "Can you think of anything else?"

She slowly shook her head. "No. That's it, step by step, I think." She paused. "It sure is a shame."

"It sure is." He paused. "You wanna get something to eat?"

"Okay."

Austin locked an accordion style folder containing their work product into a desk drawer belonging to Dean Andrews, a young deputy recently installed as a detective in Youth Aid. She picked up her sweater and adjusted the pistol on her hip.

The two walked out of the Youth Aid Division door, then into the basement garage. They walked up the ramp and out onto the sidewalk on Church Street. Edge stopped and took a deep breath. Austin began putting her arm into the sweater.

"Yes, sir. It sure is a shame," he said.

The truck that came from west to east on Church Street was not immediately familiar, but it did catch Edge's attention. It was a red F-250, and it was driving slowly.

What happened next occurred almost too fast to document. When the truck was in front of them, a blond haired man rose from lying down in the bed and began to discharge an Uzi machine pistol in the direction of the two investigators.

Edge dropped to one knee and reached with his right hand for the forty five in the holster in the small of his back, while at the same time reaching out his left hand toward Austin.

"Watch out!" he yelled.

Austin looked at him and smiled just as the first rounds began to strike her body. She fell backward and hit her head on the concrete.

Edge heard the whine of the bullets as they flew over his head. He got off two rounds toward the truck as it went past and three more as he ran out into the middle of the street. The vehicle sped up and then slowed, only slightly, to make the corner at Royal Street, turning north.

He didn't have to see a tag number to know who it was. Jere Sawyer was tying up loose ends. Edge looked back at Austin.

He could see that she was bleeding from wounds to her chest and arm. He reached and took a walkie talkie from off her belt.

"Double zero, double zero, at the Church Street side of the courthouse. Officer down, shots fired. I need an ambulance."

"What unit is calling?" the dispatcher said.

"This is for Deputy Austin. She's been shot."

"I'll get an ambulance in route."

"Can you copy a lookout?"

"Go ahead."

"Be on the lookout for a red Ford, model F-250 pickup truck. It was last seen northbound on Royal Street from Church, possibly enroute to eastbound Interstate 10 or to the Celeste Road area in Saraland. It'll be occupied by a white male, blond hair, armed with an Uzi machine pistol."

"10-4."

Edge knelt and took hold of Austin's hand. She blinked once but did not speak. He could see one wound in the left side of her chest, and another in the abdomen. His initial assessment was that if she could get to surgery quickly, she'd have a chance. He was looking her in the eye when the first Police Department scout car rolled to a stop.

"Let's get her in the backseat," Edge told the young officer. "You gotta better chance to save her if you leave now."

The officer nodded. "Right."

They loaded her in, and Edge shut the door as a second car arrived.

"I'll follow you," he said.

"Who are you?"

"John Edge."

Chapter 30

At the Medical Center, Edge stood in the waiting room outside of the emergency treatment area and took stock of himself. He was cold, hungry, and bleeding.

On Church Street, he'd shown the second officer his reserve deputy sheriff's badge, given him a tour of the scene, and provided him a more detailed description of the truck and the shooter; including the fact that the vehicle probably contained five or six bullet holes, souvenirs from his forty-five. The shift sergeant had one of the officers take him to the hospital after they all noticed one graze wound in the side of his head and another small puncture wound in the bottom of his upper left arm.

Edge sat down and held a towel over the bottom of his arm. After closer inspection of the wound, he pulled about an inch long sliver of concrete – no doubt the result of a ricochet – out of the hole and pronounced himself well. He transferred the towel to the left side of his head, an inch above his ear, and wiped away blood.

His own health assessment was interrupted by the insistent voice of Victor Riley as he walked from behind the clerk's counter to the left and stood in front of Edge.

"How do you feel?" Riley said as he chewed on a cigar.

"I'll live." He nodded toward the ER. "What about her?"

"She's in surgery. She was alive when she went in."

Edge nodded.

"What happened?"

Edge took a deep breath and exhaled. "We were at her office in Youth Aid going over what was left to do in the Harbin/Morgan homicides, and when we walked out of the courthouse, she stopped to put on her sweater. The truck came toward us, and a man popped up from the bed and started sprayin' bullets. I got off about six rounds. I think I hit the truck."

"Do you know who it was?"

"I think it was Jere Sawyer."

"You can make an ID?"

"Close enough."

"Who was driving?"

"That, I didn't see."

"What about the truck?"

"It matched the description of Sawyer's truck; the one we saw in Tampa. It's either half way to Tallahassee or burnt to a crisp by now."

"I'll get it on the wire." He pulled out his pad. "You know the tag number?"

"No. But it's in Austin's notes."

"That the young girl's name?"

"Yeah. Amy Austin."

"I'll draw a warrant in the morning. We'll pick him up."

"If I find him first, you'll have to dig him up."

Their conversation was interrupted when Nathan Randall walked into the waiting area in a huff. He stopped and looked at Riley, then at Edge.

"Edge, what the fuck happened?"

"Jere Sawyer tried to assassinate us."

"What were you two doing down there?"

"We were in the Youth Aid office, making this Harbin murder for you."

"Well? . . . Is that all?"

Edge snorted. "Austin's got a case made, that is, if you want to take a look at it."

"T.T. doesn't agree."

He paused. "Wise up, Randall. Just because the Sheriff's gotten money from Walter Sawyer in the past, doesn't mean you need to sweep this case under the rug. It's all in black and white, in her office, in a file. Get it, before it gets 'lost.'"

Randall was silent. Riley spoke.

"Listen to him, Nate. He's got a pretty good track record on these things."

"Well," was all he said. He turned and walked toward a large television hanging from the wall in the corner.

"By the way, how's she doin?" Edge said.

Randall turned back toward Edge. "Still in surgery. The word out from there is that it'll be touch and go for a while, but she'll make it. One bullet collapsed her left lung and the other hit the big bowel." He paused. "Good thing she got here when she did."

"Not my first rodeo."

Two hours later, the three men were still in the waiting area. T.T. Lawrence visited, spoke briefly to Randall out of earshot, and then left. They were told that Austin's father had come over from Orange Beach and was waiting upstairs.

A nurse brought Edge a band aid for his arm and an aspirin for his head. He chewed the aspirin without water.

Shortly after the Sheriff left, a doctor with bloody spots on his green scrubs walked in the waiting room. He was a tall man with pale skin and long thin fingers.

"Who is the investigating officer?" the doctor said.

"That'll be me. Vic Riley."

Randall walked forward also. They stood in front of Edge's chair.

"Mr. Riley. I'm Doctor Eisenhauer. I'm the surgeon that operated on Ms Austin." He paused and looked at Edge. "She's a very lucky girl. Her age and her physical condition are working for her. I think, barring infection, she'll recover."

"That's good news, Doctor."

"We got one bullet out of her. It'll be in Pathology if you find something to compare it to. The other, the one in her abdomen, went clear through; missed her spine by about a half inch. It might be in a wall or something out at the scene."

"The wall behind them was stone. If it hit that, it's probably in a million pieces. But, we'll take a look. I've got people out there."

Eisenhauer looked over at Edge. "You did the right thing sending her on to the hospital. Any delay waiting for the ambulance might have killed her."

Edge nodded. "Happy to be of help." His tone was almost derisive.

He was remembering back to another case, another female partner, who was beaten badly and didn't live through surgery; and another whose future and emotional health had been snatched from her by the criminal element.

Eisenhauer looked around at the normally busy, but at that time deserted, waiting room and nodded his head.

"She should be awake in a few minutes, if you want to talk to her."

Another hour past before Riley, Randall and Edge were allowed into the intensive care unit. Austin was awake and holding hands with a man believed to be her father. He was fifty, of average height, with brown hair and a mustache, and a bit of a spread. Edge surmised that his six button suit probably cost about two grand.

This was the man who had left his wife and found another woman, and who was sending his daughter into such an emotional tailspin. This is the man that Austin really loved; not the women with whom she had experimented.

Edge stood by the bed. "How ya feelin', Speedy?"

Austin's voice was tired but she managed a smile. "I couldn't outrun a bullet."

"No, you couldn't."

Riley spoke up. "Did you get a look at the guy in the truck?"

Austin shook her head. "The last thing I remember was Edge kneeling down and reaching for my arm. Then I saw his gun . . . and then it felt like somebody punched me in the stomach."

"That was me, Speedy," Edge said. "I was tryin' to knock some sense into ya."

She smirked then nodded to the man in the expensive suit.

"Edge, this is my father. Fredrick Austin."

Edge nodded at the obviously wealthy man. "Good to meet you, sir."

"I'm told our thanks are in order, Mr. Edge."

Edge nodded.

"If you hadn't gotten her on to the hospital, she could have bled to death. I and my family are in your debt."

Nathan Randall spoke up. "Mr. Austin, the Sheriff was here, but he had to leave on another matter. He said tell you that he would call you and fill you in on the situation tomorrow morning."

"Sure. Fine," Fred Austin said dismissively.

Everyone stood and said nothing for a minute. A nurse entered the room and said that the number of visitors was too large and about half of the people were going to have to leave. She asked who the immediate family was, and Fred

Austin spoke up and said that he was the only relative. Everyone else began to turn toward the door.

Edge looked back at Amy Austin lying in the hospital bed and nodded. She gave him a knowing look to indicate that she got his meaning.

"Edge? Don't do anything on my account."

"You're forgetting. They tried to kill me too."

The next morning, Edge took a trip out to Snow Road to visit Myra Leonard. The silver haired lady doctor left her muddy boots on the back porch, glided into some slippers, and then invited Edge to her examination room in the corner of her residence, off the laundry room. She smoothed back her hair then went to the sink and washed her hands.

Leonard was Edge's 'off the grid' physician, referred to him by Larry Silverstein from nearby Mauvilla. She took care of his injuries, no questions asked.

Edge hopped up on the sheet covered exam table and removed the band aid from the underside of his left arm, the arm that already bore a machete scar from a previous encounter with the serial killer Lewis Hart. He winced as it came off.

"Let me take a look," Leonard said turning to him while putting on rubber gloves.

She moved his upper arm left, then right and pushed the skin on either side of the quarter-sized wound.

"Move your fingers," she said.

He complied.

"Well, it doesn't look too bad. Might need a couple of stitches. What happened?"

"I think a piece of broken sidewalk jumped up and lodged itself in there. I pulled something out that looked like stone right before the nurse at the hospital gave me this oversized band aid."

Leonard removed a suture kit from a glass cabinet and opened it up. After washing down the wound, she began her work.

"Is this something that I should be worried about?" she said.

"No. This is the result of a longstanding family feud." He paused. "You know, forgiveness is a wonderful thing. Sometimes you just have to let things go." He paused. "I once read that not forgiving someone is like drinking a gallon of poison and expecting another person to die." He paused. "You know, forgiveness doesn't mean approval. You can forgive someone without approving of what they've done. And it doesn't mean amnesia, either. Some things are impossible to forget."

"I've never heard it put like that."

Leonard took out a needle and used the anesthesia to deaden Edge's arm. He winced at the insertion.

"And forgiving yourself," she said, "is the hardest thing to do. I was young at the time, but I remember a young boy who died in the ER because I gave him the wrong antibiotic. Turns out he was allergic to sulfa drugs, and I made the mistake of ordering them."

"Did anyone tell you?"

"No, but I didn't ask. Anyway, it didn't matter to me. All I could think about was how he died, and that it was my fault." She paused. "It was years before I got over that."

"Guilt's a powerful thing. Even if you don't deserve it, you can carry it around for years. That's what's wrong in this case."

"How so?"

"Well, there's an old man that I think feels responsible for the death of his son. He sent him out in the woods, alone, before he was old enough. But, instead of dealing with his death, and the grief that came with it, he's decided to turn the anger outward instead of inward, and he developed a colossal hate for someone else. It's lasted seven years."

Edge exhaled loudly. "I've made so many mistakes, and got so much grief, if I let every one of the things I've done wrong follow me, or if I turned that pain outward

220

toward someone else, I'd either be in a mental institution, or I'd be a homicidal maniac."

She smiled. "I suppose." She paused and nodded toward his arm. "What happened to the people that caused this?"

"Nothing . . . yet."

By ten o'clock, Edge was in Vic Riley's office on Church Street. He wore a long sleeved shirt over his arm to hide the bandage that Leonard had placed on the underside of his limb.

"Okay," Riley said, "fill me in about this thing. Why are these guys up here taking potshots at you? I couldn't get heads or tails outta Randall."

Edge recounted the case and Riley took notes, specifically the names of all the players. He chewed his cigar in the process.

"And this was Jere Sawyer that shot at you two last night?"

"I think so. I can ID him by the build, the blond hair, and the truck. I didn't get a look at his face."

"Well, the Sheriff's Department found the truck. It was abandoned and burned, out by the airport. The ID section is out there now. They've found some bullet holes, but they haven't found any of your slugs yet."

"Well, I guess that'll be another ten thousand that the old man will have to shell out."

"You think Evans was driving?"

"I have no idea." He paused. "I'm looking for a woman, Vic," Edge said.

"Aren't we all. You gotta a name?"

"Elizabeth Banks. I don't where she's from, but I'm told she was in Tampa last, dancing at a club."

Riley picked up the phone and called the records room, and after making contact, he began to take notes. Shortly, he hung up the phone.

"Well, we've never had her. She's gotta Florida DL and a criminal history down there; a couple of felony forgery charges." He paused and looked at his notes. "Have you dealt with anyone at their PD down there?"

"Yeah, a cat named Suarez. But . . ."

"But what?"

"But why don't you let me try to look this girl up before you call him."

"Why?"

"Well, he's close to one of the other dancers at the club where she works. I wouldn't put it past this broad to tip her off and get her out of town before I can get down there. Just give me the address, and I'll be there by tomorrow." He looked away. "She's gonna be the key to finding Sawyer."

Chapter 31

Edge was on a plane and in Tampa, Florida, by seven that evening. He rented a car and checked into a motel, and was prowling the streets by ten.

Without a good description of Banks, and unwilling to go to Suarez to get a mug photo of her, he was reduced to surveillance from the parking lot across from The Hollywood Palace, waiting for Evans to leave; hopefully, with Banks. On this particular night, Evans' Blazer was not to be found. Edge had Banks' address, but he didn't want to hit her apartment without a reasonably good idea that she was there.

At two AM, the majority of the vehicles and employees had left the bar. Edge watched as three women, one of them Destiny, or Tina, Suarez's girlfriend, walked toward two vehicles in the corner of the lot. He watched as Destiny and one other woman got into a Ford and the other woman leave in a Chevy Vega.

Edge didn't know what to do, but he took a chance and followed the red Ford Mustang driven by Destiny. He would know pretty quickly if it was traveling toward Banks' address.

The vehicle went south on the Dale Mabry Highway, then west, then south on Westshore Boulevard. She's going right to Banks' apartment, he thought.

Edge watched as the Mustang pulled into the apartment complex on the bay side of Westshore and stopped in front of building three, on the right. Edge and his rent a car found a space in the shadows.

A woman, averaged sized, with platinum hair, exited the Mustang and walked into the bottom apartment on the right, farthest from the lot. Edge waited until the Mustang drove away then made his move.

Edge stood in front of apartment C and knocked lightly. A female opened the door.

"What'd'ju forget . . . Oh," she said as Edge pushed his way in and clamped his hand over her mouth.

"Good evening, Billie."

He lifted the hand off her mouth slightly. "Who are you? What do you want?" she whispered.

"Just some information."

"Get out of here, or I'll scream."

Edge quickly clamped his hand back over her mouth.

"No, you won't. Now, I won't hurt you unless I have to. But I need some information. So, I'm gonna take my hand off your mouth. But if you holler, I'll put it back . . . and it won't be pleasant. Got it? I don't like hitting women, but it causes me no great heartache."

She nodded vigorously.

"Now, sit down and shut up."

He pushed her toward the couch on the south wall of the surprisingly tidy one bedroom apartment. He took a seat next to her and took out a Colt Detective Special that he had purchased from an allnight pawn shop shortly after he arrived in town.

223

"Anybody else here?"

She looked down at the gun. Her voice was a whisper.

"No."

Edge took the measure of her appearance. She was about five seven, with curves and larger than averaged sized breasts; just right for a dancer.

"Good. I'm a friend of the family of Tyrone Harbin. Now you may or may not know who that is, but you should . . . you helped kill him."

Her eyes widened, but she said nothing.

"That's right. In Mobile."

She licked her lips. "I, I wasn't there. I didn't shoot anybody."

"No, but you helped. You made the plane reservations; you rented the car; you even went with'em to hunt those kids down." He paused. "Did you know they shot a young girl? A seventeen year old who had nothing to do with it."

Banks' didn't speak.

Edge reached into the pocket of his safari vest and pulled out a cassette tape recorder. He set it on the coffee table in front of them.

"Now, start talking or things are gonna go a little dark."

She looked at the recorder and smirked. "You think I'm gonna tell you what happened?"

Edge shrugged, then stood up and backhanded the woman across her mouth. Blood seeped from her bottom lip. He didn't hit her as hard as he could have, but he felt sure he got her attention.

"Yes," he said.

She wiped her mouth as tears started to pool in the interior corners of her eyes. Her pain was real. Edge turned the tape recorder on.

"It was Johnny. He made me do it."

"Go on."

"He said that he was gonna make five thousand dollars, and one of it was mine. All I had to do was to make some calls and set up the plane reservations and rent a car."

"Why did you go?"

"I don't know. I, I haven't been anywhere in a while. I, I was bored. It was kinda like a vacation. When I found out what they were gonna do, I told'em to take me and drop me off somewhere, and then to pick me up afterwards."

"Where'd they leave you?"

"At a truck stop. I went in the restaurant and waited."

"Anybody there verify that?"

She paused. "A waitress, maybe, I don't know. I had coffee."

"Start at the beginning."

Elizabeth Banks told the story fast, trying to gloss over details of her own involvement and adding to Sawyer's. Her speech became a little muffled as her bottom lip began to swell.

"When we got to town, we went to Jere's daddy's house and got some guns."

"What kinda guns?"

"There was a, a shotgun, I think; you know, with the two barrels next to each other. I think there was two pistols. One of'em was like Johnny's, kinda square. He said it was a forty-five."

"Who picked the motel?"

"That dump? It was Jere's idea. He said it was out of the way and nobody would ever know we was there. Jere spilled some wine on the floor and had the maid come in and clean it up. I told him that was stupid, that somebody knew we were there now."

"How long were you there?"

"Just the one night. Thursday night."

"What did you guys do all day Friday?"

"We stayed in the motel 'til noon. Then we went to some mall and ate. Then we went to a bar, the Bonanza, I

225

think. Then we went back to Jere's daddy's house to eat supper."

She closed by telling that after they picked her up at the truck stop, they headed east toward Pensacola. They threw the guns into some water on the way. When they got back to Tampa, Evans left town for a week.

"Where'd he go?"

"Atlanta, I think. He's got family there."

"Where was he last night?"

"I don't know. He got his jaw broke at work. I haven't seen too much of him since."

Edge looked away. "Did you ever get your thousand?"

She blinked twice. "Two. Johnny said they got a bonus." She paused. "Look, I didn't know they was goin' up there to kill nobody. I, I was just . . . just like a travel agent."

Edge nodded, turned off the tape, rose to his feet, and put the recorder in this pocket. She stood also.

"Ain't there somethin' we can work out?" she said. She fingered at the collar of the blue pullover shirt that she wore.

"No." He paused and held up the tape recorder. "Maybe this'll save you from the electric chair."

Edge smiled and, without warning, swung his right fist and struck Banks on the jaw, knocking her unconscious and sending her sprawling on the couch.

The next morning, Edge was up at five. If Evans was home, he wanted to get to him early, before he had his coffee and was alert.

He parked in the lot near Evans' door at the complex, which turned out was not far from Banks'. Edge looked around but couldn't see his Blazer anywhere. No doubt Banks had called him and alerted him to Edge's presence, but Edge was counting on the fact that Evans would tell her that he wasn't afraid and could handle whoever was after him. It would be like Evans to tell her that he could handle anyone.

At the door, Edge made ready a can of pepper spray in his right hand. If the door opened any appreciable amount, Evans was going to get a face full of the cayenne pepper-based mixture and would be immobilized quickly.

He knocked twice, lightly. When nothing happened, he tried again, this time harder. There was no answer.

Edge stood back and thought. Evans had family in Atlanta, Banks had said. Edge dreaded a trip up there to look for him. In fact, he had no idea where to start.

There was nothing to do now but check at Sawyer's house. He made the trip in ten minutes and slowed as he circled the cul de sac. He was surprised to see a woman exit Sawyer's front door.

She wore a robe over her tank top and shorts, and she was a knockout. It was the same blonde that had interrupted Edge's clandestine entry operation, on his earlier trip to Tampa. Edge rolled down the window as she stopped to pick up the morning paper.

"Hey, is Jere home?" he said.

"No, he's not."

Edge put the car in park and stepped out. "I'm Darrell, a friend of his from Mobile. You know when he'll be back?"

She smiled and shook her head. "No. He went home to see his folks for a couple'a days."

Edge feigned exasperation. "Aw, shit. How do you like that; I come five hundred miles to see him, and he's back there where I just left."

"Well, he said he'd be back in a couple'a days. I take that to mean that he'll be back by Friday."

"Are you his wife?"

"Right. I'm Tammy." She paused and looked at him. "You wanna come in for some coffee?"

"Sure." Edge smiled as he realized his good fortune.

Inside Tammy poured coffee out of a pot into two cups on the kitchen table. Edge used cream to make his palatable. She sat down across from him.

"How is it that you know Jere?"

"Oh, we worked together for Jere's daddy, at the plumbin' company back home."

She stared at his eyes. "You look a lot older than Jere."

"I am, a few years. I went in service after high school, and I was in there for a while. I, well, I got into a couple'a scrapes."

Edge didn't know how long he could keep pretending to be Darrell Henry, a ne'er do well plumber's assistant with a pocked marked face. He'd know pretty quick whether Tammy Sawyer had ever been to Mobile and met anyone associated with her husband's family, or his past. He decided to get on the offensive.

"I don't remember hearin' Walter talk about you. You'n Jere been married long?"

"About six months. I ain't been home to meet his family yet." She paused. "Tell me about'em?"

"His family? Oh, well. They're a real nice bunch'a folks. I mean, I just work for'em. They gotta big ole house outside'a town. I guess you could say they're a really loyal bunch." He paused as he took a sip. "Jere's got a Uncle Josh, and I guess you know he's gotta brother that died."

"Yeah. He talks about him all the time. He said another boy killed him when they was out huntin'."

Edge nodded. "The whole fam'ly took it kinda hard. Don't a day go by without Walter mentions it."

"Yeah. Well, Jere, too. He talks about it all the time. He said his daddy said that Jere's brother was shot on purpose."

"How come?"

"He said that at the time his brother was usin' weed pretty heavy. He said that the kid that shot him was his dealer and that Jere's brother was into him for some money."

"I hadn't heard that. Wadn't the boy only about fifteen or something when it happened?"

"He was young, but I don't know how young."

Edge nodded. His ruse was holding up pretty good. Even if it didn't, it didn't matter. He was sure that Sawyer was the one that took shots at him and put Austin in the hospital, and if he was, then when he learned that Edge wasn't dead, he would be coming for him again."

Edge took another sip and looked at the woman across from him. Her blonde, shoulder length hair framed an oval face, and her brown eyes, and dark lashes and brows, were extraordinary. He wondered how Sawyer got a woman who looked like her. It must be the house, he thought. A woman'll give anything to get a house.

"Well," he said. "Ain't that just my luck. Jere told me when I come to town he was gonna show me around an' hook me up; I mean, him workin' at a club and all."

She looked him in the eye. "Well, if you come all this way to hook up, well, I mean, you know, I can take care'a that."

Edge looked her in the eye. "Are you sayin' what I think you're sayin'?"

Tammy smiled but said nothing.

Edge thought for a second. A long time ago he had resolved that he was willing to die by many causes, but he had made up his mind that AIDS would not be one of them.

"Look, it's temptin', but maybe I better go. Don't get your feelin's hurt, but, after all, he is my friend." He paused. "Maybe, I'll just catch your act down at the club."

She raised her brows and shrugged. "Suit yourself."

Suit yourself, he thought. He wanted to slap her.

Chapter 32

Edge was back in Mobile the next morning. He stopped by Riley's office and found the lieutenant with his nose buried in a police report. He looked up.

"You're back. You accomplish anything?"

"Well, a little." He flipped the cassette tape onto Riley's desk. "Can you hang onto that for me?"

"What is it?"

"It's Elizabeth Banks' confession. She made the arrangements for Sawyer and John Evans to come to town and was with'em when they did. I'd feel better if you kept it, as opposed to Randall. He doesn't really have a lotta confidence in me and this case – and I don't have a whole lotta confidence in him."

Riley shook his head. "This don't have nothin' to do with me. There wasn't a woman in the truck was there? She didn't confess to that, did she?"

"No." Edge reached and picked up the tape. "Just thought you'd be a pal."

"Give it to Randall. And don't sell him short. When the chips are down, he does what's right."

"Maybe." He paused. "Any luck finding Sawyer?"

"Not yet. His daddy won't say. You find out anything?"

"I got a come on from his slut of a wife. She told me he was here in town. My guess is his daddy's payin' to hold him up somewhere."

Then a thought hit Edge square. It came to him like a bolt, and whether it was a good lead or not, it certainly was a good idea.

"There is someone who I think we can lay hands on, and he may have been driving the truck."

Riley and couple of detectives took Darrell Henry into custody at Sawyer Plumbing and brought him to 457 Church

Street at ten that morning. Edge stood in the background and watched as Riley hammered him.

"Where were you two nights ago?"

"Where? I was, I was at home; asleep."

"Bullshit. We got your prints out of Jere Sawyer's truck?"

"How? It was bur . . . "

"Burnt? How'd you know that?"

"I didn't say that."

"But you did. Look, Darrell, you're lookin' at twenty years for conspiracy to commit attempted murder on a police officer. The only thing you can do is tell, and tell it all, and get the DA to cut you a deal."

Henry, suddenly very nervous, bit his lip. How could he have been so stupid?

"Okay. It was Jere. He did it. But I didn't know what he was gonna do. He just said he needed me to drive him down Church Street, and he was gonna shoot outta couple'a streetlights with his new gun and, you know, just have a little fun. I didn't know he was gonna shoot *at* anybody."

"Where's Sawyer"

"I don't know.

"Don't you lie to me."

"I don't."

Riley stood up straight and looked over at Edge. "You got anything that you want to say?"

Edge chuckled and stepped up from the shadows. He looked at Henry.

"You missed a good time in Tampa."

Around noon, Edge went to the Medical Center to see Austin. She had been moved to a private room, and her significant other, Wendy, was at her bedside reading the paper.

She was tall and lithe with soft brown hair and blue eyes. In fact, everything about her was soft; her coloring seemed to fade into several different shades of pastels. Her thin bones gave her a lean look, and her hands and feet were long and thin. Her lips, over straight teeth were thin also. She wore slacks, a silk shirt, and sandals. She looked up at Edge, sat up in the chair, and smiled slightly.

"Well, Edge. Where have you been?" Austin said.

"I had to take a trip."

She narrowed her brows. "To Tampa?"

"Yeah, but I got back in time to find out that the Police have made an arrest in your, that is, our case."

She sat up in the bed and grimaced. "Who?"

"Darrell Henry."

"Really? How'd you find that out?"

"My gut."

"He confessed?"

"Sure did. He'll probably get a deal, though. So, don't get your hopes up."

"Just that they identified'im is enough." Austin looked over at Wendy. "Oh, I'm sorry. Edge, this is Wendy, from Connecticut." She paused and looked slightly embarrassed. "I, I think I mentioned her."

"You did. How do you do, ma'am?"

"Fine, Mr. Edge. I've heard so much about you." Her voice was soft and feminine, and had that New England lilt.

"Nothing good, I'm sure," he said smiling. Then he looked Austin in the eye.

"So, how are you feeling?"

"Okay, I guess. I have a little congestion in my lungs and a tummy ache, but I'll get by, and," she looked over at Wendy with affection, "of course, I've got a good nurse."

"She's gettin' outta this police work just as soon as she can get to a typewriter and tap out her resignation," Wendy said.

Austin waved her hand in dismissal. "Don't listen to her."

Edge smiled. "You ought'a listen to her. I mean, you're family's got a lotta bread. What do you need this aggravation for?"

She thought for a second. "Do you remember how in Vietnam, it was only the poor kids that had to go? How if you were rich enough to go to college, or if your family had power or money, you could get a deferment? Well, I always thought about how that wasn't fair. Bein' in the cops is just my way of sayin' that rich people have got to shoulder some of the burden, just like the poor people. It's my way of doin' something, of givin' something back, in spite of my wealth."

Edge looked her and said nothing for several seconds. When he spoke he smiled slightly.

"Bullshit. You guilt-ridden liberals are all alike." He paused. "Did you ever think that maybe you could do a lot more for people *because* of your money rather than of in spite of it? I happen to have some knowledge about Vietnam and there seemed to me to be a pretty diverse mixture of economic groups there." He paused. "Why don't you try to do some good with what you have, instead trying to do for others by making yourself into something that you're not."

Austin was speechless. She looked at him with shock on her face; as if no one had ever talked to her that way before. Wendy was smiling.

"Well, I guess you told her." Wendy said, her brows raised.

"I didn't tell her anything. She's stubborn enough, so she'll do what she wants."

Edge looked at Austin and remembered the smile that was on her face right at the moment that she was shot. It was a nice smile, one of contentment; one that said I'm doing what I want to do, the way I want to do it, when and where I want to do it. He could be satisfied with that.

"Anyway," he said, "while I was in Tampa, I gotta confession from Elizabeth Banks, aka Billie Hitchcock. Riley says to go ahead and give it Randall. He says that he can be trusted to do the right thing. What do you think?"

Austin shrugged. "Well, I guess. He's the boss. We've got to roll with him, or not at all." She paused. "It wasn't coerced, was it?"

"Well, not so's anyone would notice. You can't tell it from the tape anyway."

"You got it on tape?"

"Sure. She said that she wasn't there when the murders happened; she was sittin' in the truck stop restaurant. But she made the reservations – all except the motel – went with them to get the guns, and watched when they threw'em in the drink. She says she didn't know what they were coming here for. To her, it was just a vacation."

"Please."

"By the way, what happened at Willie Rae Stanton's interrogation?"

"Oh," she chuckled. "Well, Willie Rae was so stoned, or drunk, or something, he could hardly sit in the chair. They got him to admit that he knew Ty Harbin and that he fronted him weed, and even some crack. They also got him to confess, but, hey, he would have confessed to the King assassination if they'd wanted him to. In addition to being out of his mind on dope, he's also pretty badly retarded mentally." She shook her head.

"What did you tell Randall?"

"I told him that it wasn't right. He just said it would do for now, and if we came up with some more later, they could always let Willie Rae off the hook. He said he was gonna be arrested for possession with intent to distribute anyway, and he wasn't going anywhere."

"Marvelous." He paused and looked at her. "So what do you think, Speedy? Go see Randall or not."

"Yeah. Make me look like a genius."

That afternoon, Edge met Nathan Randall on a park bench near the bank of the duck pond at Langan Park in west Mobile. It was sunny, but there was a breeze at their backs, out of the north, and in early October conditions were still not unpleasant.

Edge had brought crackers and was feeding the ducks when Randall walked up. He had to shoo the birds away in order to sit down. Edge took the package and crushed it into bite sized chunks and flung it toward the pond. The flock rushed that direction.

"So, Edge, here I am."

"Thanks for comin', Lieutenant."

"You got something for me?"

"Yeah. I do. But first, I gotta a question. When you put me and Austin together, what did you expect to happen?"

He smirked. "I expected you to get to the bottom of this case; develop enough information to make an arrest."

"Funny, I thought it was so you could keep the spigot running with donations for the Sheriff."

"Well, that *was* my first thought. But, later on, when we weren't coming up with anything, I was hoping that you'd make some progress."

"Well, we did. I think you've made a mistake with Willie Rae Stanton."

"I know. But you brought him to us."

"Sure, but he was just one of about four or five leads that Austin and I ran down. I never really thought he killed anybody. He just had a motive."

"He did." He looked toward pond. "You ever worked for a sheriff before?"

"No," he lied.

"Well, they get their jobs by political means. And, they keep them by political means. Keeping the voting public happy is the Sheriff's overriding concern. When we announced that we had somebody in jail for killing those two kids, or at least that charges were pending, that's all the public needed to hear; that the Sheriff had done his job. It didn't matter to them whether he was guilty or not. It won't matter to them if we have to drop the charges and let him go later – though with the weed we got out of his house he'll likely be tied up for a few years. It just matters that an arrest was made.

"I'm pretty sure anything he said won't hold up in court. But, by that time we'll have the real killers in jail and nobody'll even care. Heck, if they follow the case at all, when

235

it gets to court, and Wille Rae's not the man, we'll all say, 'surprise' and move on."

He took a deep breath. "I read Austin's journal, after I finally got into that desk." He chuckled. "There were three locks on the drawer. And I know that Sawyer and this John Evans are the ones. You've made a pretty good circumstantial case."

"Well, good. Take this and add it to the file." He handed him the cassette tape of Banks' confession.

"What's this?"

"It's an accomplice confession, a woman by the name of Elizabeth Banks, alias Billie Hitchcock."

"Alright. Will it stand up?"

"It doesn't have to. Just use her as a witness. She didn't shoot anybody, and if she can be believed, she wasn't there when it happened."

"I understand."

Edge looked toward the pond. "Well, what happens now?"

"I talked with Riley. I know you've got Sawyer fingered for shooting Austin. I'll put him and this Evans character in the NCIC and maybe we'll have'em soon. Meantime, Willie Rae cools his heels in jail, Austin gets well, the Sheriff's happy, and all's right with the world."

"You're not gonna tell Carla Morgan's parents about what's happened?"

"Not yet." He paused. "I know Kenneth Morgan. He's an ass. He defends drug dealers. Heck, he'd probably defend Willie Rae if the money was right. Let him go on guessing for a while."

Edge nodded. He wanted to, but he decided not to tell Randall that there was five grand riding on Morgan's knowledge of the truth about the case.

"Well, can I tell Otha Harbin?"

"I'd prefer you didn't, but if you think he can keep a secret . . ."

"He has up to now."

"Sure. Just tell him you've got the boys identified and they're just waitin' to be picked up."

"You're all heart, Lieutenant."

Chapter 33

It was three weeks later, and on into the cool of the month of November when Otha Harbin called Edge at his office. They met in the evening at the Waffle Hut in Tangerine.

"I see where they made an arrest in my boy's case," Harbin said.

"Yeah, well, they have. But don't count on that man standin' trial." He paused. "'Cause he didn't do it."

"Well . . . who did?"

"The Sheriff has warrants out on two others that actually did the shooting. This guy that they've got on drug charges was somebody who . . . who had a motive to kill your son, and he's just in jail for public relations reasons."

Edge stopped. He did not want to tell Harbin that his son was selling dope, but that was the motive that the deputies had ascribed to Stanton, and there was no way of getting around the fact that his boy was not the child that Harbin thought he was.

"Mr. Harbin, I told you not long ago that you were gonna hear some things about Tyrone that aren't gonna sound too good."

"Yeah, that's what'chu said."

"Well, get ready to start hearin'em. Willie Rae Stanton, the man in jail, is a dope dealer. He used to deal dope to your son. And, the people that killed him, they deal dope, too. In fact, I think that's how they got into his car. He invited'em in." He paused. "I know it hurts, but that's the way

237

it is." He paused again. "Just try to remember him the way he was around you."

Harbin looked away. His eyes showed his hurt. It suddenly occurred to Edge that Harbin's hurt was probably just as deep as Walter Sawyer's, but for wholly different reasons.

Edge guessed that Harbin's guilt was rooted in his own inability to provide for his son. The fact that the boy was reduced to selling drugs in order to make a better life for himself was a fact about which Otha Harbin could not be proud.

"Don't let it get you down," Edge said.

Harbin nodded. "So, who are these boys that did the shootin'?"

"Can you keep a secret?"

He nodded.

"I need to hear you say it."

"Yes."

"One of'em is Jere Sawyer."

"Sawyer?"

"The family of the boy your son shot in that huntin' accident about seven years ago."

Harbin was speechless.

"Keep that to yourself."

"So . . . when are they gonna be in jail?"

"Soon. They're looking for'em now. It'll break in the paper when it happens. But, if you say something now, they'll run to ground and it might be years before they find'em."

"Are you lookin' for'em too?"

"I've still got my eyes open."

Harbin took a deep breath. "Look, I was able to scrape up another two hundert dollars. It's yours if you'll just keep lookin'."

The man held out the money. Edge certainly felt that he was owed the money for all the work he had done, but somehow he felt guilty for taking it. That is, until it crossed his mind that a man with no visible means of support was able to show up and offer him two, crisp, new one hundred dollar bills.

Edge took the money.

"We've had a break," Austin said over the telephone. There was excitement in her voice.

It was about a week after Edge's meeting with Harbin, in the middle part of November. Austin was long past released from the hospital and was back at work on light duty, and Edge had moved on to a couple of other things.

"What's up?"

"We just gotta call from the State Police in Montgomery. They've got Evans hold up in a house on the south side of town. He's taken a hostage."

"Fantastic. When'll they have him back?"

"I don't know, but I want to go up there." She paused. "Randall says it's okay, and I feel well enough." She paused again. "Will you drive me?"

Edge exhaled loudly. "I really don't see the need."

"Please. I want to see this thing through."

Edge was reluctant. He knew these types of situations. They would only serve to get in the way.

"Okay, I'll pick you up in ten minutes. Be waiting on the curb."

Two and a half hours later Edge stopped his Impala on Woodley Road in Montgomery, approximately one mile south of the South Boulevard, in front of a wood frame house on the west side of the road. There were dozens of highway patrol vehicles and city police cars lining the side of the pavement, and what looked like a command post vehicle in the parking lot of a nursing home on the same side of the street, about twenty-five yards to the south.

Austin flashed her badge to the police officer handling crowd control and bulled her way up to a trooper lieutenant who was standing behind a car with a bullhorn in his hand. Edge stood behind her and didn't speak.

"Who are you?" the lieutenant said gruffly. "Get back."

"I'm from Mobile. I'm Amy Austin. If that's John Evans, he's a suspect in my double homicide. I came to see if you needed some assistance."

"You put out the BOLO for Evans and his Blazer?"

"Right."

"Well, our man jumped him on I-85 just outside'a Auburn. He took off and got off on 65 south. Then he got off on the South Boulevard and drove to here. You got any reason why he'd do that?"

"No. As far as we know he's from Tampa."

"Well, he ran in that house. He's hold up in there with a woman that was in the car with him, and a man that we think is the homeowner." He paused. "He's an editor at the Advocate newspaper."

Austin shook her head. "What's the editor's name?"

"Banks."

Her brows went up. "If the woman in the car is who I think it is, her name is Banks. She's supposed to be Evans' girlfriend. She's not a hostage, she an accomplice."

"What does she look like?"

Edge spoke up. "She's got platinum blonde hair, and she's a dancer in a club in Tampa. Did your man get a look at her?"

"That's her. Our man said she had white hair."

"She's a witness in the murder case. We've got her statement, and she's also a pretty big part of it."

"Is there a warrant out for her?"

"Not yet," Austin said. "But, well, I think we can get one." She looked toward Edge, then toward the house. "So, what's the plan?" Her impatience was evident.

"Well, now that we know that the homeowner and the girl are probably related, we can figure that Evans probably won't do them any harm. It's just a matter of talking him out."

Austin stepped back and stood next to Edge. They could see that officers were stationed on both sides of the house and in the rear. The home sat about hundred yards from the road in the middle of a pecan orchard.

"Are you sure he's still in there?" Edge said to the lieutenant.

"We had two troopers follow him from 65. When they stopped, one went immediately to the back and one went to the front. If he got out, he's Houdini."

The crowd of officers held their positions. They were waiting while city police officers removed every one of the elderly residents of the nursing home, loaded them in ambulances, and transported them away. It was a painstaking process that had been underway since shortly after the troopers had run the two suspects to ground. The process continued on for another forty-five minutes.

Finally, the lieutenant got the word by radio that the nursing home was empty. He put the bullhorn to his mouth.

"Okay, Evans. You and Ms Banks can come on out. Unless she's done something we don't know about, she can be on her way. There's some people from Mobile here to take you with'em."

At that moment a male voice came from inside the home. "I'm comin' out!"

The front door opened and Elizabeth Banks stepped over the threshold. There was a large forearm around her neck and a pistol to her right temple.

"I'm leavin', and I'll kill this broad if you try an' stop me."

Evans was the owner of the large forearm. His speech was still a little muffled from his broken jaw.

The lieutenant looked at Edge. "That the Banks woman?"

Edge nodded. "That's her."

Evans was fifteen steps from the driver's door of the Blazer. Edge stepped up.

"Can I talk to him?" he said to the lieutenant.

"If you think you can get him to stop."

Edge took the bullhorn. "Evans, this is John Edge."

He stopped in his tracks. Edge noticed that there was no sign of struggle from Banks.

"Who?"

"John Edge, uh, Larry Fine. I'm the guy that broke your jaw."

He was silent for a second. "What do you want?"

"Let Banks go. We know you're not gonna hurt her. We know she's your squeeze, so just let her go."

"I'll kill her if you guys don't get back."

"Look around you, Evans. There's fifty officers out here. They'll have to move their cars and . . . well, it'll take an hour. You know they're not gonna let you leave." He paused. "Did you hurt the old man inside?"

"No."

"Then all you're lookin' at is a few traffic charges and this thing in Mobile."

Evans said nothing.

"And we all know that killing those two in Mobile was Sawyer's idea. You had nothing to do with that. You were there because you needed the money."

Silence.

"Just let the girl go, drop the gun, and you can get on with your life."

Silence.

"Evans, if you try to get in that truck, they're gonna plug ya. There's a sniper trained on you right now."

Edge lowered the bullhorn and looked at the Lieutenant. "You got any snipers here?"

"No. The only one's up in St Clair County."

He turned back to Evans. "If you try to leave, you're dead. They're not gonna let you take a hostage. That's Police 101."

Evans' shoulders slumped noticeably. He appeared spent. Edge had no idea how many people he'd killed in the

242

past, but it was clear that he did not want to be the victim of his own death.

Slowly, he began to unhand Banks. His arm came off her neck, and he lowered the gun. Not surprisingly, Banks turned and put her arms around his neck and kissed him full on the lips. Evans dropped the gun.

Edge looked around at Austin. "We gotta get to a phone and call Randall. If he wants to talk to Banks, he needs to get a material witness warrant on the wire as soon as he can."

Austin nodded. As officers rushed to take Evans into custody, Banks was handcuffed also. At the front door, Arthur Banks stepped to the threshold. He appeared unhurt.

Edge turned to the lieutenant. "Where you takin'em?"

"They'll be in the Montgomery County Jail until they see a judge in the morning." He spoke to Austin. "Have your people get up here with a warrant by nine."

Austin seemed overwhelmed. "We gotta get to a phone," she said to Edge.

Three hours later, Austin picked up a faxed copy of a capital murder warrant for the arrest of John Evans at the Sheriff's office on Adams Street in Montgomery, and an hour later she and Edge had checked into the Travelers Inn on Madison Avenue, on the outskirts of downtown. After that, they repaired to Cowboy, a shitkicker disco that was leftover from the Urban Cowboy phase at the early part of the decade.

Seated at a table in the corner, Austin sipped a glass of white wine. Edge drank club soda.

"We need to talk," she said.

"About what?"

"About that day you came to my apartment."

Edge said nothing.

"I did some things, that, uh, well, I, uh, shouldn't have done."

"Yeah? Like what?"

243

"You know what. I was just overwrought; what with my father gettin' married and all. I, I just, well, I needed somebody right then." She paused. "It was nothing personal."

"Well, it all felt pretty personal to me." He paused. "How about the time before?"

"I, I don't remember that."

"Of course, you don't. You were drunk."

"Well, I'm sorry. It was my fault. I, I . . ."

Edge smirked. "Forget it. I realize you were just tryin' to stay on the case by tempting me with your body. Relax. It worked."

She recognized that he was joking, took a deep breath and exhaled, and sipped her drink. A three piece combo started playing country music in the background.

"You knew he wouldn't hurt her, didn't you," she said talking about Evans and Banks.

"It's amazing what regular, heterosexual sex will do for a man." He smiled. "He just needed a reason to end all that foolishness. I just pointed out that the alternative was death, and he realized he couldn't have any more women if he was in hell."

"Novel, but true, I guess."

He looked away. "Speaking of regular sex, how'd it go with Wendy? At the hospital, I mean."

She smirked. "Well, I've got some bad news."

"Don't tell me. She dumped you."

"How'd you know?"

"She just had that look in her eye." He paused. "Condolences," he said with a smile.

"Don't be glib." She took a deep breath and exhaled. "While I was in the hospital, we had a long talk. She said she couldn't take living in fear of me getting hurt. So, we decided to part ways."

"Was that it?"

"That and the fact that when I thought I was gonna die, I decided I wanted children. I mean, I just couldn't stand the thought of dying not having left something behind." She

244

paused. "I just want to find a man – a nice, loyal, kind hearted man, to make a family with."

"I'm sure there's one around."

"And, I thought it was about time I forgave my father for divorcing my mother."

"Forgiveness is always good."

"So, that's it."

"Feel better?"

She raised her brows and took another deep breath. "Yeah. Yeah, I do."

They looked each other in the eye and said nothing. Finally, she spoke.

She nodded. "So, what's gonna happen in the morning?"

"You'll have to get up and tell the judge that you've got a warrant for Evans' arrest, show it to him, and let'em dismiss all the speeding and reckless driving charges the troopers have on him. Then you can put handcuffs on him and we'll drive him back, or you can put him back in jail and let prisoner transport come and get him tomorrow.

She looked away and thought. "I think we'll take him back, if it's alright with you. I mean, you are still a reserve deputy sheriff, right?"

"And leave the girl here?"

"Sure. We've got her statement."

He shook his head. "Just how I wanted to spend an autumn afternoon."

The next day, after spending all morning in front of District Judge Hallie Greenbaum, Austin was finally granted custody of Evans. And because Nathan Randall had failed to send along the proper paperwork, Elizabeth Banks gave Evans a big hug, after which she walked out of court under the arm of her father, Arthur Banks. She turned and smiled back at Edge but said nothing. At least they'll know where to find her, he thought.

At one o'clock, after the noon feeding at the county jail, Austin, Edge, and Evans left Montgomery in Edge's car. Austin borrowed some leg irons from the jail, and she sat next to the handcuffed and shackled Evans in the back seat.

About ten miles south of Montgomery, Austin tried to talk to Evans. His look was sullen and tired. He was in no mood to cooperate.

"Mr. Evans," Austin began, "you know you have the right to remain silent. Anything you say can be used against you, and if you can't afford an attorney one will be appointed for you."

"Yeah, yeah," Evans said disgustedly. "I know. You guys gotta cigarette?"

Edge reached in his vest pocket and pulled out a pack of Chesterfields and some matches that he kept for just this type of occasion. He handed them over the seat to Austin who, with an experienced hand, lit Evans up.

"Now, you wanna tell me what happened with those two kids, down in Grand Bay?"

"Why should I do?"

"'Cause, I may be able to get you a deal."

"What kinda deal?" He chortled.

"Well, it's like Mr. Edge said. Killin' those kids was all Sawyer's idea. No need for you to get the electric chair for his scheme, right? Let him take the full ride for it. How's 'life without' sound? I mean, if you had wanted to die, you could've just let the snipers shoot you yesterday."

Evans looked at her and smirked. "It sounds terrible. You think I wanna spend the next thirty years in population with all them kids? If I'm acquitted, I'm home free. If they convict me of capital murder, I'll have a private cell, a TV, a desk, and a hour a day to myself in the exercise yard. I'll also have a bunch'a do gooder lawyers working on my case for me, tryin' to keep the state from killin' me. My appeals'll drag on for the next ten or fifteen years – maybe longer. I'll live the life'a Riley; the state feedin' me, buyin' me clothes, and takin' care'a my health. I can read and watch all the TV shows I wanna watch; and what's more, I don't have to work." He smiled at her. "Shit, lady. You ain't got it so good yourself."

Austin looked taken aback. Edge smiled to himself and looked at them by way of the rearview mirror. Welcome to the real world, Amy Austin, he thought.

They were back in Mobile at four, and pulling into the underground jail entrance at four thirty. Austin put Evans on docket and assisted in fingerprinting and photographing him. Edge stood outside and smoked a Tiparillo.

After booking, Evans was taken to the Sheriff's Office and questioned by Rice and Will Eubanks. Austin stood by, and Edge waited in the hall. After Evans lawyered up, they all met in the outside the Sheriff's door.

"Well, Mr. Edge," Eubanks said," looks like you and Ms Austin have wrapped this one up."

Eubanks was a tall man with large hands and thinning hair. He spoke in a slow drawl, and his eyes were tired.

"Well, it was Ms Austin mostly. She did all the work."

"Yeah. Well, congratulations to you both." He paused. "Now *you* gotta get him convicted."

Chapter 34

Warrants had been obtained for Jere Sawyer the first week in November, and he was taken into custody six weeks later, around the eleventh of December, in Tampa; oddly, seven years to the day from his brother's death. Aldo Suarez made the bust and Hawking called Austin to let her know. Hawking said they found Sawyer at his home hiding under his bed. In addition, the police seized two marijuana plants and the sawed off shotgun that, inexplicably, was still in the closet.

Suarez said that Sawyer had been hiding out back and forth between Tampa, Mobile, and Atlanta. He said that a reasonable amount of surveillance would probably have already apprehended him. Suarez has no idea how they do things in Mobile, Alabama, Edge thought.

Sawyer fought extradition, and Austin and Will Eubanks flew down to stand before the judge along with an assistant DA, Austin's journal, a transcript of Banks' confession, and little else. The judge, having no desire to burden the state of Florida with Jere Sawyer for any length of time, honored the Alabama governor's warrant, and the three Mobilians rented a car and drove back to Mobile. They were back in the city and in the County Jail before Christmas. Edge went down to visit Sawyer on Christmas Day.

He met Sawyer in the visitation room, just down the hall from the docket desk. Sawyer was being held without bond, and, after all, it was Christmas, so he agreed to meet Edge.

"How you holdin' up?" Edge said.

"What do you care?"

"I don't know, just the humanity of it, I guess. Is there anything I can get'cha?"

He took a deep breath and exhaled. "Not unless you can smuggle in some weed. Other than that, I gotta roof and three meals a day. I'll get by 'til I can get outta here."

"You think you can beat this?"

He nodded. "After the first of the year, my lawyer's gonna get the bond lowered, and I'll get out. My old man can make whatever they set it at."

"What happens then?"

"Then, maybe Johnny don't have nothin' to say; and Billie gets lost for a while. When that happens, all that so-called evidence won't hold up."

"You know what they got?"

"Most of it. Billie told me she told some PI everything." He paused. "That was you?"

Edge shrugged. "Just tryin' to make an honest dollar."

He smirked. "Yeah, she showed me her honest face. You worked her over pretty good."

Edge smiled. "Well, sometimes people are reluctant to do what's right. They have to be reminded of their obligations to their fellow man. Besides, when I left her, she was sleeping soundly."

He looked at Edge. "So, you're the one that figured out about my brother. I knew it wadn't that stupid broad that I rode back from Florida with."

"Oh, she's got her good points."

"Yeah, I saw'em underneath that sweater'a hers. Ha, ha."

Edge smiled. "We just took a look at everybody that had it in for Hardin, and your scenario seemed the most likely."

He looked at Edge. "So, just what are you doin' here?"

Edge looked away and swallowed. He didn't expect Sawyer to come right out and confess to him, but he thought that he could give him a way to fill in the blanks."

"Suppose a man was gonna come to Mobile from Tampa, Florida, and kill somebody that he had his eye on for years. Just exactly how would he go about it?"

Sawyer smiled. "You want me to confess? To you?"

Edge furrowed his brow. "Oh, no. Absolutely not. Like I said, I was just wonderin' how somebody would go about it, hypothetically, if they did."

Sawyer looked away and smiled again. "Well, he'd have to have help here in Mobile; money for travel, and guns and all. And he'd have to find somebody who knew about killin' to come with him; somebody that wadn't afraid to waste somebody, maybe get his hands a little bloody."

"That all?"

"No. He'd have to have somebody with a credit card, somebody that wadn't connected to either the man doin' the shootin' and the man gettin' shot."

"And what if this man knew the guy he was about to shoot. How would he get up next to him?"

Sawyer smirked. "He'd prob'ly meet him somewhere and tell him that he's got some good weed to move. Maybe tell him how that he can get in an organization and start makin' real money."

So, that was how he got Harbin from the Red Shed to the Interstate, Edge thought. Sawyer just appealed to the boy's sense of greed and ambition.

Edge nodded again. "So, just speculatin', wonder why they killed the girl, too?"

"He prob'ly thought that she could identify him." He paused and looked away wistfully. "It was a shame about the girl. I bet the man that killed her wished she wadn't there. But, well . . . shit happens."

"I guess."

"Besides, any slut worth'a shit wouldn't been hangin' around Ty Harbin, anyway."

"He hurt your family that bad, did he?"

"My ole man's been talkin' about it since it happened." He paused and looked away. "Every time I talked to him, he brought it up."

Edge raised his brows. "I suppose that a man plannin' something like this would think on it for a long time, right?"

Sawyer chuckled. "Oh, I don't know. 'Bout seven years, maybe."

"Was killin' Harbin his idea . . . or yours. Just speculatin', of course."

"Well, I ain't gonna say that he didn't bring it up. But, I was the only one who could make him happy. If it was gonna get done, his son was the one that was gonna have to do it."

"Your ole man blames you for it, don't he."

Sawyer said nothing for a long minute. Then, "Somehow, I think he does."

"Tell me, just how mad was he about Ty Harbin killin' your brother?"

He spoke pensively, softly, much lighter than before. He seemed to not want to cast his father in a bad light, but he wanted to tell the truth.

"He just couldn't let it go."

Having found out just exactly how the crime was committed, and hearing from Sawyer that he would deny any of his 'speculations' if Edge tried to repeat them in court, Edge decided that one last visit to his client was in order, just to set the record straight.

That evening, at Harbin's home, they settled into chairs in the living room. Otha Harbin offered Edge a drink.

"No, thank you, sir. I can't stay long. I just wanted to come by and let you know that both the boys that shot your son and his girlfriend are in jail."

Annie Harbin immediately broke down in tears. They weren't the tears of grief that she had displayed in the past. They were either sobs of relief, or they were a byproduct of the type of refreshment that her husband had offered Edge.

"Oh!" she said as she covered her face with a dish towel.

"You think they'll get convicted?" Otha Harbin said ignoring his wife.

"Well, you never can tell what a jury'll do, and it'll depend a lot on how good'a lawyer he gets, but I think they can make it stick."

"Do you know what happened?" Annie Harbin said through her sobs.

"I think so. It looks like Sawyer called over here and found out where Ty was. They met him after the ballgame down at the Red Shed over in Mississippi. Sawyer told your son that he had some weed to show him; he gave him some story about wanting him to get in the marijuana business with a south Florida connection. They met on the side of the interstate, away from the crowd at the bar, and that's where . . ."

"Oh!" Annie Harbin said as she broke into another paroxysm.

Otha Harbin sat in his recliner and seethed. Edge didn't know if he was upset that his son was being slandered as a drug dealer, or if he too was developing a hate for his son's killers in the same way that Walter Sawyer had done for Tyrone Harbin. Either way, Edge knew that Otha Harbin was going to be disappointed, and it would lead to no good.

Harbin finally spoke and offered Edge the money he had left out of the initial two thousand, a little over a hundred dollars. Edge declined. Even though he thought Harbin had plenty, he just couldn't see taking the man's last few dollars for something that the Sheriff's Department should have done for free.

The next morning, Edge visited the parents of Carla Morgan. It was just before noon, and he was surprised to find Kenneth Morgan at home.

As at their last meeting, the Morgans continued to be much more reserved in their grief than the Harbins. They met this time on the patio in the rear of the home. Edge was offered iced tea, but declined.

"You've been reading the papers," Edge said.

"I have. There are two men in custody for my daughter's murder," Kenneth Morgan said.

"That's right. There's a female that was involved, but I don't know if she'll be charged or simply used as a witness."

"What was her involvement?"

"She made the plane reservations and booked the rent a car that got'em to Mobile. She claimed to me that she didn't know what they were about to do, and when she found out, she made'em let her out of the car." Edge paused. "I don't believe her."

"Did you testify at the Grand Jury?"

"No. Amy Austin, a deputy was with me throughout my part of the investigation. She was able to take care of things."

252

"And this was all about a hunting accident," Helen Morgan said, "that happened seven years ago?" Her voice choked back a sob.

Edge nodded. "That's what my investigation has shown."

Everyone sat in silence for what seemed like five minutes. Kenneth Morgan, Edge thought, looks like he's got some kind of legal maneuvering up his sleeve.

"So, my daughter was killed for no reason," Helen Morgan said.

"That's about the size of it. The fact that she was killed because she was a witness does make this a capital case and therefore the men are eligible for the death penalty."

They all sat and looked at each other. With one hand Helen Morgan wiped her eyes, and with the other she held tightly onto his husband's arm, another picture of the grief of a mother who had to bury a dead child.

"Well, I guess you're here to get your reward," Morgan said.

Edge looked at him but said nothing.

"Just exactly how big a part in this case did you play?"

Edge was taken aback. He should have known that Morgan was not serious when he offered the five thousand. Edge decided to push the rich lawyer as far as he could to try to get some of the man's dirty drug money.

"Well, if I hadn't brought them the information, they wouldn't have known about the hunting accident."

"I see."

Edge leaned forward and narrowed his eyes. "Mr. Morgan, you wouldn't be considering holding out on me, would you?"

Helen Morgan sat up. "Oh, pay him, Ken. He's done more than that sheriff has."

Morgan smirked. "Do you want cash, or will you take a check?"

Edge sat back. "Cash, please."

Chapter 35

Three weeks later, Jere Sawyer's preliminary hearing was held on the second floor of the Mobile County Courthouse. Edge had purchased a new suit with the Morgan reward money and decided to do something he ordinarily did not do: attend a judicial proceeding.

Courtroom number two, the largest in the building, sat on the northwest corner of the second floor. It was made dark by the stained wood paneling on the walls, and the furniture and other appointments on and around the room. The jury box sat to the left, and a wood carving of Moses carrying the Ten Commandments hung on the wall high above the bench.

Edge took a seat on the end of the rear pew near the middle aisle. The thirty or forty other people in the room included the Morgans and the Harbins who sat immediately behind the prosecution table; the gallery being separated from the front of the courtroom by a short wooden railing.

Otha Harbin wore a bad sport jacket and blue jeans, and Annie Harbin was in a threadbare housedress and low heeled pumps. The Morgans looked like a couple fresh off the pages of a fashion magazine.

Walter Sawyer and his wife sat behind the defense table. Sawyer had on a four button suit, and his shoes looked as if they'd been spit shined.

Austin and Will Eubanks sat on the opposite side behind the prosecution table. Austin wore a blue dress and pumps and held a large accordion style folder. Her hair was perfect, and she appeared to have lost weight as a result of her injuries. Eubanks wore a gray suit with a maroon tie, and a bored look.

Dennis Knotts, the priciest defense lawyer in town, stood immediately in front of the bench and talked with an assistant district attorney, Carlton Grady. The bailiff was at the door next to the bench, the clerk was in her place next to the judge's seat, and the clock on the wall in the rear said nine o'clock.

In a minute, the door next to the bench opened and Judge Frank McInnis entered. He was an elderly white man with silver hair and horn rimmed glasses. He took his seat, banged his gavel one time, after which Grady and Knotts took their places.

"This court will come to order," he said. McInnis was handed a file by the clerk.

"First case is State v. Jere Sawyer. I see here it's set for a preliminary hearing. Are you ready Mr. Prosecutor?"

"Ready, Judge."

"Mr. Knotts?"

"Just waiting on my client, Judge."

McInnis turned to the bailiff. "Bring him in, Harold."

The door on the opposite side opened, and the bailiff summoned two of T.T. Lawrence's brown shirted deputies who walked on either side of a jumpsuited and handcuffed Jere Sawyer, as he shuffled into the room. After he was seated at the defense table, the deputies took up positions on either side of the courtroom. One stood beside the court clerk, the other was next to Grady's table.

"Mr. Knotts, has your client been advised of his rights?" McInnis said.

"He has, Your Honor."

"I see he pleaded 'not guilty' at the arraignment. Does he wish to change his plea?"

"No, Judge."

"Okay, then we shall proceed with this preliminary hearing. Call your first witness, Mr. Grady."

"State calls Amy Austin."

Austin rose from the gallery and walked through a short gate up to the witness stand. She was sworn by the judge and took a seat.

After the preliminary questions – Who are you? What do you do for a living? etc. – Grady slowly led Austin through her time with Edge. She told of gathering the information from the airlines, the rent a car company, the Tampa Police Department, and also the SBI. She produced the state's file on the death of Terry Sawyer from all the way back in 1977, and told the court of the case and the motive for Harbin's and Morgan's death.

When Grady was finished, he passed the witness. Knotts rose to his feet.

"Judge, we have no questions for this witness."

"Mr. Grady, any other witnesses?"

Edge tensed. He didn't expect to be called, but there was always a chance.

"No, Judge. We believe we have met the burden. The prosecution rests in this proceeding."

"Mr. Knotts, do you have any witnesses?"

"No, Your Honor. The only thing that we really want to do here today is to set a date for a comprehensive discovery; hopefully, sometime next week."

McInnis looked at Grady. "Can you be ready by next week, Mr. Grady?"

Grady looked as if he was caught off guard. "Well, uh, yes, Judge. I think we can."

"Good. You two work that out. Okay, I order this case bound over the Grand Jury for consideration." He paused and looked down. "Is there any other business?"

Knotts rose. "Judge, we'd like to be heard on bail."

"Mr. Grady?"

"Judge, the defendant lives out of state. I don't know if we let him go whether or not we can get him back." He paused. "In addition, there are other charges pending; namely the attempted murder of Detective Austin back here."

Knotts spoke up. "Judge, my client has family here in town, they are prepared to make his bond, and they are prepared to ensure that he returns to court."

"Your Honor, the state would object. We can offer testimony that Mr. Sawyer is a drug user, and, well, Judge, due to the gravity of this crime, the heinousness of it, we would submit that Mr. Sawyer should remain in jail."

"Judge, this man is innocent until proven guilty."

"Okay, okay, okay." He paused. "I'm gonna set a bond at five hundred thousand dollars on each charge; how many are there?"

"There are four, Judge, at this time: two counts of capital murder and two counts of conspiracy to commit murder."

"Okay, that'll be a total of five hundred thousand dollars on each charge, for a total of two million; cash, property, or corporate surety."

Edge could see Walter Sawyer smile broadly. Jere Sawyer turned to him and smiled, also. It was apparent that very shortly Jere Sawyer would be getting out of jail.

What happened next was almost too unexpected to believe. Edge was looking at his watch when Otha Harbin rose from his seat and walked toward the gate in the partition that separated the gallery from the defense table. When Edge looked up, he saw Harbin's hand come out of his right hand coat pocket with some type of thin cord or wire in it. As he went through the gate he unrolled it.

Harbin had never struck Edge as a particularly agile or energetic man, but he moved like a cat to a position behind Jere Sawyer. Then he wrapped the cord around Sawyer's neck twice with the skill of a Mafioso. He yanked it tight, and the struggle was on.

Both deputies, who were unarmed, as well as Grady, Knotts, Austin, and Eubanks all descended on Harbin and knocked him and Sawyer to the floor. They fought bravely, hitting Harbin over the head repeatedly with any hard object they could lay their hands on, but they were unable to either get the garrotte from around Sawyer's neck, or to immobilize Harbin. Edge stood and watched as the face of Jere Sawyer turned red, then blue. Thirty seconds later he collapsed. Harbin held on for another minute or two before his hands were pried from what Edge could now see was a wire. He was pulled away from Sawyer's body and thrown to the floor.

Sawyer lay motionless as his mother knelt by his side. Harbin, now handcuffed and sitting with his back to the wall, was wide-eyed and yelling hysterically.

"He killed my boy! He killed my boy!" he yelled at the top of his lungs.

Jere Sawyer was pronounced dead at the emergency room of the Medical Center forty minutes after the attack. Harbin was taken away to jail.

That night, Edge went back to his apartment and opened a bottle of a very nondescript Merlot that he kept in his pantry for emergencies. He sat in his recliner and drank the whole bottle.

He slept soundly in his chair that night, and in the morning, his head hurt, just like he knew it would.

Film of the murder had been taken by a local television camera stationed out in the hall, whose lens was pointed through a small glass window in the door; and the footage was ultimately forwarded to CNN, a new cable news network, and thereafter rerun – albeit with Sawyer's death mask blurred – for three days.

Not long after, the presiding Circuit Judge ordered that all deputies at the courthouse be armed with pistols. T.T. Lawrence said that it should always have been so.

Chapter 36

A month later, Edge picked up Timmy Hankins at his trailer in Creola, at noon on a Friday, and took him to a buffet lunch in Saraland. As usual, the skinny young man filled his plate full and went back for thirds.

"I gotta thank you, Timmy. If you hadn't put me on to that hunting accident, we never would have found out what happened to Ty."

"Oh, yeah. Right. Is that why they killed him?"

"It is. Once we eliminated everybody else, it had to be the Sawyers." He paused. "I guess you heard Jere Sawyer got an early death penalty."

"Yeah. I did."

"The other guy, John Evans, is going to trial in a week. In light of what happened, I expect him to get the death penalty, too." He paused. "There was a woman, uh, Banks is her name. She was involved, too. She's expected to take a plea and do three years.

"So, eat all you want, son. This one's on me." He paused and reached into his pocket. "And to help out in the future, here's a little bit'a pocket money."

Edge slid ten, crisp, new one hundred dollar bills across the table to Hankins who laid his hand on the currency while he kept on eating. It was part of the Morgan reward money.

"And," Edge said. "order something' for your mother."

The End

Caleb Lott, who was once a homicide detective, and a private investigator, is the pseudonym for the author who lives and writes in Alabama.